metric equivalents

linear

US	Metric
⅛ IN	3 MM
¼ IN	6 MM
½ IN	1.5 CM
¾ IN	2 CM
1 IN	2.5 CM
6 IN	15 CM
12 IN (1 FT)	30 CM
39 IN	1 M

weight

US	Metric
¼ OZ	7 G
½ OZ	15 G
¾ OZ	20 G
1 OZ	30 G
8 OZ (½ LB)	225 G
12 OZ (¾ LB)	340 G
16 OZ (1 LB)	455 G
35 OZ (2.2 LBS)	1 KG

volume

US	Metric
1 TBSP (½ FL OZ)	15 ML
¼ CUP (2 FL OZ)	60 ML
⅓ CUP	80 ML
½ CUP (4 FL OZ)	120 ML
⅔ CUP	160 ML
¾ CUP (6 FL OZ)	180 ML
1 CUP (8 FL OZ)	235 ML
1 QT (32 FL OZ)	950 ML
1 QT + 3 TBSPS	1 L
1 GAL (128 FL OZ)	4 L

temperature

US	Metric
0°F (FREEZER TEMPERATURE)	−18°C
32°F (WATER FREEZES)	0°C
98.6°F	37°C
180°F (WATER SIMMERS*)	82°C
212°F (WATER BOILS*)	100°C
250°F (LOW OVEN)	120°C
350°F (MODERATE OVEN)	175°C
425°F (HOT OVEN)	220°C
500°F (VERY HOT OVEN)	260°C

*AT SEA LEVEL

ALL NUMBERS HAVE BEEN ROUNDED. FOR MORE EXACT NUMBERS, USE METRIC CONVERSION CHART AT LEFT

Dec 5. 2003.

Reader's Digest
Low Calorie
Cookbook

Reader's Digest

Low Calorie Cookbook

Published by
The Reader's Digest Association, Inc.,
Pleasantville, New York • Montreal

Contents

Introduction

A healthy diet helps you to look good and feel great. *Low-Calorie Cookbook* is packed with delicious calorie-counted dishes so you can make a daily choice to suit your tastes and energy needs. Nutrition fads come and go, but the key to eating well remains the same: enjoy a balance of varied foods that supply all the nutrients your body requires.

Getting It into Proportion

Current Dietary Guidelines for North Americans are that most people should eat more starchy foods, more fruit and vegetables, and less fatty meat products and sugary foods. However, it is almost impossible to give exact amounts that you should eat, because every person's requirements vary, depending on size, age, and the amount of energy expended during the day.

However, nutrition experts have suggested an ideal balance of the foods that provide energy (calories) and the nutrients needed for good health. The number of daily servings of each of the food groups they specify will vary from person to person—for example, an active teenager might need up to 11 portions of bread, cereals, rice and pasta every day, whereas a sedentary adult would require only 6 or 7 portions. But the proportions of the food groups in relation to each other should ideally stay the same.

Food on the Plate

As a simple way to get the balance right, nutritionists have devised a food guide for healthy eating. (For specific information see the U.S Food Guide Pyramid [www.nutrition.gov] or Canada's guide [www.hc-sc.gc.ca/hppb/nutrition/pube/foodguid/index.html].) Try to eat a wide variety of foods with an emphasis on bread, cereals, rice, pasta, fruit and vegetables, lesser amounts of milk, yogurt, and cheese; and meat, poultry, fish, dry beans, eggs and nuts. And limit your intake of fats, oils and sweets. The groups listed below show the balance of foods to aim for.

It isn't essential to eat the ideal proportions at every meal, or even every day—balancing them over a week or two is just as good to ensure you get all the nutrients you need. The healthiest diet for you and your family is one that is generally balanced and sustainable.

Daily Energy Requirements in Adult Life

Daily calorie needs vary according to age, sex and lifestyle. To maintain an ideal body weight, we need to balance the calories we consume with the energy we expend.

	Less active women and older adults	Active women and less active men	Teen boys and active men
Calories	About 1,600	About 2,200	About 2,800
Bread Group	6	9	11
Vegetable Group	3	4	5
Fruit Group	2	3	4
Milk Group	2 to 3*	2 to 3*	2 to 3*
Meat Group	2 for a total of 5 ounces	2 for a total of 6 ounces	3 for a total of 7 ounces

* Women who are pregnant or breast feeding, teenagers, and young adults (up to age 24 years) need 3 servings

Recommended Food Groups

Bread, Cereals, Rice, and Pasta:

Eat 6 to 11 servings a day

Bread, cereals, rice, and pasta are the foundation of a healthy diet. They provide complex carbohydrates, which are an important source of energy, especially in lowfat diets, and they also supply protein, and essential vitamins and minerals, particularly those from the B group.

Eat a variety of starchy foods, choosing wholewheat or wholegrain types whenever possible, because the fiber they contain helps to prevent constipation, bowel disease, heart disease, and other health problems.

Starchy foods are not, in themselves, fattening. It is often what is added to them, such as butter, cream, or cheese that contributes most of the calories.

Examples of 1 serving:

1 ounce ready to-eat cereal
½ cup cooked cereal, rice, or pasta
½ bagel, hamburger roll, or pita bread
1 slice bread
1 x 6 inch tortilla
3 or 4 small crackers
½ cup cooked barley
½ cup quinoa, bulgur, millet, or other wholegrain

Vegetables:

Eat 3 to 5 servings a day

Vegetables provide vitamin C for immunity and healing, and other "antioxidant" vitamins and minerals for protection against cardiovascular disease and cancer. They also offer several "phytochemicals" that help protect against cancer, and B vitamins, especially folate, which is important for women planning a pregnancy, to prevent birth defects. All of these, plus other nutrients in vegetables, work together to boost well-being.

Different vegetables supply different nutrients and phytochemicals. Deep yellow, orange, and dark green leafy vegetables, such as carrots, sweet potatoes, and spinach, are great sources of the antioxidant beta-carotene, which the body converts to vitamin A. Bell peppers, watercress, and tomatoes provide vitamin C.

The best way to make sure you get the full range of these nutrients is to eat a wide variety of vegetables.

Examples of 1 serving:

½ cup raw, nonleafy vegetables
1 cup leafy raw vegetables (lettuce, spinach, watercress, or cabbage)
½ cup cooked vegetables
½ cup legumes (beans, pulses, or lentils)
1 small baked potato
¾ cup vegetable juice

Fruit:

Eat 2 to 4 servings a day

Citrus fruits and kiwi are a great source of vitamin C. Deep yellow fruits, such as cantaloupe, apricots, peaches, and mangoes, are rich in beta-carotene. Fruits that are eaten with their skin on, such as apple and pears, provide useful amounts of fiber. Many fruits are also a good source of potassium and folate.

Antioxidant nutrients (for example, vitamin C and beta-carotene, which are mainly derived from both fruit and vegetables) and vitamin E help to prevent harmful free radicals in the body initiating or accelerating cancer, heart disease, cataracts, arthritis, general aging, sun damage to skin, and damage to sperm. Free radicals occur naturally as a by-product of normal cell function but are also caused by pollutants, such as tobacco smoke and overexposure to sunlight.

Examples of 1 serving:

1 medium fruit (apple, orange, banana, or peach)
½ grapefruit, mango, or papaya
¾ cup fruit juice
½ cup berries or cut-up fruit
½ cup canned, frozen, or cooked fruit
¼ cup dried fruit

Fats, Oils, and Sweets:

No minimum requirement

It is recommended that you limit your intake of foods such as salad dressings, cream, butter, oil, sugar, soft drinks, jams and jellies, candies, sherbet, and gelatin desserts. In small amounts they add flavor and pleasure to meals and snacks. Because there are no minimum requirements for them, fats, oils, and sweets are not considered to be part of a food group and, therefore, no serving sizes are specified.

Fatty foods should not exceed 30% of the day's calories in a balanced diet, and only 10% of this should be from saturated fat. This quantity of fat may seem like a lot, but it isn't—fat contains more than twice as many calories per gram as either carbohydrate or protein.

Overconsumption of fat is a major cause of weight and health problems. A healthy diet must contain a certain amount of fat to provide fat-soluble vitamins and essential fatty acids, needed for the development and function of the brain, eyes, and nervous system, but we only need a small amount each day—just 1 ounce is required, which is much less than we consume in most Western diets.

Although many foods naturally contain sugars (for example, fruit contains fructose; milk has lactose), health experts recommend that we limit "added" sugars, such as table sugar, which provide only calories. They contain no vitamins, minerals, or fiber to contribute to health, and it is not necessary to eat them.

Sweet foods, however, can be a pleasurable part of a well-balanced diet, provided they are eaten in moderation.

In assessing how much sugar you consume, don't forget that it is also a major ingredient of many processed and ready-to-eat meals.

Meat, Poultry, Fish, Dry Beans, Eggs, and Nuts:

Eat 2 to 3 servings a day

Lean meat, fish, eggs, and vegetarian alternatives provide protein for growth and cell repair, as well as iron to prevent anemia. Meat also provides B vitamins for healthy nerves and digestion, especially vitamin B_{12}, and zinc for growth and healthy bones and skin. Only moderate amounts of these protein-rich foods are required.

The total amount of any day's serving should be the equivalent of 5 to 7 ounces of cooked lean meat, poultry, or fish. The examples below also show what amounts of other foods are required to eat the protein equivalent of 1 ounce of meat.

Examples of 1 serving:

2 to 3 ounces cooked lean meat, poultry, or fish (4 ounces raw meat, poultry, or fish)

1 small chicken leg or thigh

1 medium pork chop

1 unbreaded 3 ounce fish fillet

2 to 3 ounces lean sliced deli meat (turkey, ham, or bologna)

2 to 3 ounces canned tuna or salmon, packed in water

Count as 1 ounce of meat:

½ cup cooked lentils, peas or dried beans

1 egg or ½ cup egg substitute

2 tablespoons peanut butter

⅓ cup nuts

4 ounces tofu

Milk, Yogurt, and Cheese:

Eat 2 to 3 servings a day

Dairy foods, such as milk, cheese, and yogurt, are the best sources of calcium for strong bones and teeth, and important for the nervous system. They also provide some protein for growth and repair, vitamin B_{12} and B_2, and vitamin A for healthy eyes.

They are particularly valuable foods for young children, who need full-fat versions at least up to age 2. Dairy foods are also especially important for adolescent girls to prevent the development of osteoporosis later in life, and for women throughout life generally.

To limit fat intake, wherever possible adults should choose lower-fat dairy foods, such as skim milk and lowfat yogurt.

Examples of 1 serving:

1 cup milk or buttermilk

1 cup yogurt

⅓ cup dry milk

1½ ounce natural cheese (Cheddar, Swiss, Monterey Jack)

½ cup ricotta cheese

2 ounces processed cheese

½ cup frozen yogurt

1 cup cottage cheese

½ cup evaporated milk

Too Salty

Salt (sodium chloride) is essential for a variety of body functions, but we tend to eat too much through consumption of salty processed foods, "fast" foods and prepared foods, and by adding salt in cooking and at the table. The end result can be rising blood pressure as we get older, which puts us at higher risk of heart disease and stroke. Eating more vegetables and fruit increases potassium intake, which can help to counteract the damaging effects of salt.

Alcohol in a Healthy Diet

In recent research, moderate drinking of alcohol has been linked with a reduced risk of heart disease and stroke among men and women over 45. But because of other risks associated with alcohol, particularly in excessive quantities, no doctor would recommend taking up drinking if you are a teetotaler. The healthiest pattern of drinking is to enjoy small amounts of alcohol with food, to have alcohol-free days, and always to avoid getting drunk. A well-balanced diet is vital because nutrients from food (vitamins and minerals) are needed to detoxify the alcohol.

Water—the Best Choice

Drinking plenty of nonalcoholic liquids each day is an often overlooked part of a well-balanced diet. The drinks should not all be tea or coffee, because these are stimulants and diuretics, which cause the body to lose liquids, including water-soluble vitamins. Water is the best choice. Other good choices are fruit or herb teas or tisanes, fruit juices—diluted with water, if preferred—or low-fat (2%) or skim milk (whole milk for very young children). Fizzy sugary or acidic drinks such as cola are more likely to damage tooth enamel than other drinks.

As a guide to the vitamin and mineral content of foods and recipes in the book, we have used the following terms and symbols, based on the percentage of the daily RDA provided by one serving for the average adult man or woman aged 19 to 49 years:

✓✓✓	or excellent	at least 50% (half)
✓✓	or good	25–50% (one-quarter to one-half)
✓	or useful	10–25% (one-tenth to one-quarter)

Note that recipes contribute other nutrients, but the analyses only include those that provide at least 10% RNI per portion. Vitamins and minerals where deficiencies are rare are not included.

Ⓥ denotes that a recipe is suitable for vegetarians.

Breakfast

A nourishing start sets you up for the day, so breakfast should never be skipped. This chapter is packed with delicious ideas, from a light Strawberry-Yogurt Smoothie—a mere 55-calorie treat—to a substantial dish of Scrambled Eggs with Smoked Salmon and Dill—still quite acceptable at 363 calories. With healthy muesli, granola, pancakes, popovers, and brioches as well, you will find plenty of breakfast ideas to enjoy.

Banana and Mango Shake

A thick banana-flavored milk shake with a tropical touch, this will appeal to children and adults alike. It is an ideal drink for busy breakfast times, because it is packed with nourishment and very quick to prepare.

Serves 2

½ ripe mango
1 small ripe banana, sliced
⅔ cup low-fat (2%) milk
½ cup orange juice
2 teaspoons fresh lime juice
1 teaspoon sugar
2 heaped tablespoons vanilla frozen yogurt
Sprigs of fresh lemon balm (optional)

Preparation time: 5 minutes

1 Peel the mango and cut the flesh away from the seed. Chop the flesh roughly. Put it into a blender with the banana.

2 Add the milk, orange juice, lime juice, sugar, and frozen yogurt and blend on maximum speed for about 30 seconds or until mixed and frothy.

3 Pour into glasses and serve immediately, decorated with sprigs of lemon balm, if you like.

Some More Ideas

● Use skim milk instead of low-fat. An 8 ounce cup skim milk contains only 0.4 g fat, as compared with 8.9 g for whole milk and 4.7 g for low-fat (2%) milk, but still has similar levels of vitamins and minerals.
● Those who do not eat dairy products or who have a lactose (milk sugar) intolerance can substitute 1¼ cups soy milk for the cow's milk, and omit the frozen yogurt; or use 1 cup soy milk with 2 tablespoons soy ice cream.
● Use a ripe peach instead of the mango half.
● For a shake rich in fiber, use 1 cup pitted ready-to-eat prunes instead of the mango, with lemon juice instead of lime juice.

Plus Points

● Milk is an excellent source of several important nutrients—protein, calcium, and phosphorus (important for strong bones and teeth), along with many of the B vitamins, particularly B_1, B_2, B_6, and B_{12}.
● Bananas are a useful source of the mineral potassium, a good intake of which might help to prevent high blood pressure.
● Mangoes are rich in vitamin C and carotenoid compounds, both antioxidants that are believed to protect the body against damage by free radicals.

Each serving provides Ⓥ

cals 150, **protein** 5 g, **fat** 2 g (of which saturated fat 1 g), **carbohydrate** 30 g (of which sugars 29 g), **fiber** 3 g

✓✓✓ C

✓　　A, B_1, B_6, B_{12}, niacin, calcium, potassium

Strawberry-Yogurt Smoothie

This refreshing drink is perfect for summer when strawberries are plentiful and full of flavor. It provides a healthy start to the day, with its high vitamin C content and natural sweetness. Dilute it with extra orange juice if you want a thinner drink.

Serves 4

1 pound ripe strawberries, hulled

Grated zest and juice of 1 large orange

⅔ cup plain low-fat yogurt

1 tablespoon sugar, or to taste (optional)

To decorate (optional)

4 small strawberries

4 small orange slices

Preparation time: 5 minutes

1 Tip the strawberries into a food processor or blender and add the orange zest, orange juice, and yogurt. Blend to a puree, scraping down the sides of the container once or twice. Taste the mixture and sweeten with the sugar, if necessary.

2 For a really smooth consistency, press through a nylon sieve to remove the strawberry pips, although this is not essential.

3 Pour into glasses. If you like, decorate with small strawberries and slices of orange, both split so they sit on the rim of the glass.

Some More Ideas

● Add a sliced banana to the strawberries. This will thicken the texture of the smoothie and will also add natural sweetness, so be sure to taste before adding sugar—you might not need any.

● Swap the dried apricots for strawberries, to make a smoothie with a useful amount of beta-carotene and a good amount of soluble fiber. Gently simmer 1⅓ cups dried apricots in 1 quart strained Earl Grey tea until tender, about 30 minutes. Cool, then pour the apricots and liquid into a blender. Add the orange zest, juice, and yogurt and blend until smooth. Taste and sweeten with sugar, if required. Serve sprinkled with a little Blueberry and Cranberry Granola (see page 22).

Plus Points

● Strawberries are low in calories and are an excellent source of vitamin C.

● Most yogurt is "live," which means it contains high levels of active cultures. Although all yogurt is made by heating milk to destroy harmful bacteria, many brands contain active cultures of beneficial bacteria added after pasteurization. The balance of bacteria in the gut is easily upset by stress, a poor diet, and medication, such as antibiotics, but a regular intake of "good" bacteria, such as that provided by the active cultures in yogurt, help to maintain a healthy digestive tract. Look for labels that contain the words "with active cultures," "living yogurt cultures," or "contains active cultures."

Each serving provides Ⓥ

cals 55, **protein** 3 g, **fat** 0.5 g (of which saturated fat 0.2 g), **carbohydrate** 11 g (of which sugars 11 g), **fiber** 2.5 g

✓✓✓ C

✓ folate, calcium

Breakfast

Mango, Peach and Apricot Fizz

A luscious combination of fruit pureed together with ginger ale, or with tonic water, bitter lemon, or sparkling mineral water, makes a wonderfully refreshing breakfast drink. Choose perfectly ripe fruit for the smoothest, low-calorie drink.

Serves 4

1 ripe mango
1 ripe peach
2 large ripe apricots
2¼ cups ginger ale
Fresh mint or lemon balm leaves (optional)

Preparation time: 5 to 10 minutes

1 Peel the mango and cut the flesh away from the central seed. Roughly chop the flesh and put it into a blender or food processor. (Alternatively, if you are using a stick blender, put the mango in a large tall jug.)

2 Cover the peach and apricots with boiling water and leave for about 30 seconds, then drain and cool under cold water. Slip off the skins and roughly chop the flesh, discarding the pits. Add to the mango in the blender or food processor.

3 Pour enough of the ginger ale over just to cover the fruit, then process until smooth. Pour in the remaining ginger ale and process again.

4 Quickly pour into tall glasses, preferably over crushed ice. Decorate with fresh mint or lemon balm leaves, if you like. Serve immediately with wide straws or swizzle sticks.

Some More Ideas

● Use low-calorie ginger ale to reduce the calorie content.

● So many different fruit and fizz combinations are possible. Using about 1 pound fruit in total, try: raspberry, peach, and melon with bitter lemon; strawberry, banana, and orange segments with tonic water.

● When soft fruit are not in season, use fruit canned in juice, rather than syrups, as a substitute. A delicious combination is fresh melon, banana, and canned apricots with sparkling mineral water.

Plus Points

● With their easily digested flesh, these golden fruits provide a feast of vitamins. Peaches are full of vitamin C; essential for healthy skin, healing wounds, and fighting infections; apricots are a good source of the B vitamins (B_1, B_6, and niacin); and mangoes are an excellent source of vitamin A, which is important for vision and might help the prevention of heart disease and some cancers.

Each serving provides Ⓥ
cals 55, **protein** 1 g, **fat** 0 g, **carbohydrate** 14 g (of which sugars 13 g), **fiber** 2.5 g

✓✓✓ C
✓ A

Breakfast

Berry Salad with Passion Fruit

Berries are the fresh, healthy flavor of summer. Naturally tart, sweet, and juicy, they range from delicate raspberries to fleshy strawberries, plump blueberries, and rich blackberries. The passion fruit adds a fragrant edge to this breakfast salad.

Serves 6

1 pound strawberries, hulled and cut in half

1 heaping cup raspberries

⅔ cup blackberries

⅔ cup blueberries

⅔ cup mixed red currants and black currants, removed from their stems

2 passion fruit

1 tablespoon sugar

Fresh juice of ½ lemon or lime

Preparation time: 10 to 15 minutes

1 Mix the strawberries, raspberries, blackberries, blueberries, red currants, and black currants together in a medium-size bowl.

2 Cut the passion fruit in half. Holding a sieve over the bowl of berries, spoon the passion fruit flesh and seeds into the sieve. Rub the flesh and seeds briskly to press all the juice through the sieve onto the berries. Reserve a few of the passion fruit seeds left in the sieve and discard the rest.

3 Add the sugar and lemon or lime juice to the berries. Gently toss together. Sprinkle the reserved passion fruit seeds over. Serve right away or cover and chill briefly.

Some More Ideas

• Instead of passion fruit, use 3 tablespoons crème de cassis. Chill until ready to serve.

• Omit the passion fruit and instead serve the berry salad with a Peach and Apricot Sauce: Peel and puree 2 ripe peaches. Flavor with 2 to 3 tablespoons sugar, the juice of ¼ lemon, and a dash of pure almond extract. Finely dice 8 ready-to-eat dried apricots and add to the peach puree. Serve the berries on plates in a pool of the sauce.

• Serve the berry salad spooned over vanilla frozen yogurt.

Plus Points

• Comparing the same weight of each fruit, black currants come out top of the table for vitamin C, with 200 mg in each 3½ ounce serving, while strawberries have 77 mg, raspberries 32 mg, and blackberries 15 mg. These days vitamin C is recognized as essential for maintaining the immune system and as an antioxidant, preventing the damaging processes that can lead to heart disease and cancer.

• To this feast of summer fruit, rich in dietary fiber and vitamin C, passion fruit also adds vitamin A, which is essential for healthy skin and good vision, and blackberries add vitamin E, another important antioxidant. The effects of vitamin E are enhanced by other antioxidants like vitamin C, so the combination of fruits in this berry salad recipe is particularly healthy.

Each serving provides ⓥ

cals 55, **protein** 1 g, **fat** 0 g, **carbohydrate** 12 g (of which sugars 12 g), **fiber** 5 g

✓✓✓	C
✓	E, folate

Breakfast

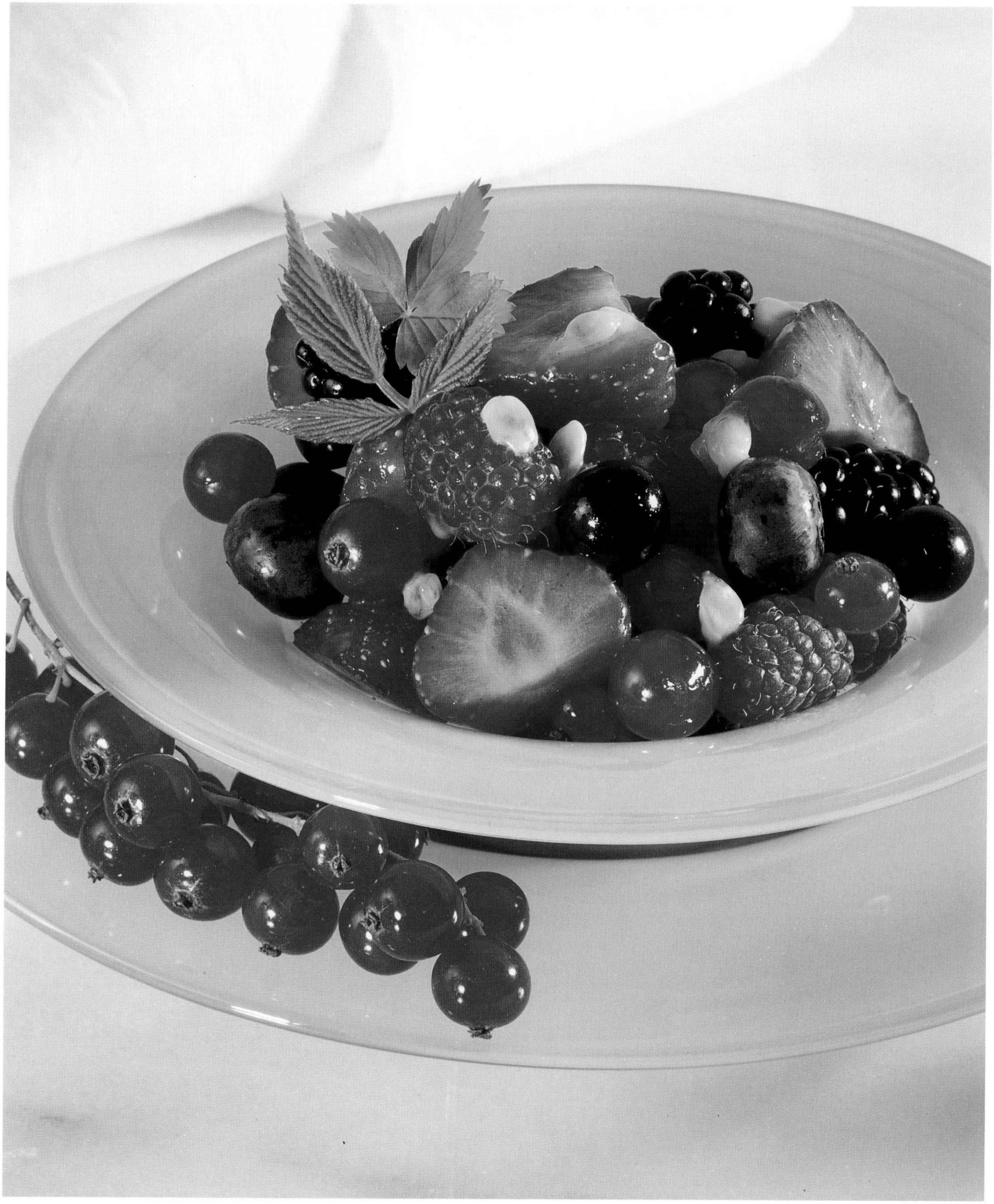

Fruity Bircher Muesli

This is an entire meal in one bowl. The original recipe for this nutritious breakfast cereal was developed more than a century ago by Dr. Bircher-Benner at his clinic in Zurich. Soaking the cereal overnight makes it easier to digest.

Serves 4

1½ cups oatmeal
⅔ cup golden raisins
1 cup low-fat (2%) milk
1 crisp dessert apple
2 teaspoons fresh lemon juice
2 tablespoons roughly chopped hazelnuts
1 tablespoon pumpkin seeds
1 tablespoon sesame seeds
⅔ cup strawberries, hulled and chopped
4 tablespoons plain low-fat yogurt with active cultures
4 teaspoons honey

Preparation time: 10 minutes, plus overnight soaking

1 Place the oats and golden raisins in a large bowl. Add the milk and stir to mix evenly. Cover and place in the refrigerator; leave to soak overnight.

2 The next day, just before eating, grate the apple, discarding the core. Toss the apple with the lemon juice to prevent browning.

3 Stir the hazelnuts, pumpkin seeds, and sesame seeds into the oat mixture, then stir in the grated apple and strawberries.

4 To serve, divide the muesli between 4 cereal bowls, and top each with a spoonful of yogurt and honey.

Another Idea
● To make a mixed-grain muesli, soak ⅓ cup oatmeal, 1½ cups malted wheat flakes, ¼ cup flaked rice, and ¾ cup raisins in 1 cup buttermilk. Just before eating, stir in 2 tablespoons roughly chopped almonds and 4 tablespoons sunflower seeds. Add 1 roughly mashed banana and 1 chopped mango. Serve topped with plain low-fat yogurt.

Plus Points
● Look for yogurt with active cultures. These yogurts are believed to be more effective at keeping a healthier balance of bacteria in the gut than other yogurts. You will find them in supermarkets and natural food stores.
● Oats have a low glycaemic index, which means they are digested and absorbed slowly, producing a gentle, sustained rise in blood glucose levels.
● Hazelnuts are a particularly good source of vitamin E and most of the B vitamins, apart from B_{12}. Like most other nuts, except for chestnuts, they have a high fat content. This is, however, mostly the more beneficial monounsaturated fat.

Each serving provides Ⓥ
cals 366, **protein** 11 g, **fat** 12 g (of which saturated fat 2 g), **carbohydrate** 56 g (of which sugars 37 g), **fiber** 5.7 g

✓✓	B_1, C, E, calcium, copper, zinc
✓	B_2, B_6, B_{12}, folate, niacin, iron, potassium

Breakfast

Blueberry and Cranberry Granola

This delicious toasted cereal is made from a mix of grains, nuts, seeds, and colorful berries.
Stirring maple syrup and orange juice into the granola helps to keep the oil content down,
making this version much lower in fat than most "crunchy" cereals you buy.

Makes about 1 pound 2 ounces

2¾ cups oatmeal

½ cup wheat germ

7 tablespoons millet flakes

2 tablespoons sunflower seeds

2 tablespoons slivered almonds

1 tablespoon sesame seeds

½ cup dried blueberries

½ cup dried cranberries

1 tablespoon soft light brown sugar

2 tablespoons maple syrup

2 tablespoons sunflower oil

2 tablespoons orange juice

Preparation time: 40 to 50 minutes, plus
cooling

1 Preheat the oven to 325°F. In a large bowl, combine the oats, wheat germ, millet flakes, sunflower seeds, almonds, sesame seeds, dried berries, and sugar. Stir until well mixed.

2 Put the maple syrup, oil, and orange juice in a measuring jug and whisk together. Pour this mixture slowly into the dry ingredients, stirring until the liquid is evenly distributed and coats everything lightly.

3 Spread out the mixture evenly in a nonstick roasting pan. Bake until slightly crisp and lightly brown, 30 to 40 minutes, stirring every 10 minutes to encourage even browning.

4 Remove the roasting pan from the oven and leave the granola to cool. Store in an airtight container up to 2 weeks. Serve with plain yogurt, milk, or fruit juice.

Plus Points

• This is a delicious way to eat plenty of fiber, B vitamins, and essential fatty acids. Wheat germ is especially rich in B vitamins.

• A special feature of this recipe is the use of sunflower seeds, which not only add flavor, but are also a rich source of nutrients. They are rich in polyunsaturated fat, and also provide plenty of magnesium, copper, iron, and several B vitamins. Both sesame seeds and sunflower seeds provide useful amounts of calcium, which is particularly important for people who do not include milk or cheese in their diet.

Some More Ideas

• For a chunkier granola, replace the millet with barley flakes and the berries with a mixture of roughly chopped dried apples or apricots, prunes, and dates. A little shredded coconut can also be added, if liked.

• The maple syrup can be replaced with honey, and the slivered almonds with chopped hazelnuts.

• If you prefer, use all dried blueberries or cranberries, or replace some or all of the berries with dried cherries.

A 2 ounce serving provides

cals 250, **protein** 7 g, **fat** 11 g (of which saturated fat 0.8 g), **carbohydrate** 32 g (of which sugars 7 g), **fiber** 5 g

✓✓✓	E
✓✓	B₁
✓	B₂, B₆, folate, niacin

Breakfast

Apple and Hazelnut Pancakes

These thicker-than-usual pancakes make an almost instant sweet start to the day. The batter is made by simply stirring together a few basic ingredients, with hazelnuts and apples added for extra goodness. Top the pancakes with maple syrup.

Makes 16 pancakes

⅓ cup chopped skinned hazelnuts

1⅔ cups all-purpose flour

½ teaspoon baking soda

Pinch salt

2 tablespoons sugar

1 extra large egg

1 cup buttermilk

1 dessert apple, about 5 ounces, cored and finely chopped

1 tablespoon sunflower oil

4 tablespoons maple syrup

Preparation time: 15 minutes
Cooking time: 20 minutes

Each pancake provides Ⓥ

cals 106, **protein** 3 g, **fat** 3 g (of which saturated fat 0.5 g), **carbohydrate** 18 g (of which sugars 8 g), **fiber** 0.9 g

✓✓　E

1 Heat a small, nonstick skillet. Add the hazelnuts and dry-fry until golden brown, stirring and tossing constantly: Take care not to overcook the nuts because they burn easily. Tip the nuts into a small bowl.

2 Sift the flour, baking soda, salt, and sugar into a large mixing bowl and make a well in the middle. Lightly beat the egg with the buttermilk. Pour into the well and gradually whisk the flour mixture into the buttermilk mixture to make a smooth, thick batter. Stir in the apple and toasted hazelnuts.

3 Lightly brush a griddle or heavy-bottomed skillet with a little of the sunflower oil, then heat over medium heat. Depending on the size of the griddle or skillet, cook about 4 pancakes at the same time. For each one, drop a heaped tablespoon batter onto the hot surface. Bubbles will rise to the surface and burst. Gently slip a small metal spatula under the pancakes to loosen, then cook until the undersides are golden brown, about 1 minute longer. Turn the pancakes over and cook the other sides until golden, 1 to 2 minutes.

4 Remove the pancakes from the griddle or skillet and keep warm under a clean cloth. Cook the rest of the batter in the same way.

5 When all the pancakes are cooked, quickly warm the maple syrup in a small saucepan over medium heat. Drizzle the syrup over the warm pancakes.

Some More Ideas

● For Apricot and Walnut or Pecan Pancakes, use ½ cup chopped ready-to-eat dried apricots instead of the apple, and ⅓ cup walnuts or pecans instead of the hazelnuts.

● Make Fresh Berry Pancakes by adding ⅔ cup blackberries or raspberries to the batter in place of the apple, and seasoning with a good pinch of apple-pie spice. Omit the hazelnuts, if you prefer.

Plus Points

● Buttermilk is the liquid left over after cream has been turned into butter by churning. Contrary to its name, buttermilk does not contain butterfat, but it does provide protein, minerals, and milk sugar or lactose, as well as a delightfully piquant taste.

● Eating apples with their skins offers the maximum amount of fiber. Research has shown that apples can also help the teeth because they appear to prevent gum disease.

● Hazelnuts are rich in the essential fatty acids, that are vital for normal tissue growth and development.

Breakfast

Blueberry Popovers

A sweet version of this all-American classic is perfect for breakfast or brunch. The batter is baked in muffin pans, or special popover pans available in cookware stores. Serve the popovers with sweet, fresh berries to add extra vitamin C.

Serves 4 (makes 8 popovers)

1 teaspoon butter
1 cup all-purpose flour
Pinch salt
1 teaspoon sugar
2 large eggs
1 cup low-fat (2%) milk
½ cup blueberries
1 tablespoon confectioners' sugar

Mixed Berry Salad

Heaping 1 cup raspberries
⅔ cup blueberries
1⅓ cups strawberries, hulled and thickly
    sliced
1 tablespoon confectioners' sugar

Preparation time: 20 minutes
Cooking time: 25 to 30 minutes

Each serving provides Ⓥ

cals 275, **protein** 10 g, **fat** 6 g (of which saturated fat 2 g), **carbohydrate** 45 g (of which sugars 19 g), **fiber** 7.5 g

✓✓✓	C
✓✓	B₁₂
✓	A, B₁, B₂, folate, niacin, calcium, copper, iron, potassium, zinc

1 Preheat the oven to 425°F. Using a piece of crumpled paper towel and the butter, lightly grease 8 of the cups in a nonstick muffin tray.

2 To make the popovers, sift the flour, salt, and sugar into a large mixing bowl and make a well in the middle. Break the eggs into the well, add the milk, and beat together with a fork.

3 Using a wire whisk, gradually work the flour into the liquid to make a smooth batter that has the consistency of light cream. Pour into a large measuring jug.

4 Divide the batter evenly between the prepared muffin cups—they should each be about two-thirds full. Drop a few of the blueberries into the batter in each cup, dividing the berries equally between the popovers.

5 Bake in the middle of the oven until the popovers are golden brown, well risen, and crisp around the edges, 25 to 30 minutes.

6 Meanwhile, make the berry salad. Puree two-thirds of the raspberries by pressing them through a nylon sifter into a bowl. Add the remainder of the raspberries to the bowl, together with the blueberries and strawberries. Sift the confectioners' sugar over the fruit and fold gently together so all the ingredients are mixed.

7 Unmold the popovers using a round-bladed knife, and dust with the confectioners' sugar. Serve hot, with the berry salad.

Some More Ideas

● Use frozen blueberries, thawed and well drained. You can also use thawed frozen raspberries and blueberries for the berry salad.
● For a baked sweet batter dessert, make the batter as in the main recipe. Add 4 tablespoons sparkling mineral water or cold water. Pour into a 1 to 1¾ quart shallow baking dish that has been lightly greased with butter; omit the blueberries. Bake at 425°F until crisp and well risen, 30 to 35 minutes. Spoon the berry salad into the middle of the hot pudding, scatter 2 tablespoons toasted slivered almonds over, dust with the confectioners' sugar, and serve.

Plus Points

● Blueberries, like cranberries, contain antibacterial compounds called anthocyanins. These are effective against the *E. coli* bacteria that cause gastrointestinal disorders and urinary tract infections.
● Eating raspberries is believed by many to be beneficial in cleansing and detoxifying the digestive system. It is also thought to help with the discomfort of indigestion.

Apple and Blackberry Brioches

An irresistible start to the day—toasted brioche slices topped with caramelized apple rings and fresh blackberries, with a hint of cinnamon. Brioche has a slightly higher fat content than white bread, but it is still a deliciously healthy source of starchy carbohydrate.

Serves 4

2 tablespoons butter

4 apples

½ teaspoon cinnamon

4 individual brioches

1⅓ cups fresh blackberries

4 teaspoons soft light brown sugar

Preparation and cooking time: 15 minutes

1 Preheat the broiler to high. Line the broiler pan with foil, put the butter on it, and position it under the broiler to melt; do not turn off the broiler. Meanwhile, core the apples and slice each one into 6 rings, discarding the outer edge pieces. Dip the apple rings in the melted butter to coat both sides, then lay them in a single layer on the foil and sprinkle with the cinnamon.

2 Broil the apple rings until they are starting to brown, turning them over once, about 4 minutes. Remove the apples from the broiler pan; set aside.

3 Slice each brioche horizontally into 3 slices. Arrange the slices in the broiler pan and toast lightly on both sides. Place 2 apple rings on top of each brioche slice, add a few blackberries, and sprinkle with sugar. Broil 4 inches from the heat to warm the berries, for 2 to 3 minutes. Serve hot.

Some More Ideas

• For another breakfast that is higher in energy, make delicious Banana and Raspberry Toasts. Toast 4 slices of white, wholewheat or challah bread. Arrange 2 large sliced bananas and ¾ cup raspberries on top, covering the toast right up to the edges. Top with 2 tablespoons diced butter and sprinkle each with 1 teaspoon soft light brown sugar. Broil them until they start to brown and caramelize.

• Try Orange and Strawberry-topped Muffins. Toast 4 split wholewheat muffins, then top with 2 segmented oranges, and halved strawberries. Sprinkle each muffin with 2 teaspoons soft brown sugar. Broil until the fruit sizzles.

• Pancakes can also be topped with sliced kiwi fruit and orange, or strawberries and grapes.

Plus Points

• Apples contribute pectin, a soluble fiber that helps to reduce the highs and lows in blood sugar levels, and also helps to lower blood cholesterol. This makes apples a great start to the day.

• Blackberries are a useful source of the antioxidant vitamin E, which might help to protect against heart disease and keep skin in good condition. They are also a good source of fiber and bioflavonoid compounds.

• A recent study of more than 2,500 middle-age men living in Britain found that those who ate 5 or more apples per week had stronger lungs than those men who did not eat any apples. Apples contain high levels of a flavonoid called quercetin (also found in onions, tea, and red wine), which is thought to have a strong antioxidant effect and might help to protect the lungs from damage.

Each serving provides ⓥ

cals 280, **protein** 5 g, **fat** 10 g (of which saturated fat 6 g), **carbohydrate** 44 g (of which sugars 31 g), **fiber** 7 g

✓✓	C, E
✓	B₆

Breakfast Muffins

Muffins are perfect for breakfast, providing the energy boost the body needs to get going. This particular recipe is packed full of good ingredients that add fiber, vitamins, and minerals, too, but still keep the muffins low in calories.

Makes 12 muffins

⅔ cup wholewheat flour

¾ cup plus 2 tablespoons all-purpose flour

2 teaspoons baking soda

Pinch salt

¼ teaspoon cinnamon

¼ cup packed dark brown sugar

5 tablespoons wheat germ

1 cup packed raisins

1 cup plain low-fat yogurt

4 tablespoons sunflower oil

1 large egg

Grated zest of ½ orange

3 tablespoons orange juice

Preparation time: 15 minutes
Cooking time: 15 to 20 minutes

1 Preheat the oven to 400°F. Grease a 12-cup muffin tray.

2 Sift the wholewheat and all-purpose flours, baking soda, salt, and cinnamon into a large bowl, tipping in any bran left in the sieve. Stir in the sugar, wheat germ, and raisins, and make a well in the middle.

3 Lightly whisk together the yogurt, oil, egg, and orange zest and juice. Pour the liquid ingredients into the well in the flour mixture and stir together, mixing only enough to moisten the dry ingredients: Do not beat or overmix.

4 Spoon the batter into the muffin tray, dividing it equally between the cups. Bake until the muffins are well risen and just firm to the touch, 15 to 20 minutes. Leave them to cool in the tray 2 to 3 minutes, then turn out onto a wire rack. The muffins are best eaten freshly baked, preferably still slightly warm from the oven, but can be cooled completely and stored in an airtight container up to 2 days.

Some More Ideas

• Substitute chopped prunes or dried dates for the raisins.

• For Carrot and Spice Muffins, replace the cinnamon with 1½ teaspoons apple-pie spice. Stir 1 cup grated carrot into the flour mixture with the wheat germ, and reduce the amount of raisins to packed ⅔ cup.

• To make Blueberry and Walnut Muffins, use 1⅓ cups blueberries, add ¾ cup chopped walnuts, and omit the raisins.

Plus Points

• Breakfast is a good opportunity to kick-off your fiber intake for the day, which is why eating a high-fiber cereal is usually recommended. These muffins are another good choice, as they offer plenty of dietary fiber from the wholewheat flour, wheat germ, and raisins.

• Wheat germ is the embryo of the wheat grain and as such it contains a high concentration of nutrients, intended to nourish the growing plant. Wheat germ is a good source of folate, vitamin B_6, vitamin E, zinc, and magnesium. (Once you open a container, store it in the refrigerator and use within 6 months to prevent it spoiling.)

Each muffin provides

cals 180, **protein** 4 g, **fat** 5 g (of which saturated fat 1 g), **carbohydrate** 31 g (of which sugars 17 g), **fiber** 2 g

✓ B_1, B_6, E, calcium, iron, selenium, zinc

Scrambled Eggs with Smoked Salmon and Dill

Here's a healthy way to scramble eggs—cook them in the top of a double saucepan or in a bowl over simmering water, without any butter, and then stir in crème fraîche. You get a deliciously creamy result that is lower in calories than conventionally scrambled eggs.

Serves 4

6 large eggs

3 tablespoons low-fat (2%) milk

6 plum tomatoes, halved lengthwise

4 thick slices wholewheat bread

3 tablespoons cultured crème fraîche

2½ ounces sliced smoked salmon, cut into thin strips

1 teaspoon fresh lemon juice

1 tablespoon chopped fresh dill

Salt and fresh-ground black pepper

Fresh dill sprigs

Preparation time: 10 minutes

Cooking time: 10 minutes

Each serving provides

cals 363, **protein** 22 g, **fat** 21 g (of which saturated fat 9 g), **carbohydrate** 24 g (of which sugars 6 g), **fiber** 6 g

✓✓✓	A, B₁₂
✓✓	C, E, niacin, selenium, zinc
✓	B₁, B₂, B₆, folate, calcium, copper, iron, potassium

1 Lightly beat the eggs together with the milk in the top of a double saucepan or a heatproof bowl. Set over a saucepan containing barely simmering water—the bottom of the pan or bowl should just touch the water. Cook until the eggs begin to thicken, stirring frequently, 6 to 8 minutes.

2 Preheat the broiler to high. While the eggs are cooking, arrange the tomatoes, cut side up, on the broiler pan rack and sprinkle them with a little salt and pepper. Add the bread slices to the rack. Broil until the tomatoes are lightly brown and the bread is toasted on both sides, 4 to 5 minutes, turning the bread over after about 2 minutes.

3 Add the crème fraîche to the eggs, and season with salt and pepper to taste. Cook, stirring constantly, until the mixture is softly scrambled, about 1 minute longer. Sprinkle the smoked salmon with the lemon juice, then add this to the eggs together with the chopped dill. Immediately remove the scrambled eggs from the heat.

4 Place the toast on warm serving plates and divide the smoked salmon scramble between them. Garnish each with a sprig of dill. Add 3 broiled tomato halves to each plate, and serve.

Some More Ideas

• Serve on slices of pumpernickel bread.

• For a ham and egg scramble, replace the salmon with smoked ham, and use chopped fresh flat-leaf parsley instead of dill.

• Make Indian Scrambled Eggs, a spicy version. Melt 1 tablespoon butter in a nonstick saucepan over medium heat. Add 2 teaspoons grated fresh ginger, 1 seeded and finely chopped fresh red chile, and ¼ teaspoon each ground cumin and ground coriander and sauté 1 minute. Stir in the egg and milk mixture, and cook over low heat, stirring constantly, until softly scrambled. Stir in 3 tablespoons thick plain yogurt, 4 chopped and seeded tomatoes and 1 tablespoon chopped fresh cilantra. Serve hot, with warm naan bread.

Plus Points

• Salmon contains omega-3 fatty acids, a type of polyunsaturated fat that might help to protect against heart disease and strokes.

• Crème fraîche is a slightly tangy thickened cream, widely available in Europe but less so here. To make it, mix 1 tablespoon buttermilk per 1 cup cream (or lower fat cream—15% milk fat), and let ferment for 24 hours at 80°F (22°C), or use sour cream instead.

Breakfast

Herbed French Toast

Give breakfast a twist with this savory version of French toast. Triangles of bread are dipped into a herb-and-egg mixture, then pan-fried until golden. Serve with tasty "meaty" mushrooms and lean bacon, both broiled to limit the calorie intake.

Serves 4

4 extra large eggs
4 tablespoons low-fat (2%) milk
1 tablespoon finely chopped parsley
1 tablespoon finely snipped fresh chives
½ tablespoon chopped fresh thyme, or a
   pinch of dried thyme
Pinch paprika (optional)
4 large portobella mushrooms or large flat
   mushrooms, about 8 ounces in total
3 tablespoons sunflower oil
4 slicers Canadian bacon, trimmed of fat
5 thick slices white bread
Salt and fresh-ground black pepper

Preparation and cooking time: about 25 minutes

Each serving provides

cals 349, protein 19 g, fat 19 g (of which saturated fat 4 g), carbohydrate 28 g (of which sugars 2 g), fiber 3.2 g

✓✓✓	B₁₂, copper, selenium
✓✓	B₁, B₂, E, niacin, zinc
✓	A, B₆, folate, calcium, iron, potassium

1 Combine the eggs, milk, most of the parsley, the chives, thyme, and paprika, if using, in a shallow dish. Season to taste; set aside.

2 Preheat the broiler to medium-high. Remove the stems from the mushrooms. Using 1 tablespoon of the oil, lightly brush the gill sides of the mushroom cups. Place them gill side up on the broiler rack. Add the bacon to the broiler rack. Broil the mushrooms until tender, and the bacon until crisp, 6 to 7 minutes for the mushrooms and about 10 minutes for the bacon, turning the slices over after about 5 minutes. When they are all cooked, remove them from the broiler pan and keep warm.

3 Meanwhile, cut each slice of bread into 4 triangles. Heat a large, nonstick skillet over medium heat. Add 1 tablespoon of oil. Dip about one-third of the bread triangles into the egg mixture to moisten both sides, then put into the hot pan. Cook until golden brown on both sides, 1 to 2 minutes. Remove from the pan and keep warm while you cook the rest of the bread, adding the remaining oil as needed.

4 To serve, arrange 5 triangles of French toast on each plate. Cut the mushrooms into thick slices and add to the plates, together with the bacon. Sprinkle with the remaining parsley.

Another Idea

● For Sweet Orange French Toast, first make a fresh fruit compote to serve alongside, in place of the bacon and mushrooms. Combine 2 cups raspberries and 2 thinly sliced ripe peaches in a bowl; cover and set aside. Gently whisk 3 large eggs with 3 tablespoons low-fat (2%) milk and the finely grated zest of 1 large orange. Cut 8 slices of brioche loaf, each about ¼ inch thick, then cut each slice in half. Dip into the egg mixture and cook in batches as in the main recipe. Serve the hot French toast topped with the fruit compote and 1 tablespoon thick plain yogurt per serving.

Plus Points

● This hearty breakfast dish contains fewer calories than the traditional version, which is often served with melting butter and maple syrup.

● Wholewheat bread is often considered to be healthier than white bread, but, in fact, all breads are important sources of starchy carbohydrate. Also, white bread has calcium added and so contains more of this important mineral than wholewheat bread.

Breakfast

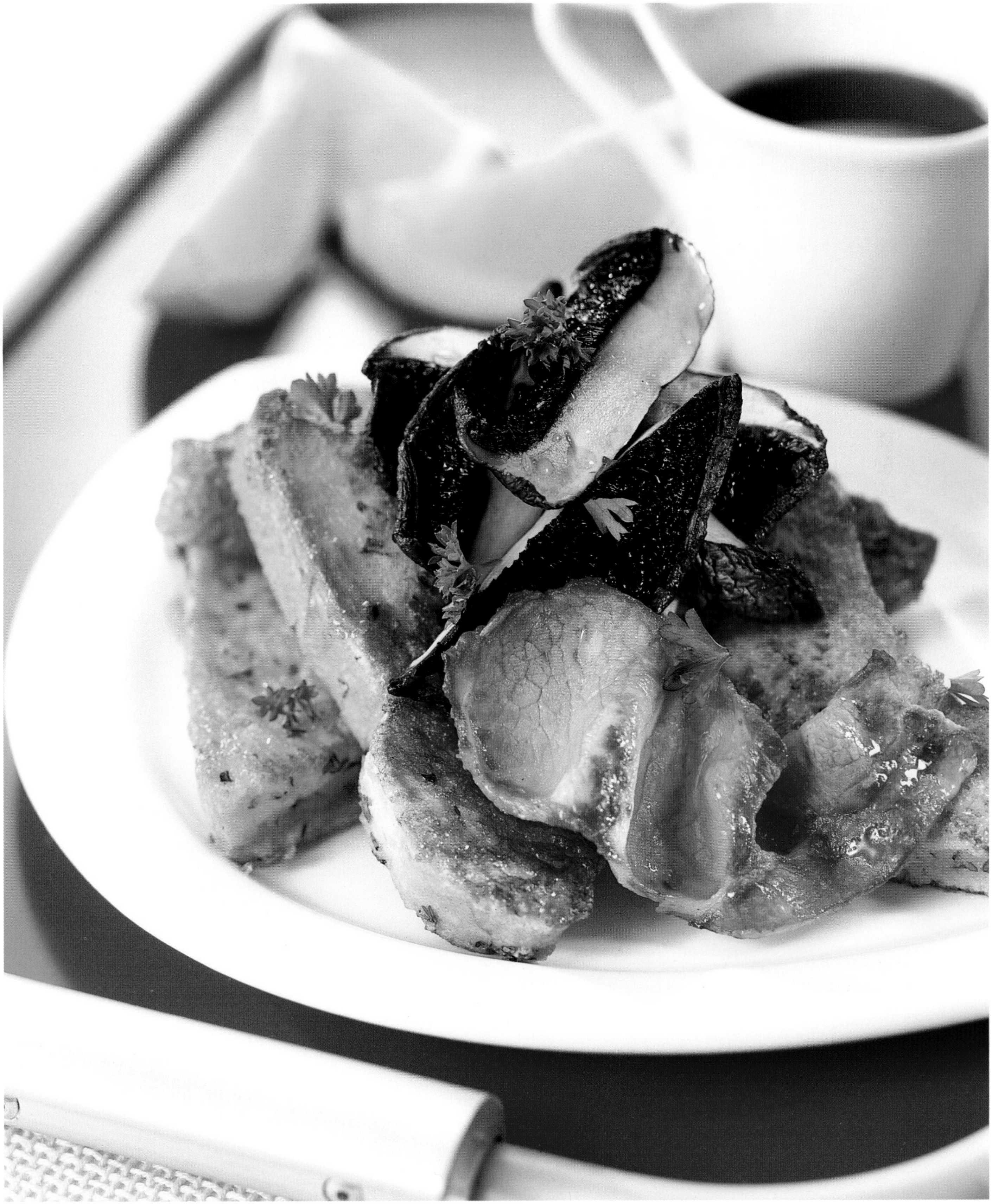

Snacks

Good news for snackers. A recent study suggests grazing might be healthy, because eating more frequently can lower blood cholesterol levels. So there is no need to feel guilty when sampling goodies, such as Ginger Cookies or even Double Chocolate Chunk and Nut Cookies, provided you eat them within a balanced diet. Nutritious savory treats include crispy Sesame-Cheese Twists, Baked Potato Skins with Smoked Salmon and Fresh Dill, and Tuscan Bean Crostini.

Cereal Bars

Naturally sweet and moist, these delicious bars provide a great energy boost at any time of the day. They are also a good way of coaxing family members to try more unusual grains and seeds, adding new, healthy ingredients to their daily diet.

Makes 14 bars

2 tablespoons sunflower seeds

2 tablespoons pumpkin seeds

2 tablespoons flaxseeds

2 bananas, about 10 ounces in total, weighed with their skins on

7 tablespoons unsalted butter

3 tablespoons light corn syrup

7 tablespoons millet flakes

1¼ cups oatmeal

⅔ cup roughly chopped pitted dates

Preparation time: 25 minutes

Cooking time: 30 minutes

1 Preheat the oven to 350°F. Grease an 11 x 7 x 1½ inch cake pan and line the bottom with parchment paper; set aside. Roughly chop the sunflower seeds, pumpkin seeds, and flaxseeds. Peel and roughly mash the bananas.

2 Melt the butter in a large saucepan over medium heat. Stir in the corn syrup. Add the seeds and bananas, together with the millet flakes, oatmeal, and dates and stir together. Spoon the mixture into the pan and smooth the surface.

3 Bake until golden brown, about 30 minutes. Leave to cool in the pan for 5 minutes, then mark into 14 bars and leave to cool completely. The bars keep in an airtight container up to 2 days.

Some More Ideas

• Instead of dates, use chopped ready-to-eat dried apricots or prunes, or a mixture of chopped dried fruits.

• Replace the millet flakes with all-purpose or wholewheat flour.

• The cereal bars can be frozen up to 2 months. Wrap them individually in freezer wrap or foil. Then, if you simply pack a frozen bar into a plastic container along with wrapped sandwiches, it will have thawed by lunchtime.

Plus Points

• Naturally occurring fruit sugars found in bananas and dates are released slowly into the blood stream by the body, giving a more sustained energy boost. Extrinsic or "added" sugars (such as table sugar, honey, and corn syrup), on the other hand, are quickly absorbed and burned up by the body.

• Seeds are a rich source of protein and are particularly valuable for those following a vegetarian diet.

• Flaxseeds are an excellent source of omega-3 fatty acids, essential for brain and eye development in a fetus.

Each bar provides Ⓥ

cals 190, **protein** 3 g, **fat** 10 g (of which saturated fat 4 g), **carbohydrate** 24 g (of which sugars 9 g), **fiber** 1.6 g

✓ A, B$_1$, B$_6$, E, copper, zinc

Snacks

Ginger Cookies

Here's a healthier, less-fatty version of a traditional favorite cookie. Bake simple round cookies, or use fancy cutters and encourage children to stamp out gingerbread figures and shapes. Whatever the shape, these spicy, crunchy cookies taste terrific.

Makes 12 cookies

⅔ cup all-purpose flour

⅔ cup wholewheat flour

½ teaspoon baking soda

2 teaspoons ground ginger

½ teaspoon ground cinnamon

3 tablespoons butter

4 tablespoons light corn syrup

Preparation time: 15 minutes

Cooking time: 8 to 10 minutes

1 Preheat the oven to 375°F. Grease a cookie sheet; set aside. Sift the all-purpose and wholewheat flours, baking soda, ginger, and cinnamon into a large bowl, tipping in any bran left in the sieve.

2 Melt the butter with the corn syrup in a small saucepan over low heat, stirring occasionally. Pour the melted mixture onto the dry ingredients and stir to bind them together into a firm dough.

3 Break off a walnut-sized lump of dough and roll it into a ball on the palm of your hand. Press it flat into a thick cookie, about 2½ inches in diameter, and place on the cookie sheet. Repeat with the remaining dough. (Or roll out the dough and stamp out decorative shapes; see Some More Ideas, right.)

4 Bake the cookies until they are slightly risen and brown, 8 to 10 minutes. Leave to cool on the cookie sheet until they are firm enough to lift without breaking, 2 to 3 minutes. Transfer the cookies to a wire rack to cool completely. The cookies will keep in an airtight container up to 5 days.

Some More Ideas

• Instead of shaping the cookies by hand, roll out the dough on a lightly floured board until ¼ inch thick, and use shaped cutters to stamp out cookies. Bake 5 to 7 minutes.

• For Oat and Orange-Ginger Cookies, replace half the wholewheat flour with ½ cup oatmeal. Add the grated zest of 1 orange with the melted mixture, and use 1 to 2 tablespoons orange juice to bind the mixture into a dough. Roll into balls, shape, and bake as in the main recipe.

• For Fruity Ginger Cookies, peel, core, and coarsely grate 1 dessert apple, and add to the flour mixture with ⅓ cup golden raisins and the grated zest of 1 lemon. Shape and bake as in the main recipe.

Plus Points

• Making your own cookies means you can include some wholewheat flour and control the amount of fat and sugar you use. Commercial cookies are often very sugary and might also be high in hydrogenated fats.

• Ginger is a traditional remedy for nausea and can sometimes ease morning sickness in pregnancy. It is also known as an aid to digestion and circulatory problems.

Each biscuit provides

cals 90, **protein** 2 g, **fat** 4 g (of which saturated fat 2 g), **carbohydrate** 14 g (of which sugars 4 g), **fiber** 1.5 g

Apple and Muesli Mounds

A small amount diced apple makes these snacks moist and fruity, and a perfect replacement for store-bought cookies. Easy to prepare, these cookies are ideal to make with children, who will enjoy making these nutritious treats as much as eating them.

Makes 24 cakes

1¾ cups self-rising flour

7 tablespoons unsalted butter, cut into small pieces

¼ cup packed soft light brown sugar, plus a little extra to sprinkle

1 teaspoon cinnamon

2 dessert apples, peeled and diced

¾ cup sugar-free muesli

1 large egg, beaten

4 to 5 tablespoons low-fat (2%) milk, as needed

Preparation time: 20 minutes
Cooking time: 15 minutes

1 Preheat the oven to 375°F. Lightly grease 2 cookie sheets; set aside. Put the flour into a bowl. Add the butter and rub it in with your fingertips until the mixture resembles fine bread crumbs.

2 Stir in the sugar, cinnamon, apples, and muesli. Add the egg and stir it in with enough milk to bind the dough together roughly.

3 Drop generous tablespoonfuls of the dough onto the cookie sheets, leaving space around each mound, and sprinkle with a little extra sugar. Bake until golden and firm to the touch, about 15 minutes.

4 Transfer to a wire rack to cool, and serve warm or cold. The rock cakes keep in an airtight container up to 2 days.

Some More Ideas

● Replace the muesli with a mixture of 3 tablespoons oatmeal, 2 tablespoons sesame or sunflower seeds, and 4 tablespoons roughly chopped hazelnuts or almonds.

● For Tropical Mounds, replace the apples, muesli, and cinnamon with ⅔ cup shredded coconut and 1 cup chopped ready-to-eat exotic dried fruits, including pineapple, papaya, and mango.

Plus Points

● Apples are a good source of vitamin C and soluble fiber (in the form of pectin), as well as offering a flavonoid called quercetin, which is thought to have a potent antioxidant effect.

● Adding muesli to baked goods is a good way to increase their fiber content.

● Children need healthy snacks to boost their energy and nutritional needs, and these mounds are much better than sugar-laden commercial cookies or salty potato chips.

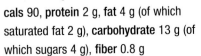

Each cake provides

cals 90, **protein** 2 g, **fat** 4 g (of which saturated fat 2 g), **carbohydrate** 13 g (of which sugars 4 g), **fiber** 0.8 g

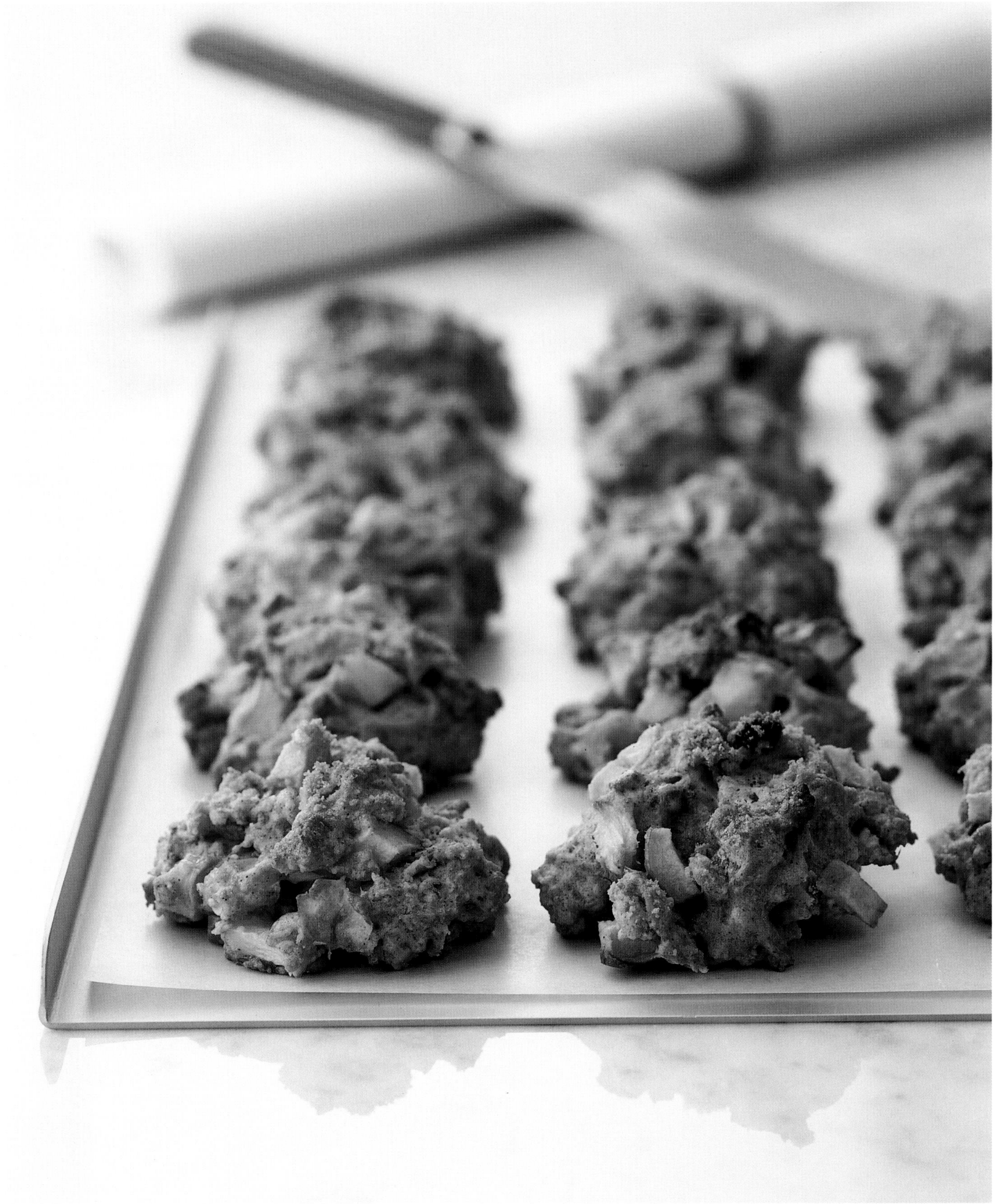

Orange and Pecan Cookies

These are "slice-and-bake" cookies—the roll of dough can be prepared in advance and kept in the refrigerator. Then, whenever you want these energy-boosting cookies, simply slice the roll, top with pecan nuts, and bake.

Makes 24 cookies

½ cup plus 1½ tablespoons wholewheat flour, plus extra for kneading

½ cup plus 1 tablespoon self-rising flour

⅓ cup packed soft light brown sugar

½ cup ground rice

¼ cup chopped pecan nuts

Grated zest of 1 orange

4 tablespoons sunflower oil

1 extra large egg

24 pecan nut halves to decorate

Preparation time: 15 minutes, plus 2 hours chilling

Cooking time: 8 to 10 minutes

1 Put the wholewheat and self-rising flours, sugar, ground rice, chopped pecan nuts, and orange zest in a medium bowl, and stir until combined.

2 In a small bowl, beat the oil and egg together with a fork. Add this mixture to the dry ingredients and mix with a fork until a dough forms.

3 Knead the dough very lightly on a floured surface until smooth, then roll into a rope shape about 12 inches long. Wrap in plastic and chill at least 2 hours. (The dough can be kept in the refrigerator 2 to 3 days before slicing and baking.)

4 Preheat the oven to 350°F. Unwrap the roll of dough and lightly reshape to a neat rope, if necessary.

5 Using a sharp knife, slice the roll crosswise into 24 slices. Arrange the slices, spaced apart, on 2 large nonstick cookie sheets. Top each with a pecan half, pressing it in slightly.

6 Bake until firm to the touch and lightly golden, about 10 minutes. Transfer the cookies to a wire rack to cool completely. They keep in an airtight container up to 5 days.

Some More Ideas

● Instead of the sunflower oil, use ¼ cup (½ stick) melted butter.

● Chopped hazelnuts can be used in place of the pecans, with whole hazelnuts to decorate.

● To make Almond-Polenta Cookies, mix ½ cup instant polenta with ¾ cup confectioners' sugar and 1 cup less 1 tablespoon self-rising flour. Cut in ¼ cup (½ stick) butter until the mixture resembles bread crumbs. Beat 1 extra large egg with ½ teaspoon almond extract, add to the mixture and mix into a soft dough. Roll, wrap, and chill as in the main recipe. Before baking, scatter ¼ cup slivered almonds over the slices.

Plus Points

● Like other nuts, pecans are rich in fat— up to 70 g per 3 ounces—but little of this is saturated fat, the majority being present as monounsaturated fat. Pecans also provide generous amounts of vitamin E, in addition to dietary fiber.

● Sunflower oil is one of the most widely used vegetable oils in baking because of its mild flavor, and it works well in cookies and other baked goods in place of saturated fats such as butter. It is a particularly good source of vitamin E, a powerful antioxidant. Always read the label carefully, however, several types of sunflower oil have different fat compositions.

Each cookie provides

cals 106, **protein** 2 g, **fat** 7 g (of which saturated fat 1 g), **carbohydrate** 9 g (of which sugars 4 g), **fiber** 0.5 g

✓✓	E
✓	copper

Snacks

44

Fruit and Nut Bread

This fruited German-style loaf is especially good served thickly sliced, or lightly toasted and buttered. It contains no added fat (the fat present comes from the nuts), but the dried fruits give it a rich, moist texture and good keeping qualities.

Makes 1 round loaf (cuts into about 10 slices)

3¼ cups bread flour

½ teaspoon salt

Fresh-grated zest of ½ lemon

1 envelope (¼ ounce) quick-rising yeast

⅔ cup roughly chopped dried apricots

⅔ cup roughly chopped dried pears

½ cup roughly chopped pitted prunes

⅓ cup roughly chopped dried figs

½ cup chopped mixed nuts, such as almonds, hazelnuts, and cashews

1 cup water (120° to 130°F)

Preparation time: 50 minutes, plus 2½ to 3 hours rising

Cooking time: 30 to 40 minutes

Each slice provides Ⓥ

cals 220, **protein** 6 g, **fat** 3 g (of which saturated fat 0.2 g), **carbohydrate** 44 g (of which sugars 14 g), **fiber** 6 g

✓ B₁, B₆, E, folate, copper, iron, potassium, zinc

1 Stir the flour with the salt, lemon zest, and yeast in a large bowl. Stir in the chopped fruits and nuts. Stir in the water and work the mixture with your hand to make a soft-textured, heavy dough.

2 Turn out the dough onto a lightly floured work surface and knead until it feels pliable, about 10 minutes. Place the dough in a lightly greased bowl, cover with a damp dishtowel, and leave to rise in a warm place until double in size, 1½ to 2 hours, depending on the temperature.

3 Turn out the risen dough onto the floured work surface and punch it down with your knuckles to return it to its original size. Gently knead the dough into a neat ball shape, then set it on a well-greased baking sheet. Cover with a damp dishtowel and leave to rise in a warm place until double in size, about 1 hour depending on the temperature.

4 Toward the end of the rising time, preheat the oven to 400°F. Uncover the loaf and bake until it is lightly brown and sounds hollow when tapped on the bottom, 30 to 40 minutes; cover with foil if the top is becoming too brown. Transfer to a wire rack and leave to cool. This bread keeps well up to 5 days.

Another Idea

• To make Spicy Fruit Buns, add 2 teaspoons apple-pie spice and ¼ teaspoon fresh-grated nutmeg to the flour with the salt. Omit the lemon zest. After the first rising, divide the dough into 12 equal portions. Shape them into neat balls (see Basic loaf, Some more ideas, page 211), then set them, spaced well apart, on greased baking sheets and leave to rise until double in size, about 45 minutes. Bake until they sound hollow when tapped on the bottom, about 25 minutes.

Plus Points

• Dried apricots are an excellent ingredient to have on hand in the cupboard, because they are very nutritious—an excellent source of beta-carotene and a useful source of calcium—and versatile. They can be used in cakes, cookies, quick breads, and sweet yeasted breads, as well as making a delicious addition to many breakfast cereals, stews, and casseroles. And they are ideal for a healthy snack.

• Like all nuts, cashews are rich in protein and unsaturated fats. Cashews also provide useful amounts of iron, zinc, and folate.

Double Chocolate Chunk and Nut Cookies

These cookies are simply irresistible when eaten warm while the chocolate chunks are still soft and melting. Macadamia nuts, with their buttery flavor, add a crunchy texture. Like the chocolate, the nuts should be used in fairly large pieces.

Makes 12 cookies

½ cup (1 stick) unsalted butter, softened

6 tablespoons packed soft light brown sugar

½ teaspoon vanilla extract

1 large egg, beaten

⅔ cup self-rising white flour

½ cup wholewheat flour

3½ tablespoons unsweetened cocoa powder

¼ teaspoon baking powder

¼ teaspoon salt

4 ounces semisweet chocolate (at least 70% cocoa solids), roughly chopped

½ cup roughly chopped macadamia nuts

3 tablespoons low-fat (2%) milk

Preparation time: 20 minutes
Cooking time: 15 minutes

1 Preheat the oven to 375°F. Line 2 cookie sheets completely with parchment paper.

2 Beat the butter with the sugar and vanilla extract in a large bowl until light and fluffy. Gradually add the egg, beating well after each addition.

3 Sift the self-rising and wholewheat flours, cocoa powder, baking powder, and salt over the creamed mixture, tipping in any bran left in the sifter. Add the chocolate, nuts, and milk, and mix everything together.

4 Place tablespoons of the batter on the cookie sheets, arranging the cookies 1½ inches apart so there is space for them to spread during baking. Flatten the cookies slightly with the back of a fork. Bake until they feel soft and springy, about 15 minutes.

5 Leave on the cookie sheets for a few minutes, then transfer to a wire rack. Serve while still slightly warm or leave until cold. The cookies will keep in an airtight container up to 5 days.

Some More Ideas

● Use walnuts or pecan nuts instead of macadamia nuts.

● For cherry and almond cookies, use all-purpose flour instead of the cocoa powder, and substitute ½ cup dried sour cherries and ½ cup silvered almonds for the chocolate chunks and macadamia nuts. If you want a pronounced almond flavor, use ¼ teaspoon pure almond extract instead of the vanilla.

Plus Points

● Semisweet chocolate is a good source of copper and provides useful amounts of iron. The scientific name of the cocoa bean tree is *Theobroma cacao*, which means "the food of the gods." Casanova was reputed to drink hot chocolate before his nightly conquests—in fact, he was said to prefer chocolate to champagne.

● Butter contains useful amounts of the important fat-soluble vitamins A and D. Vitamin A is essential for healthy vision and skin, while vitamin D is needed for the formation of strong, healthy bones.

Each cookie provides ⓥ

cals 240, **protein** 3 g, **fat** 15 g (of which saturated fat 8 g), **carbohydrate** 22 g (of which sugars 13 g), **fiber** 1 g

✓   A, copper

Snacks

Sesame-Cheese Twists

These crisp cheese sticks are delicious served fresh from the oven. Enriched with egg yolks and flavored with Parmesan cheese, they are made with a combination of wholewheat and all-purpose flours, so they are substantial without being at all heavy.

Makes 40 sticks

½ cup plus 2 tablespoons wholewheat flour, preferably stoneground

⅔ cup all-purpose flour, plus extra for rolling

¼ teaspoon salt

3 tablespoons butter

½ cup freshly grated Parmesan cheese

1 extra large egg

2 tablespoons low-fat (2%) milk

1 teaspoon paprika

1 tablespoon sesame seeds

Preparation time: 10 to 15 minutes
Cooking time: 15 minutes

1 Preheat the oven to 350°F. Line a cookie sheet with parchment paper. Sift the flours and salt into a bowl, tipping in the bran left in the sifter. Rub in the butter until the mixture resembles fine bread crumbs. Stir in the Parmesan cheese.

2 Beat the egg and milk together. Reserve 1 teaspoon of the egg mixture, and stir the rest into the dry ingredients to make a firm dough. Knead on a lightly floured surface until smooth, a few seconds.

3 Sprinkle the paprika over the floured surface, then roll out the dough on it to form an 8 inch square; trim the edges to make them straight. Brush the dough with the reserved egg mixture and sprinkle the sesame seeds over. Cut the square of dough in half, then cut into forty 4 inch sticks that are about ½ inch wide.

4 Twist the sticks and place on the cookie sheet. Lightly press the ends of the sticks down so they do not untwist during baking.

5 Bake until lightly brown and crisp, about 15 minutes. Cool on the cookie sheet for a few minutes, then serve warm, or transfer to a wire rack to cool completely. The sticks will keep in an airtight tin up to 5 days.

Some More Ideas

● Use finely grated sharp cheddar cheese instead of the Parmesan.

● For Blue Cheese and Walnut Cookies, mash 1 ounce blue cheese, such as Gorgonzola, Stilton, or Danish blue, with 4 tablespoons softened butter. Sift ⅓ cup wholewheat flour, ¼ cup plus 1 tablespoon all-purpose flour, and 3½ tablespoons ground rice over, tipping in the bran left in the sifter. Add ¼ cup chopped toasted walnuts. Rub together, then knead lightly to form a dough. Shape into a roll about 5 inches long. Wrap in plastic wrap and chill for about 30 minutes. Cut into thin slices, arrange on a cookie sheet lined with parchment paper. Bake in a preheated 375°F oven 15 minutes. Transfer to a wire rack to cool. Makes about 16 cookies.

Plus Points

● Sesame seeds are a good source of calcium, as well as providing iron and zinc.

● Wholewheat flour has a lot to offer: Dietary fiber, B vitamins, and vitamin E, together with iron, selenium, and magnesium. Stoneground wholewheat flour has slightly more B vitamins than factory-milled wholewheat flour, because stonegrinding keeps the grain cool. Milling with metal rollers creates heat, which spoils some of the nutrients.

Each stick provides   Ⓥ

cals 32, **protein** 1 g, **fat** 2 g (of which saturated fat 1 g), **carbohydrate** 3 g (of which sugars 0.1 g), **fiber** 0.3 g

Snacks

Crudités with Three Dips

Few foods can be healthier than raw vegetable sticks, so make the most of them by serving them with tempting low-fat dips for a snack. You can also offer a selection of fruit and warm pita bread for dipping, as well as vegetables.

Serves 8

Pesto-Yogurt Dip

1 cup fresh basil leaves

1 garlic clove, crushed

1 tablespoon pine nuts

1 cup plus 2 tablespoons plain low-fat yogurt with active cultures

Fresh Herb Dip

¾ cup quark

1 scallion, minced

2 tablespoons chopped parsley

1 tablespoon finely snipped fresh chives

1 teaspoon tarragon vinegar

Italian-Style Tomato Dip

2 ounces sun-dried tomatoes (dry-packed)

⅓ cup packed cottage cheese

⅓ cup plain low-fat yogurt

½ cup fresh basil leaves

Salt and fresh-ground black pepper

To serve

1 pound mixed vegetable crudités, such as baby carrots, zucchini sticks, baby sweetcorn (blanched in boiling water for 1 minute), green beans (blanched for 1 minute), bell pepper strips, Belgian endive, and broccoli flowerets

Preparation time: 25 minutes, plus 30 minutes soaking

1 For the Pesto-Yogurt Dip, use a mortar and pestle to crush the basil, garlic, and pine nuts to a paste. Work in the yogurt a spoonful at a time, until thoroughly combined. Add seasoning to taste. Alternatively, purée all the ingredients together in a food processor or blender. Transfer to a bowl, cover, and chill until required.

2 For the Fresh Herb Dip, stir all the ingredients together in a bowl until blended. Cover tightly and chill until required.

3 For the Italian-Style Tomato Dip, place the sun-dried tomatoes in a heatproof bowl and pour boiling water to cover over. Leave to soak until the tomatoes are plump and tender, about 30 minutes. Drain the tomatoes well, then pat them dry and finely chop them.

4 Puree the cottage cheese with the yogurt in a food processor or blender. Alternatively, press the cheese through a sifter and stir in the yogurt. Transfer to a bowl and stir in the tomatoes. Cover and chill until required.

5 Just before serving the Italian-Style Tomato Dip, finely shred the basil and stir in with seasoning to taste.

6 Serve the bowls of dips on a large platter with the crudités arranged around them.

Plus Points

• Pine nuts are rich in a variety of minerals: Magnesium, potassium, iron, zinc, and copper.

• Dairy products, such as yogurt, quark and cottage cheese, are valuable sources of calcium. This mineral is essential for the structure of bones and teeth, which contain 99 percent of the body's calcium.

Some More Ideas

• There is a wide choice of vegetables for making crunchy, delicious crudités. Others to try include: Celery or cucumber sticks, whole radishes, baby plum tomatoes halved lengthwise, small cauliflower flowerets (raw or briefly cooked), and baby new potatoes cooked until tender.

Each serving (3 dips alone) provides ⓥ
cals 115, **protein** 6 g, **fat** 8 g (of which saturated fat 2 g), **carbohydrate** 6 g (of which sugars 5 g), **fiber** 0.7 g

✓✓	B_{12}, E
✓	B_2, calcium

Cheese and Watercress Biscuits

The wonderful tastes of peppery watercress and sharp cheddar cheese flavor these tempting and nutritious savory biscuits. Packed full of fiber, both soluble and insoluble, these bicuits also make a good protein contribution to your daily diet.

Makes 8 biscuits

1 cup plus 2 tablespoons self-rising white flour

1 cup plus 1½ tablespoons wholewheat flour

2½ teaspoons baking powder

2½ tablespoons butter, cut into small pieces

⅔ cup oatmeal

3 ounces watercress without coarse stems, chopped

¾ cup sharp cheddar cheese, grated

7 tablespoons low-fat (2%) milk, plus a little extra to glaze

Salt and fresh-ground black pepper

Preparation time: 20 minutes
Cooking time: 10 to 15 minutes

Each biscuit provides ⓥ

cals 230, **protein** 8 g, **fat** 10 g (of which saturated fat 5 g), **carbohydrate** 30 g (of which sugars 1 g), **fiber** 3.3 g

✓✓	A
✓	B$_1$, B$_6$, B$_{12}$, C, folate, calcium, copper, iron, selenium, zinc

1 Preheat the oven to 450°F. Lightly grease a cookie sheet. Sift the all-purpose and wholewheat flours and the baking powder into a bowl, tipping in any bran left in the sifter. Rub in the butter with your fingertips until the mixture resembles fine bread crumbs.

2 Add the oatmeal, watercress, about three-quarters of the cheese, and a little salt and pepper. Use a fork to stir in the milk. Scrape the dough together with a spatula and turn out onto a well-floured surface. Pat together into a smooth, soft ball: It will be a little softer than a standard biscuit dough.

3 Pat or roll out the dough until it is about ¾ inch thick. Using a 3 inch round cutter, stamp out the biscuits. Press the trimmings together lightly, reroll, and stamp out more biscuits to make 8 in total.

4 Place the biscuits on the cookie sheet, arranging them so they are not touching. Brush the tops lightly with milk and sprinkle with the remaining grated cheese. Bake until risen and golden brown, 10 to 15 minutes. Cool on a wire rack. These biscuits are at their best eaten on the day they are made, but will still be good the next day; store in an airtight container.

Some More Ideas

• To make biscuit wedges, place the smooth ball of dough on a greased cookie sheet and press it out into a flat circle ¾ to 1 inch thick. Use a sharp knife to cut the dough into 8 wedges, leaving them in place. Bake until risen and golden, about 15 minutes.

• For cheese and celery biscuits, replace the watercress with 2 finely chopped celery stalks.

• To make carrot and poppy seed biscuits, instead of watercress and cheese, add ½ cup finely grated carrot and 1 tablespoon poppy seeds with the oatmeal. Before baking, sprinkle the top of the biscuits with 1 tablespoon poppy seeds instead of cheese.

Plus Points

• These biscuits are a good fiber source—both the insoluble type found in wholewheat flour and soluble fiber from the oatmeal.

• Cheddar cheese is a good source of protein and a valuable source of calcium, phosphorus, and vitamins B$_{12}$ and niacin.

• Watercress, one of the healthiest of fresh salad vegetables, provides beta-carotene, vitamin C, and vitamin E, nutrients that act as protective antioxidants. It also contains a compound that has been shown to have antibiotic properties.

Snacks

Pissaladière

The Provençal relative of Italian pizza, Pissaladière has a thick bread base, enriched with olive oil, topped with a tomato and onion mixture, then finished with a lattice of anchovies and olives. Serve warm or cool for a snack high on flavor, but low in calories.

Makes 64 bite-sized squares

Dough

3⅔ cups strong white flour, plus extra for kneading

1 teaspoon salt

1 envelope (¼ ounce) quick-rising yeast

3 tablespoons extra virgin olive oil

1¼ cups 120°-130°F water

Topping

3 tablespoons extra-virgin olive oil

4 onions, about 1 pound 10 ounces in total, thinly sliced

2 garlic cloves, crushed

1 can (14½ ounces) crushed tomatoes in tomato juice

2 tablespoons tomato paste

1 tablespoon chopped fresh oregano

2 cans (2 ounces) anchovy fillets, rinsed and halved lengthwise

16 pitted black olives, about 2 ounces in total, quartered

Fresh-ground black pepper

Preparation time: 1½ hours, plus 1 hour rising
Cooking time: 40 minutes

Each square provides

cals 44, **protein** 1.5 g, **fat** 1.5 g (of which saturated fat 0.2 g), **carbohydrate** 6.5 g (of which sugars 1 g), **fiber** 0.7 g

1 To make the dough, sift the flour and salt into a bowl, then stir in the yeast. Make a well in the middle and pour in the oil and water. Gradually mix the dry ingredients into the liquids, using a spoon at first and then by hand, to make a soft, slightly sticky dough.

2 Turn out the dough onto a lightly floured surface and knead until the dough is smooth and springy, about 10 minutes. Place in a lightly greased bowl, cover with plastic wrap, and leave in a warm place to rise until doubled in size, about 45 minutes depending on the room temperature.

3 Meanwhile, make the topping. Heat the oil in a large saucepan, over low heat. Add the onions and garlic and sauté over a low heat until very soft and lightly golden, but not brown, about 40 minutes. Add the tomatoes with their juice, the tomato paste, oregano, and pepper to taste and simmer, stirring occasionally, 10 minutes. Remove from the heat and leave to cool.

4 Meanwhile, lightly grease a cookie sheet. When the dough has risen, punch it down and knead again gently. Roll it out on a floured surface into a 12 inch square and place on the cookie sheet.

5 Preheat the oven to 400°F. Spread the onion mixture evenly over the dough square. Make a crisscross pattern on top with the anchovy fillets. Place the olive quarters in the squares. Leave the pissaladière to rise at room temperature for about 15 minutes.

6 Bake the pissaladière until the crust is golden and firm, about 30 minutes, then reduce the oven temperature to 375°F and bake 10 minutes longer. Leave to cool slightly before cutting into squares for serving.

Plus Points

• This pissaladière is made with a thick bread base, providing generous starchy carbohydrate. As the law requires all flour that doesn't contain wheat germ to be fortified with reduced iron and the B vitamins, B_1, B_2, folate, and niacin, the bread base also makes a nutrient contribution.

• Canned tomatoes are a nutritious cupboard ingredient. The canning process enhances the lycopene content of the tomatoes. Lycopene is a phytochemical with powerful antioxidant properties.

Snacks

Some More Ideas

• For an onion and pancetta pissaladière, leave the tomatoes and tomato puree out of the onion mixture. Cut 3½ ounce thin slices of smoked pancetta in half lengthwise, twist them, and lay them on top of the onion mixture in a crisscross pattern. Place rinsed capers in the squares in between.

• Make a tomato and red bell pepper pissaladière. Cover the dough base with a thin layer of tomato puree, then arrange a mixture of sliced fresh tomatoes, strips of sun-dried tomatoes, and coarsely chopped, broiled and peeled red bell peppers over the top. Brush with a little extra-virgin olive oil, sprinkle fresh-ground black pepper over, and bake as in the main recipe. Serve with fresh basil leaves scattered over the top.

Baked Potato Skins with Smoked Salmon and Fresh Dill

Potato skins are often deep-fried, but brushing with a mixture of olive oil and butter and then baking gives just as good a flavor and crisp texture. Here, the potato skins are topped with herby, low-fat quark, smoked salmon, and dill.

Serves 8

8 small baking potatoes, such as russet or Idahos, about 7 ounces each

2 tablespoons extra-virgin olive oil

1⅓ tablespoons butter

4 ounces smoked salmon

1 tablespoon fresh lemon juice

⅔ cup quark

1 tablespoon capers, rinsed and chopped

2 tablespoons chopped fresh dill

Salt and fresh-ground black pepper

Small sprigs fresh dill

Preparation and cooking time: 1¾ to 2 hours

Each serving provides

cals 162, **protein** 7 g, **fat** 7 g (of which saturated fat 3 g), **carbohydrate** 18 g (of which sugars 2 g), **fiber** 2.8 g

✓ B₁, B₆, B₁₂, C, folate, niacin, potassium

1 Preheat the oven to 400°F. Scrub the potatoes and dry them with paper towels. Thread the potatoes onto metal skewers—this helps them to cook more quickly. Brush the skin of the potatoes with 1 tablespoon of the oil, then sprinkle with a little salt. Arrange on a cookie sheet and bake until tender, 1 to 1¼ hours.

2 Remove the potatoes from the skewers and cut them in half lengthwise. Scoop out the flesh, leaving a layer of potato next to the skin about ½ inch thick. (Use the scooped-out potato flesh for fish cakes, or mash.) Cut each piece in half lengthwise again, and place, flesh side up, on a large, clean cookie sheet.

3 Melt the butter with the remaining 1 tablespoon oil in a small saucepan over medium heat. Season with salt and pepper to taste. Lightly brush this mixture over the flesh side of the potato skins. Return the potato skins to the oven and bake until golden and crisp, 12 to 15 minutes.

4 Meanwhile, cut the smoked salmon into thin strips and sprinkle with the lemon juice. Mix together the quark, capers, and dill in a small bowl, then stir in the salmon.

5 Leave the potato skins to cool for 1 to 2 minutes, then top each one with a little of the salmon and quark mixture. Garnish each with a small sprig of dill. Serve while the potato skins are still warm.

Plus Points

• Baking potatoes in their skins helps to retain their vitamins and minerals—many nutrients are found just beneath the skin. Eating the skins also boosts the intake of dietary fiber.

• Salmon is an oily fish and a rich source of essential omega-3 fatty acids, a type of polyunsaturated fat that is thought to help protect against heart disease. Smoking the salmon doesn't destroy the beneficial oils.

• Capers, the pickled buds of a shrub mostly grown in southern Europe, are commonly used to add a salt-sour taste to dishes, and can reduce the need for salt as a flavoring.

Snacks

Some More Ideas

● For a salmon and tomato topping, mix together 2 drained cans (5 ounces) salmon, 2½ cups diced ripe tomatoes, ½ diced cucumber, 6 sliced scallions, and 12 chopped black olives. Whisk 2 tablespoons extra-virgin olive oil with 2 teaspoons red-wine vinegar, 1 teaspoon Dijon mustard, and salt and fresh-ground black pepper. Add to the mixture.

● For a guacamole topping, peel and dice 2 avocados. Mix with 3 tablespoons lime juice, 3 tablespoons plain yogurt, 4 finely chopped tomatoes, 1 seeded and finely chopped fresh red chile, or a dash of hot-pepper sauce, and salt and fresh-ground black pepper.

● Instead of making potato skins, bake 12 small potatoes, about 4 ounces each, at 200°F until tender, about 50 minutes. Halve the potatoes and scoop out most of the flesh, then fill with the smoked salmon and quark mixture, or one of the other toppings.

Tuscan Bean Crostini

Here's an appetizing snack to be enjoyed hot or cold—toasted slices of baguette topped with a creamy white-bean puree flavored with garlic and thyme, and finished with tomato slices and arugula leaves. These are ideal to serve with predinner drinks.

Makes 22 crostini

2 teaspoons extra-virgin olive oil

1 small onion, minced

1 garlic clove, crushed

1 can (15 ounces) cannellini beans, rinsed

2 tablespoons cultured crème fraîche

1 tablespoon chopped fresh thyme

1 thin baguette, about 20 inches long and
  weighing 8 ounces

3 plum tomatoes, thinly sliced

Salt and fresh-ground black pepper

Arugula or fresh herb sprigs

Preparation and cooking time: about 25 minutes

1 Heat the oil in a small skillet over medium heat. Add the onion and garlic and sauté until soft, stirring occasionally, about 5 minutes.

2 Meanwhile, place the cannellini beans in a bowl and mash with a potato masher or fork. Remove the saucepan of onion and garlic from the heat and stir in the mashed beans, crème fraîche, and thyme. Season with salt and pepper and mix well; keep warm.

3 Preheat the broiler to high. Cut the crusty ends off the baguette and discard. Cut the loaf into 22 equal slices, each about ¾ inch thick. Broil the baguette slices about 4 inches from the heat, turning once, until toasted. (The toasts can be left to cool and then kept in an airtight tin. When ready to serve, top with the bean mixture, cooled to room temperature, and the tomato slices and arugula or herbs.)

4 Thickly spread some bean mixture over each slice of toast. Top with a tomato slice and arugula or fresh herb sprigs.

Some More Ideas

● Instead of cannellini beans, use other canned legumes, such as flageolet or fava beans, or chickpeas.

● Top the bean mixture with broiled zucchini slices, lightly cooked white mushrooms, or halved cherry tomatoes.

● Herbs such as fresh basil, oregano, sage, or parsley can be used instead of the thyme.

● Use different types of bread, such as ciabatta, Pugliese, or wholewheat.

● Make Tuna Crostini. Drain and flake 2 cans (6 ounces) water-packed tuna. Mix with 1½ tablespoons each mayonnaise and plain low-fat yogurt, 2 tablespoons snipped fresh chives, and fresh-ground black pepper to taste. Spread each slice of toast with ½ teaspoon tomato relish, top with the tuna mixture, and garnish with tiny watercress sprigs or arugula leaves.

Plus Points

● Cannellini beans belong to the same family as the haricot bean and have a similar floury texture when they are cooked. Although an excellent source of dietary fiber, beans can produce side effects such as bloating and wind. These can be minimized by thoroughly rinsing canned beans before use.

● The tomato, which is indigenous to the Andes, was first cultivated in Mexico. It is a good source of antioxidants vitamin C and beta-carotene, and several important phytochemicals.

● Crème fraîche—see Plus Points, p32.

Each crostini provides

cals 62, **protein** 2 g, **fat** 2 g (of which saturated fat 1 g), **carbohydrate** 9 g (of which sugars 1 g), **fiber** 2.3 g

Snacks

Soups and Appetizers

From light broths to thick pottages packed with nutritious
ingredients, soups are a very versatile food. Classic Gazpacho,
Celery Root and Spinach Soup, or Shrimp Bisque, for example,
are excellent to start a meal with, as none are high in calories,
while Hearty Mussel Soup or Borscht with Mashed Potatoes
can be meals in themselves when served with bread. The light
and varied appetizers in this chapter include Goat Cheese Toasts,
Jumbo Shrimp with Pepper Salsa, and Dolmades (Greek rice-
stuffed grape leaves).

Classic Gazpacho

This traditional Spanish soup is full of fresh flavors and packed with vitamins, because all the vegetables are raw. Cool and refreshing, it is ideal for a simple lunch or supper, served with some crusty country-style bread, or as a delicious first course in an evening meal.

Serves 4

18 ounces full-flavored tomatoes, quartered and seeded

¼ cucumber, peeled and coarsely chopped

1 red bell pepper, seeded and coarsely chopped

2 garlic cloves

1 small onion, quartered

1 slice bread, about 1 ounce, torn into pieces

2 tablespoons red-wine vinegar

½ teaspoon salt

2 tablespoons extra-virgin olive oil

1¼ cups tomato juice

1 tablespoon tomato paste

To serve

1 red bell pepper

4 scallions

¼ cucumber

2 slices bread, made into croutons (See Some More Ideas, right)

Preparation time: 20 minutes, plus 2 hours chilling

Each serving provides Ⓥ

cals 215, **protein** 6 g, **fat** 9 g (of which saturated fat 1.5 g), **carbohydrate** 30 g (of which sugars 17 g), **fiber** 6 g

✓✓✓ A, B₁, B₆, C, niacin, potassium

1 Mix all the ingredients in a large bowl. Ladle batches of the mixture into a blender and puree until smooth. Pour the soup into a large, clean bowl, cover, and chill at least 2 hours.

2 Meanwhile, prepare the vegetables to serve with the soup toward the end of the chilling time: Seed and finely dice the red bell pepper; thinly slice the scallions; and finely dice the cucumber. Place these vegetables and the croutons in separate serving dishes.

3 Taste the soup and adjust the seasoning, if necessary. Ladle the soup into bowls. Serve at once, offering the accompaniments so they can be added to taste as the soup is eaten.

Some More Ideas

• For a milder flavor, use 2 chopped shallots instead of the onion.

• In very hot weather, add a few ice cubes to the soup just before serving, to keep it chilled. This will also slightly dilute it.

• To make a fresh green soup, use 3½ cups chopped zucchini instead of tomatoes and cucumber. Add 2 cups vegetable stock, preferably homemade, instead of the tomato juice. Use a green bell pepper instead of a red one. Add ¼ cup fresh basil leaves and ½ cup pitted green olives. Mix, puree, and chill the soup as above. Serve with a diced green bell pepper instead of red.

Plus Points

• Up to 70 percent of the water-soluble vitamins— B and C—can be lost in cooking. In this classic soup the vegetables are eaten raw, which means they retain maximum levels of vitamins and minerals.

• Peppers have a naturally waxy skin that helps to protect them against oxidation and prevents loss of vitamin C during storage. As a result, their vitamin C content remains high even several weeks after harvesting.

Croutons

To make crispy croutons, brush both bread slices on both sides with 1 tablespoon extra-virgin olive oil. Heat a dry skillet over medium heat. Add the bread and brown, about 2 minutes on each side. Remove the bread from the pan and cut into ½ inch cubes. Return the bread cubes to the pan and sauté until crisp, about 3 minutes.

Soups and Appetizers

Celery Root and Spinach Soup

With celery root you can create a rich soup with lots of character and a creamy texture, so there is no need for other calorie-rich thickeners. Young leaf spinach complements the celery root beautifully, bringing color and a light, fresh taste.

Serves 4

2 tablespoons extra-virgin olive oil

1 large onion, thinly sliced

1 garlic clove, crushed

1 celery root, about 1 pound 5 ounces, peeled and grated

4¼ cups boiling water

2 vegetable bouillon cubes, crumbled

18 ounces young leaf spinach

Grated nutmeg

Salt and fresh-ground black pepper

To Serve

4 tablespoons light cream

Fresh chives

Preparation time: 10 minutes

Cooking time: about 20 minutes

1 Heat the oil in a large saucepan over medium heat. Add the onion and garlic and sauté until the onion is soft, but not brown, about 5 minutes. Add the celery root. Pour in the boiling water and stir in the bouillon cubes. Bring to a boil over high heat, then reduce the heat and cover the saucepan. Simmer the soup until the celery root is tender, about 10 minutes.

2 Add the spinach to the soup and stir well. Increase the heat and bring the soup to a boil, then remove the pan from the heat. Leave the soup to cool slightly before pureeing it, in batches, in a blender or food processor until smooth. Alternatively, puree it in the saucepan using a stick blender: The soup will be fairly thick.

3 Reheat the soup, if necessary, then stir in nutmeg, and salt and pepper to taste. Ladle the soup into warm bowls. Swirl a tablespoon of cream into each portion and garnish with fresh chives.

Some More Ideas

- For a hearty winter soup, substitute shredded greens for the spinach.
- Crispy bacon makes a delicious garnish for the soup. While the soup is cooking, broil 4 lean Canadian bacon slices until crisp and golden. Drain on paper towels, then chop the bacon into small pieces.

- For a more substantial dish, add a poached egg to each bowl of soup.
- To make a delicious potato and watercress version of this soup, use peeled, diced potatoes instead of celery root, and watercress instead of spinach. Add extra stock or low-fat (2%) milk if the pureed soup is too thick.
- For a vegetarian main-course soup, top with broiled tofu. While the soup is cooking, broil a 7 ounce block firm tofu under the broiler, preheated to medium, until brown, about 3 minutes on each side. Cut the tofu into small dice; set aside. Toast 2 tablespoons sesame seeds in a dry skillet, stirring frequently, until golden. Ladle the soup into bowls, divide the tofu between the bowls, and sprinkle with the sesame seeds.

Plus points

- Celery root, a relative of celery, complements both the flavor and texture of spinach, making the most of the modest amount of cream used to enrich this soup. It also provides potassium.
- Onions have many health benefits. They contain sulfur compounds, which give onions their characteristic smell and make your eyes water. These compounds transport cholesterol away from the artery walls.

Each serving provides

cals 150, **protein** 6 g, **fat** 10 g (of which saturated fat 3 g), **carbohydrate** 9 g (of which sugars 7 g), **fiber** 11.9 g

✓✓✓	A, folate
✓✓	C, B$_6$, calcium, iron
✓	E

Soups and Appetizers

Shrimp Bisque

This classic seafood soup is ideal for impressing guests. A last-minute addition of chopped red pepper brings a delightful flourish of flavor, texture and extra vitamins instead of the fat found in the traditional swirl of cream.

Serves 6

1 pound raw jumbo shrimp, without heads
4 tablespoons dry white wine
4 lemon slices
4 black peppercorns, lightly crushed
2 sprigs fresh parsley, stems bruised
1 fennel bulb
1 teaspoon fresh lemon juice
1 tablespoon butter
1 tablespoon sunflower oil
1 shallot, minced
⅓ cup fine white bread crumbs, made from day-old bread slices
Pinch paprika
1 red bell pepper, seeded and finely diced
Salt and fresh-ground black pepper
Chopped leaves from the fennel bulb, or herb fennel

Preparation time: about 45 minutes, plus cooling
Cooking time: about 35 minutes

Each serving provides

cals 113, **protein** 14 g, **fat** 4 g (of which saturated fat 1.5 g), **carbohydrate** 3.5 g (of which sugars 2 g), **fiber** 0.5 g

✓✓✓	A, B₆, B₁₂, C, phosphorus, selenium
✓✓	copper, iron, zinc
✓	B₂, folate, calcium, potassium

1 Shell the shrimp; set aside. Place the shells in a large saucepan. Pour in 5 cups cold water and add the white wine, lemon slices, peppercorns, and parsley. Bring to a boil over high heat. Reduce the heat and simmer 20 minutes, skimming off any scum that rises to the surface.

2 Use a small, sharp knife to make a shallow slit along the curved back of each shrimp. With the tip of the knife remove the black vein and discard. Cover and chill the shrimp until they are required.

3 Leave the shrimp-shell broth to cool slightly, then pick out and discard the lemon slices. Line a sieve with cheesecloth and place it over a large bowl or measuring jug. Process the broth in a blender or food processor until the shells are finely ground, then strain the broth through the cheesecloth-lined sieve; discard the residue from the shells.

4 Coarsely chop ⅔ cup of the fennel, then finely chop the remainder of the bulb. Place the finely chopped fennel in a medium bowl, add the lemon juice, and toss well; cover closely with plastic wrap and set aside.

5 Melt the butter with the oil in the washed saucepan over medium heat. Add the chopped fennel and the shallot and sauté, stirring frequently, until the vegetables are soft, but not brown, 5 to 8 minutes. Stir in the bread crumbs, paprika and stock. Bring slowly to a boil, then reduce the heat so the soup simmers. Add the shrimp and continue simmering 3 minutes.

6 Use tongs or a slotted spoon to remove 6 shrimp for garnishing the soup; set them aside. Season the soup with salt and pepper to taste and simmer 15 minutes longer.

7 Puree the soup in a blender or food processor until smooth. Return to the saucepan and add the finely chopped fennel and the red bell pepper. Reheat the soup until piping hot. Serve with the reserved shrimp and chopped fennel leaves.

Plus Points

• Shrimp are a good source of low-fat protein. They are an excellent source of vitamin B₁₂, selenium, and phosphorus.
• Making the broth with the shrimp shells gives the bisque a full flavor, and at the same time boosts its calcium content.

Some more ideas

• To add extra fiber, sprinkle the soup with garlic-flavored rye bread croutons just before serving. Cut 2 ounces light rye bread into ½ inch cubes and toss these with 1 tablespoon garlic-flavored olive oil. Transfer to a baking sheet and bake in an oven preheated to 350°F until crisp, about 10 minutes.

• To serve the soup as a filling main course, make the broth with 1½ quarts water and add 1½ cups frozen corn kernels with the red bell pepper and fennel. Serve with a simple side salad of mixed leaves, cucumber, and green bell pepper, and plenty of crusty bread.

• A variety of vegetables can be added with or instead of the red bell pepper. For example, try a mixture of small broccoli flowerets, finely chopped celery, and frozen peas.

Golden Lentil Soup

This velvety-smooth soup owes its rich color to a combination of lentils, parsnips, and carrots. The sherry and a horseradish-flavored cream adds a piquant taste and a luxurious touch. Serve with crunchy melba toast.

Serves 6

2 tablespoons butter

1 large onion, minced

5 medium parsnips, peeled and diced

3 medium carrots, scrubbed and diced

⅔ cup dry sherry

½ cup red lentils

5 cups vegetable stock, preferably homemade

Salt and fresh-ground black pepper

Fresh chives to garnish

To serve

2 teaspoons grated horseradish

6 tablespoons cultured crème fraîche

Preparation time: about 15 minutes

Cooking time: about 1¼ hours

1 Melt the butter in a large saucepan over low heat. Add the onion, stir well, and cover the saucepan. Sweat the onion until soft, about 10 minutes. Stir in the parsnips, carrots, and sherry. Bring to a boil, then cover the saucepan, and leave to simmer very gently 40 minutes.

2 Add the lentils, stock, and salt and pepper to taste. Return to a boil, then reduce the heat and cover the pan. Simmer until the lentils are tender, 15 to 20 minutes longer. Puree the soup in a blender until smooth, or use a stick blender to puree the soup in the saucepan. Return the soup to the saucepan if necessary, and reheat it slowly until boiling. If it seems a bit thick, add a little stock or water.

3 Stir the grated horseradish into the crème fraîche. Snip some of the chives for the garnish and leave a few whole. Ladle the soup into warm bowls and top each portion with a tablespoon of the horseradish cream. Scatter snipped chives over the top and add a few pieces whole chive across the top of each bowl. Serve at once.

Some More Ideas

• Use celery root instead of parsnips, and rutabaga instead of carrots. Prepare and cook the soup as in the main recipe. Dry white vermouth or white wine can be added in place of the sherry for a lighter flavor.

• For a lower-fat version, top each portion with 1 teaspoon creamed horseradish, instead of the horseradish and crème fraîche mixture. Scatter chopped parsley over the soup.

Plus Points

• Lentils are a good source of protein and an excellent source of fiber. High-fiber foods are bulky and make you feel full for longer, so they are very satisfying. A diet high in fiber and low in fat is good for weight control.

• Root vegetables are an excellent source of vitamins and minerals during the winter.

• Children who are reluctant to eat plainly cooked vegetables will not even realize they are eating them in this tasty, colorful soup.

• Crème fraîche—see Plus Points, p32.

Each serving provides   Ⓥ

cals 250, **protein** 6 g, **fat** 11 g (of which saturated fat 3 g), **carbohydrate** 25 g (of which sugars 11 g), **fiber** 7 g

✓✓✓	A
✓✓	B₁, B₆, folate, potassium
✓	calcium, iron

Soups and Appetizers

Salmon and Tomato Chowder

Chowder is a classic meal-in-a-bowl soup. This delicious version is flavored with lean bacon, leeks, and tomatoes and thickened with potatoes, all of which provide the perfect background for the protein-packed salmon. Try it with sourdough bread.

Serves 4

One 7 ounce piece skinless salmon fillet

1 bay leaf

1¼ cups fish or vegetable stock

2½ cups low-fat (2%) milk

1 tablespoon unsalted butter

1 teaspoon sunflower oil

1 large onion, finely chopped

1 leek, chopped

1 thick slice Canadian bacon, about 1 ounce, rinded and chopped

2 medium potatoes, peeled and diced

2 large tomatoes, skinned, seeded, and diced

3 tablespoons chopped parsley

4 tablespoons nonfat sour cream

Salt and fresh-ground black pepper

Preparation time: 15 minutes
Cooking time: 30 minutes

Each serving provides

cals 315, **protein** 20 g, **fat** 12 g (of which saturated fat 5 g), **carbohydrate** 29 g (of which sugars 12 g), **fiber** 3.3 g

✓✓✓	B$_6$, B$_{12}$, C, E
✓✓	A, B$_1$, B$_2$, folate, niacin, calcium, potassium, selenium, zinc
✓	copper, iron

1 Put the salmon fillets and bay leaf in a large saucepan. Pour the stock over and add some of the milk, if needed, so the fish is completely covered with liquid. Slowly bring the liquid to a boil over medium heat. Reduce the heat, cover, and simmer until the fish flakes easily, 6 to 7 minutes. Remove the salmon with a slotted spoon and break into large flakes; discard any bones and set aside. Pour the cooking liquid (with the bay leaf) into a measuring jug or large-size bowl and reserve.

2 Melt the butter with the oil in the saucepan over low heat. Add the onion, leek, and bacon and sauté, until soft, about 10 minutes. Add the potatoes and sauté the mixture 2 minutes longer, stirring constantly.

3 Pour the reserved cooking liquid over and add the remaining milk. Bring to a boil, half-cover the saucepan and simmer, stirring occasionally, 8 minutes. Add the diced tomatoes and simmer until the potatoes have become tender, but have not started to disintegrate, 3 to 4 minutes longer.

4 To thicken the soup, remove a ladleful or two and puree it in a bowl with a stick blender, or in a food processor. Return to the soup in the saucepan and mix well.

5 Stir in the flaked salmon and 2 tablespoons of the parsley. Simmer until the soup is piping hot, 1 to 2 minutes longer; discard the bay leaf. Season with salt and pepper to taste.

6 Ladle the soup into warm serving bowls. Top each serving with 1 tablespoon nonfat sour cream, swirling it around, and add a sprinkling of the remaining chopped parsley.

Plus points

• Salmon, like most fish, is an excellent source of protein, as well as of vitamins B$_6$ and B$_{12}$ and the minerals selenium and potassium. It also offers heart-healthy fats.

• Milk provides several important nutrients, most notably protein, calcium, phosphorus, and many of the B vitamins. These nutrients are found in the nonfat part of milk, so lower fat varieties, such as 2% milk, actually contain more than whole milk.

Soups and Appetizers

Some More Ideas

• For a Corn and Blue Cheese Chowder, soften 1 chopped onion and 1 chopped celery stalk in 1 tablespoon butter. Stir in 2 medium peeled and diced potatoes, 2 cups low-fat (2%) milk, 1¼ cups vegetable stock, and 1 bay leaf. Half-cover and simmer until the potatoes are tender, about 12 minutes. Puree one-third of the soup in a food processor or with a stick blender, then stir it into the rest of the soup. Stir in 1 can (15 ounces) cream-style corn, 3 tablespoons snipped fresh chives, and salt and pepper to taste. Simmer 2 to 3 minutes to heat through. Ladle into serving bowls and top each one with 1 tablespoon quark and 1 ounce crumbled blue cheese.

• Make a quick clam chowder. Soften 1 bunch sliced scallions in 1 tablespoon butter. Add 2 medium peeled and diced potatoes, 2 cups fish stock, and 1¼ cups low-fat (2%) milk. Half-cover and simmer until the potatoes are tender, about 12 minutes. Mash a few of the potatoes on the side of the saucepan to thicken the soup, then stir in 2 well-drained cans (6 ounces each) clams, 1 can cream-style sweetcorn, ½ can (14½ ounces) crushed tomatoes, with juice, 3 tablespoons chopped parsley, 2 tablespoons dry sherry, and salt and pepper to taste. Simmer until piping hot, about 5 minutes.

Borscht and Mashed Potatoes

This healthy beet soup is a hearty version of the Russian favorite, which is often strained and served as a clear broth. Here the soup is pureed and accompanied by creamy mashed potatoes mixed with crunchy raw vegetables.

Serves 4

1 tablespoon extra-virgin olive oil

1 onion, chopped

1 large carrot

½ teaspoon lemon juice

1 fennel bulb

18 ounces raw beets

4½ cups vegetable stock, preferably homemade

1¾ pounds potatoes, such as russet, peeled and cut diced

½ cup low-fat (2%) milk

4 tablespoons nonfat sour cream

2 scallions, minced

Salt and fresh-ground black pepper

Chopped leaves from the fennel bulb, herb fennel, or parsley

Preparation time: about 35 minutes
Cooking time: about 50 minutes

Each serving provides Ⓥ

cals 300, **protein** 11 g, **fat** 4 g (of which saturated fat 1 g), **carbohydrate** 56 g (of which sugars 21 g), **fiber** 7.5 g

✓✓✓	A, folate
✓✓	B₁, B₆, C
✓	iron

1 Heat the oil in a large saucepan over medium heat and add the onion. Set aside one-third of the carrot for the mashed potato, then chop the rest and add it to the pan. Stir well, cover, and sauté until the onion is soft, about 5 minutes.

2 Place the lemon juice in a small bowl. Cut the bulb of fennel into quarters. Finely grate one-quarter into the lemon juice and toss well. Finely grate the reserved carrot and add it to the grated fennel; cover and set aside.

3 Chop the remaining fennel and add to the saucepan. Peel and dice the beets, and add to the saucepan. Pour in the stock and bring to a boil. Reduce the heat, cover, and simmer until all the vegetables are tender, about 30 minutes.

4 Meanwhile, bring another saucepan of water to a boil. Add the potatoes and boil until very tender, about 10 minutes. Drain the potatoes and return them to the saucepan. Place over low heat to dry, shaking the saucepan occasionally to prevent the potatoes from sticking, about 1 minute. Remove from the heat and cover; set aside.

5 Puree the soup in a blender or food processor until smooth, or puree in the saucepan using a stick blender. Return the soup to the saucepan, if necessary, and reheat. Taste and adjust the seasoning.

6 While the soup is reheating, set the saucepan of potatoes over a medium heat and mash until smooth, gradually working in the milk. Stir in the sour cream, grated fennel and carrot, scallions, and seasoning to taste.

7 Divide the mashed potatoes between 4 bowls, piling it up in the middle. Ladle the soup around the mashed potatoes and sprinkle with chopped fennel or parsley.

Plus Points

• Beets are a particularly rich source of the B vitamin folate, which might help to protect against heart disease and spina bifida. They also provide useful amounts of iron. The characteristic deep-red color comes from a compound called betacyanin, which has been shown to prevent the growth of tumors in animal studies.

• Adding grated raw vegetables to mashed potatoes is a good way of including them in a hot meal, especially for children.

• Fennel contains phytoestrogen, a naturally occurring plant hormone that encourages the body to excrete excess estrogen. A high level of estrogen is associated with increased risk of breast cancer. Fennel also contains useful amounts of folate.

Some More Ideas

• Other delicious raw vegetable additions to mashed potatoes are finely chopped celery, grated peeled celery root, finely shredded red or savoy cabbage, and shredded brussels sprouts. They all contribute extra vitamins and minerals.

• Serve the borscht chunky instead of pureed, and add 2 tablespoons hazelnut oil to the mashed potatoes instead of the sour cream.

• Instead of spooning the borscht around a pile of mashed potatoes, garnish each bowl simply with 1 tablespoon plain yogurt, sour cream, or creamed horseradish, then sprinkle with chopped fresh fennel or parsley.

Vietnamese Broth with Noodles

Punchy flavors and aromatic ingredients transform this light broth into an exotic dish. Unlike many oriental soups, the ingredients are not fried first so the fat content remains low. Select prime-quality lean steak, that tastes excellent when poached.

Serves 2

Scant 1 ounce dry shiitake mushrooms

3 ounces fine rice noodles, such as vermicelli

6 ounces lean top round steak, diced

1¼ cups beef stock

2 tablespoons fish sauce

1 heaped teaspoon grated fresh ginger

1 ounce bean sprouts

½ small onion, thinly sliced

2 scallions, thinly sliced

2 small fresh red bird's-eye chiles or 1 medium red chile, deveined, seeded, and minced

1 tablespoon shredded fresh mint

1 tablespoon shredded fresh cilantro

1 tablespoon shredded fresh basil

To serve

Lime wedges

Soy sauce (optional)

Preparation time: 20 minutes, plus 20 minutes soaking

Cooking time: 10 to 15 minutes

Each serving provides

cals 300, **protein** 23 g, **fat** 4 g (of which saturated fat 1.5 g), **carbohydrate** 42 g (of which sugars 2 g), **fiber** 0.8 g

✓✓✓	B_1, B_6, B_{12}, E, niacin
✓✓	iron, zinc

1 Rinse the shiitake mushrooms and put them in a small heatproof bowl. Place the rice noodles in a large heatproof bowl. Cover the mushrooms with boiling water and leave to soak 20 minutes. Cover the rice noodles with boiling water and soak 4 minutes, or according to the packet instructions. Drain the noodles and set aside until they are needed.

2 Drain the mushrooms and pour the soaking liquid into a large saucepan. Trim and discard any tough stems from the mushrooms, then slice them and add to the pan along with the steak, stock, fish sauce, and ginger. Bring to a boil, then reduce the heat and simmer until the steak is cooked and tender, 10 to 15 minutes; skim any scum that rises to the surface during cooking.

3 Divide the noodles, bean sprouts, and sliced onion between 2 large, deep soup bowls. Use a slotted spoon to remove the steak and mushrooms from the broth, then divide them between the bowls. Ladle the broth into the bowls. Scatter the scallions, chiles, mint, cilantro, and basil over the tops.

4 Serve immediately, with the lime wedges—the juice can be squeezed into the broth to taste. Soy sauce can also be added, if liked.

Plus Points

- In common with other red meats, beef is a good source of iron and zinc, and the iron in meat is far more easily absorbed by the body than iron from vegetable sources.
- Beef is now far leaner than it used to be. Top round steak, used in this recipe, is one of the leanest cuts available, with 4.2 g fat each 3 ounce serving.

Some More Ideas

- For a vegetarian version of this soup, use tofu and vegetable stock instead of beef and beef stock, and soy sauce or dry sherry instead of the fish sauce. Cook the tofu gently only until heated through, about 2 minutes.
- The bean sprouts can be replaced by carrot shavings and chopped celery. Vary the quantities of scallions, chile, and herbs to taste.
- Any thin oriental noodles can be used in place of rice noodles, including the readily available Chinese egg noodles. Cook or soak the chosen noodles according to the package directions.
- For a warm, spicy flavor, add a good pinch of cinnamon with the ginger.

Hearty Mussel Soup

This soup tastes fabulous and is packed full of healthy, fresh vegetables. The diced potatoes absorb the flavors and add body to the soup. Warm soda bread is an ideal partner, delicious for dunking and mopping up the last of the soup.

Serves 4

2¼ pounds live mussels in shells, scrubbed

2 tablespoons extra-virgin olive oil

1 onion, minced

2 garlic cloves, minced

2 leeks, thinly sliced

3 celery stalks, thinly sliced

2 carrots, diced

1 large potato, peeled and diced

1 quart vegetable stock, preferably
   homemade

⅔ cup dry white wine

1 tablespoon lemon juice

1 bay leaf

1 sprig fresh thyme

4 tablespoons chopped fresh parsley

2 tablespoons snipped fresh chives

Salt and fresh-ground black pepper

Preparation time: 30 minutes

Cooking time: 40 to 50 minutes

Each serving provides

cals 260, **protein** 17 g, **fat** 8 g (of which saturated fat 1 g), **carbohydrate** 24 g (of which sugars 7 g), **fiber** 4.5 g

✓✓✓	A
✓✓	B₆, B₁₂, C, folate
✓	B₁, B₂, selenium

1 Discard any mussels with broken shells or those that do not close when tapped. Put the wet mussels into a saucepan and cover tightly. Cook over a medium heat 4 minutes, occasionally shaking the pan. Check if the mussels are open—if not, cover and cook 1 to 2 minutes longer. Drain the mussels, reserving the juices. Keep some mussels in their shells for garnish, but remove the remainder from their shells and set aside. Discard the shells and any unopened mussels.

2 Heat the oil in the washed saucepan. Add the onion, garlic, leeks, celery, and carrots and sauté, stirring frequently, until the vegetables are soft but not brown, 5 to 10 minutes. Add the potatoes, stock, wine, reserved mussel juices, lemon juice, bay leaf, thyme, and salt and pepper to taste. Bring to a boil, then reduce the heat to low. Cover the saucepan and simmer the soup until the vegetables are tender, 20 to 30 minutes.

3 Remove the bay leaf and thyme. Add the shelled mussels, parsley, and chives to the pan. Heat gently for about 1 minute: Do not let the soup boil or cook longer because the mussels will become tough.

4 Ladle the soup into warm bowls and top with the reserved mussels.

Another Idea

● Cooked fresh mussels are available in supermarkets, usually vacuum packed and displayed in chill cabinets. Use 10 ounces shelled mussels.

Plus points

● Like other shellfish, mussels are a good low-fat source of protein. They are an extremely good source of vitamin B₁₂, and provide useful amounts of copper, iodine, iron, phosphorus, and zinc.

● Vitamin C from the potatoes, parsley, and chives aids the absorption of iron from the mussels.

● Celery is said to have a calming effect on the nerves.

Soups and Appetizers

Goat Cheese Toasts

Indulge your taste buds with these morsels of toasted, crusty baguette topped with slices of plum tomato and tangy goat cheese, sprinkled with pine nuts and fresh herbs. Choose your favorite type of goat cheese: delicate or strong in flavor, soft or firm in texture.

Makes 16 toasts

1 baguette, about 10 ounces, cut into 16
   1 inch slices
4 tablespoons tomato puree
2 tablespoons sun-dried tomato paste
4 plum tomatoes, about 8 ounces in total
5 ounces goat cheese
1½ tablespoons extra-virgin olive oil
1 tablespoon pine nuts
Few fresh thyme or oregano sprigs, plus
   extra to garnish

Preparation time: 15 minutes
Cooking time: 4 to 5 minutes

1 Preheat the broiler to medium. Place the baguette slices on a rack in the broiler pan and lightly toast on both sides.

2 Mix together the tomato puree and tomato paste and spread a little on top of each toast, covering the surface.

3 Slice the tomatoes lengthwise, discarding a slim slice from the ends, to cut 4 flat slices from each tomato. Lay a slice of tomato on top of each toast.

4 Place 1 small slice of firm goat cheese or about 1 teaspoon of soft goat cheese on top of each tomato slice. Drizzle a little olive oil over. Scatter each with a few pine nuts and thyme or oregano leaves.

5 Broil 4 inches from the heat until the cheese is beginning to melt and the pine nuts are golden, 4 to 5 minutes. Serve the toasts hot, with sprigs of thyme or oregano.

Some More Ideas

• Use a goat cheese flavored with garlic and herbs.

• Serve the toasts on a bed of mixed soft salad leaves as an appetizer or light lunch. Allow 4 toasts per serving.

• Make Fruity Goat Cheese Toasts. Instead of the tomato topping, mix together 2 tablespoons each cranberry sauce and mango, peach, or another fruit chutney. Spread this over the toasts, top with the goat cheese, and scatter a few slivered almonds over. Broil as in the main recipe.

• For Tapenade Goat Cheese Toasts, put ⅔ cup pitted black olives, 1 can (2 ounces) rinsed anchovy fillets, 3 tablespoons rinsed capers, 3 tablespoons extra-virgin olive oil, fresh juice of ½ lemon, and 2 crushed garlic cloves in a blender or food processor and blend to a paste (or pound to a paste with a mortar and pestle). This makes 1 scant cup tapenade: It can be kept, covered, in the refrigerator 2 weeks. Spread onto 4 large, thick slices toasted bread, then top with the goat cheese. Broil 3 to 4 minutes. Cut each slice into 8 fingers or triangles and serve warm, sprinkled with chopped parsley. Makes 32 toasts.

Each toast provides

cals 89, **protein** 3 g, **fat** 4 g (of which saturated fat 1 g), **carbohydrate** 11 g (of which sugars 1 g), **fiber** 1.1 g

✓   E

Plus Points

• Pine nuts are commonly found in Middle Eastern rice dishes and stuffings. They are also an important ingredient in the classic Italian pesto sauce.

• Goat cheese is a tasty source of protein and calcium, as well as B vitamins (B_1, B_6, B_{12}, and niacin) and phosphorus. Medium-fat goat cheese contains about half the fat of cheddar cheese.

Soups and Appetizers

Chicken and Vegetable Phyllo Rolls

These phyllo pastry rolls make an excellent appetizer. The filling is a colorful mixture of low-fat ground chicken and plenty of vegetables, with a little smoked ham and fresh herbs to add extra flavor. The rolls are served with a piquant cranberry relish.

Serves 8 (makes 8)

1 large carrot, about 3 ounces, cut into very fine matchsticks

1 cup finely shredded savoy cabbage

2 scallions, cut into fine shreds

8 ounces ground chicken

2 ounces lean smoked ham, finely chopped

½ small onion, minced

2 tablespoons fresh white bread crumbs

2 teaspoons chopped fresh sage

2 teaspoons chopped fresh thyme

4 large sheets phyllo pastry dough, each about 18 x 11 inches, thawed if frozen

2 tablespoons extra-virgin olive oil

1 tablespoon butter, melted

1 teaspoon sesame seeds

Salt and fresh-ground black pepper

Cranberry Relish

3 tablespoons cranberry sauce

1 tablespoon extra-virgin olive oil

1 tablespoon red-wine vinegar

1 teaspoon Dijon mustard

To serve

4 ounces mixed salad leaves

Preparation time: 40 minutes
Cooking time: 30 minutes

1 Bring a large saucepan of water to a boil over high heat. Add the carrot, cabbage, and scallions and blanch for 1 minute. Drain, then plunge into a bowl of cold water to refresh. Drain again and pat dry with paper towels. Put the vegetables in a large mixing bowl with the chicken, ham, onion, bread crumbs, herbs, and seasoning. Mix together well; set aside.

2 Preheat the oven to 375°F. Halve each phyllo dough sheet lengthwise and then trim to strips measuring 15 x 5 inches. Mix the oil and butter together.

3 Brush one dough strip lightly with the butter mixture. Place one eighth of the filling at one end, shaping it into a log. Roll up the filling inside the dough, folding in the long sides as you roll, to make a spring-roll-shape. Place on a cookie sheet and brush with a little of the butter and oil mixture. Repeat to make another 7 rolls.

4 Score 3 diagonal slashes on top of each roll. Sprinkle the sesame seeds over. Bake until the pastry is golden, about 30 minutes.

5 Meanwhile, put all the relish ingredients in a screw-top jar, season to taste, and shake well.

6 Arrange the salad leaves on serving plates. Place a phyllo roll on each and drizzle the relish around.

Plus Points

- Unlike most other types of pastry, phyllo, which is similar to strudle dough, contains very little fat—in 3½ ounces phyllo there are 2 g fat and 300 cals.

- Phyllo pastry dough is traditionally brushed with all butter. Using a mixture of oil and butter to brush the sheets of phyllo, however, reduces the amount of saturated fat. Brushing it on sparingly also keeps the overall fat content down.

- By bulking out the poultry with vegetables you reduce the fat content of the dish, and provide extra vitamins and dietary fiber.

Each roll provides

cals 130, **protein** 8.5 g, **fat** 7.5 g (of which saturated fat 2 g), **carbohydrate** 7 g (of which sugars 4 g), **fiber** 1 g

✓ A, B$_6$

Some More Ideas

- Use ground turkey instead of chicken.
- For Greek-Style Chicken rolls, cook 2 tablespoons long-grain rice in boiling water until tender, about 12 minutes; drain and rinse with cold water. Meanwhile, soften 1 finely chopped onion in 1 teaspoon extra-virgin olive oil, 5 minutes; set aside to cool. Put the rice and onion in a bowl with 8 ounces ground chicken or turkey, 2 tablespoons toasted pine nuts, 2 tablespoons raisins, 2 tablespoons chopped fresh mint, and 2 tablespoons chopped fresh dill. Season to taste. Mix and divide into 8 equal portions. Cut the sheets of phyllo pastry dough into 8 strips as before. Brush each dough strip with the olive oil and butter mixture, then put one portion of the filling at one end. Fold the dough over the filling into a triangle. Continue folding along the dough strip to make a triangle bundle. Brush all the bundles with the oil and butter mixture, and scatter 1 teaspoon poppy seeds over. Bake 30 minutes. Serve on a tomato and onion salad: Thickly slice 3 large tomatoes and scatter 1 sliced red onion, 15 small black olives, and 1 tablespoon chopped fresh dill over. Season with salt and pepper and drizzle 1 tablespoon extra-virgin olive oil over.

Jumbo Shrimp with Pepper Salsa

A salsa is a Mexican-style vegetable or fruit sauce with a fresh, zingy flavor. A tomato, pepper, and chile salsa makes a wonderful accompaniment for broiled shrimp kabobs, here served with sweet melon and crusty bread.

Serves 4

32 raw jumbo shrimp, shelled, but with tails left on

1 Canteloupe melon, seeded and cut into cubes

Marinade

2 tablespoons fresh lime juice

1 teaspoon chopped garlic

1 teaspoon chopped ginger

Salsa

6 vine-ripened tomatoes, chopped

1 small red onion, minced

1 red bell pepper, seeded and chopped

1 teaspoon chopped garlic

1 fresh green chile, deveined, seeded and finely chopped

2 tablespoons fresh lime juice

2 tablespoons chopped fresh cilantro

Salt and fresh-ground black pepper

Shredded scallions

Preparation and cooking time: 30 minutes

Each serving provides

cals 150, protein 24 g, fat 1.5 g (of which saturated fat 0.5 g), carbohydrate 11 g (of which sugars 10 g), fiber 3.5 g

✓✓✓	A, B$_{12}$, C
✓✓	B$_6$, iron
✓	folate, niacin, potassium, selenium, zinc

1 Preheat the broiler to high. Soak 8 bamboo skewers in cold water (this will prevent them from burning under the broiler). Combine all of the ingredients for the marinade in a shallow dish. Add the shrimp and stir to coat with the marinade. Cover and chill while preparing the salsa.

2 Mix together all the salsa ingredients and season with salt and pepper to taste. Spoon into a serving bowl. Thread the cubes of melon onto 8 unsoaked wooden skewers and place on a serving dish; set aside.

3 Thread 4 shrimp onto each of the soaked skewers, piercing them through both ends (this will help to keep them flat). Broil 4 inches from the heat until the shrimps are pink, turning them once, 3 to 4 minutes: Do not overcook or they will become tough.

4 Garnish the salsa with the shredded scallions. Place the shrimp kabobs on the serving dish with the melon. Serve with the salsa alongside.

Some More Ideas

• Make Broiled Chicken Kabobs and serve with a fresh citrus salsa. Cut 1¼ pounds skinless, boneless chicken breast halves into cubes and marinate as described in the main recipe. Broil the chicken on skewers until tender and cooked through, about 10 minutes. For the salsa, chop the flesh from 1 pink grapefruit, 1 orange, and 1 crisp juicy apple. Mix with 2 chopped scallions, 1 finely chopped fresh green chile, and 1 tablespoon chopped fresh mint.

• Cubes of fresh pineapple can be speared onto skewers to accompany the shrimp or chicken kabobs in place of melon.

Plus Points

• The raw fruit and vegetables in the salsa are packed with vitamins. The tomatoes and red bell peppers are excellent sources of the antioxidants beta-carotene and vitamin C. Red bell peppers, in particular, are an excellent source of vitamin C. Weight for weight, they provide over twice as much vitamin C as oranges.

• Shrimp are a high-protein, low-fat food.

Soups and Appetizers

Chicken Liver Mousse

A splash of brandy adds a special touch to this light mousse. Poaching the chicken livers with vegetables and herbs, instead of frying them, keeps the fat content low, and quark adds the richness that would traditionally have come from butter.

Serves 4

8 ounces chicken livers, thawed if frozen, well trimmed

1 onion, minced

1 garlic clove, crushed

2½ cups vegetable stock or water

Several sprigs parsley

Several sprigs fresh thyme

1 bay leaf

1 to 1½ tablespoons quark

2 teaspoons garlic vinegar or white-wine vinegar

2 teaspoons brandy or Calvados, or to taste

1 tablespoon pink or green peppercorns in brine, rinsed and patted dry

2 tablespoons finely chopped fresh parsley

Salt and fresh-ground black pepper

Preparation time: 10 minutes, plus at least 4 hours chilling

Cooking time: about 15 minutes

Each serving provides

cals 80, **protein** 12.5 g, **fat** 1.5 g (of which saturated fat 0.4 g), **carbohydrate** 3.5 g (of which sugars 2.5 g), **fiber** 0.2 g

✓✓✓	A, B$_2$, B$_6$, B$_{12}$, folate, iron
✓✓	C, copper, zinc
✓	B$_1$, niacin

1 Place the chicken livers, onion, and garlic in a saucepan over medium heat. Add stock or water to cover. Tie the parsley, thyme, and bay leaf into a bouquet garni and add to the pan. Slowly bring to a boil, skimming the surface as necessary, then reduce the heat and simmer gently until the livers are cooked through, but still slightly pink in the middle when you cut into one, 5 to 8 minutes.

2 Drain and discard the bouquet garni. Tip the livers, onions, and garlic into a food processor. Add 1 tablespoon of the quark, the vinegar, and brandy, and process until smooth, adding the remaining ½ tablespoon quark, if necessary, for a lighter texture. Season the mixture to taste, then stir in the peppercorns. Alternatively, tip the livers, onions, and garlic into a bowl and mash with a fork to a slightly coarse paste. Add the quark, vinegar, and brandy and mix. Season and stir in the peppercorns.

3 Spoon the mousse into a serving bowl, or individual ramekins, and smooth the top. Sprinkle with a layer of parsley. Cover with plastic wrap and chill at least 4 hours, but preferably overnight.

4 Before serving, leave the mousse to return to room temperature. Serve with slices of hot toast.

Some More Ideas

● Replace the brandy with fresh orange juice and add the finely grated zest of ½ orange.

● If you can't find pink or green peppercorns, substitute finely chopped rinsed capers.

● For a smooth mousse, made without a food processor, omit the onion, and push the cooked livers and garlic through a fine sifter. Add 2 minced scallions with the peppercorns.

● For a less rich mousse to serve 6, omit the brandy and add ⅔ cup rinsed canned cannellini beans to the food processor with ½ tablespoon finely chopped fresh sage. This mousse is excellent on toasted slices of country-style bread, or spread on slices of baguette and then topped with sliced gherkins.

● Vary the herbs—snipped fresh chives, tarragon, and mint all go well with chicken liver mousse.

Plus Points

● Chicken livers are one of the richest iron sources—as well as providing high amounts of resistance-building vitamin A.

● Many traditional recipes for chicken liver mousse and pâté seal the surface with a layer of melted or clarified butter for storage. In this version the fat is replaced by the chopped fresh herbs, which makes the pâté much lower in calories.

Soups and Appetizers

Dolmades

Here's a healthy twist on these delicious Greek grape-leaf rolls. To boost the fiber content, brown rice is used instead of white. The filling is flavored with garlic and herbs, with sweetness from the raisins and crunch from the walnuts.

Serves 8 (makes 24)

1 cup long-grain brown rice

24 large grape leaves preserved in brine, about 4 ounces in total when rinsed

3 tablespoons extra-virgin olive oil

1 onion, minced

1 large garlic clove, minced

1 tablespoon chopped parsley

1 tablespoon chopped fresh mint

1 tablespoon chopped fresh dill

Grated zest and fresh juice of 1 lemon

⅓ cup raisins

½ cup walnuts, chopped

Salt and fresh-ground black pepper

To serve

Lemon wedges

Fresh dill, parsley, or mint sprigs

Preparation time: 1 hour
Cooking time: 10 to 15 minutes

Each serving provides   Ⓥ

cals 199, **protein** 4 g, **fat** 9 g (of which saturated fat 1 g), **carbohydrate** 27 g (of which sugars 6 g), **fiber** 1.9 g

✓✓✓ copper

✓ A, B₁, C, folate, calcium, iron, zinc

1 Put the rice in a large saucepan over medium heat with 2½ cups water. Bring to a boil. Stir, then cover with a tight-fitting lid, and simmer until the rice is tender and absorbs all the water, 30 to 40 minutes. Remove the saucepan from the heat.

2 While the rice is cooking, drain the grape leaves, rinse with cold water, and pat dry with paper towels; set aside.

3 Heat 2 tablespoons of the oil in a large saucepan over medium heat. Add the onion and garlic, and sauté, stirring occasionally, until soft, but not brown, 5 to 8 minutes. Remove from the heat and stir in the parsley, mint, dill, lemon zest, and raisins.

4 Put the walnuts in a small dry skillet over medium heat. Toast them, stirring constantly, until lightly brown and aromatic, about 1½ minutes.

5 Add the toasted walnuts to the onion mixture. Stir in the cooked rice and add the lemon juice (you might not need all of it), and salt and pepper to taste. Stir together.

6 Place one of the grape leaves flat on the countertop and put about 2 teaspoons of the rice mixture in the middle. Fold up the stem end, then fold in the sides. Roll up the leaf into a cylinder shape. Repeat with the remaining grape leaves and filling.

7 Place the rolls, seam sides down, in a steamer and brush the tops with the remaining 1 tablespoon olive oil. Cover and steam until piping hot, 10 to 15 minutes. Serve hot or at room temperature, with lemon wedges and fresh herb sprigs.

Plus Points

• Brown rice has only the outer husk removed and, therefore, contains all the nutrients in the germ and outer layers of the grain. A ½ cup serving cooked brown rice contains 1.7g fiber, while the same amount of white rice only contains 0.2g. Brown rice also contains more B vitamins than white.

• Walnuts are high in unsaturated fats, especially linoleic acid. Recent studies have suggested that regular consumption of walnuts might help to protect against heart attacks.

• Raisins, currants, and golden raisins are all types of dried grapes. They are rich in sugars, mostly as glucose and fructose, and a useful source of iron, potassium, and fiber.

Another Idea

• To make Stuffed Cabbage Rolls, use 12 large savoy cabbage leaves instead of the grape leaves. Blanch them for 1 minute in boiling water, then refresh under cold water and pat dry. Cut out the tough cores. Cook the onion and garlic as in the main recipe, then add 1 tablespoon chopped fresh thyme, the grated zest of 1 orange, and ⅓ cup each chopped dried apricots and chopped toasted almonds. Stir in the rice and the fresh juice of ½ orange, then season with salt and pepper to taste. Roll up the filling in the cabbage leaves as directed for the grape leaves. Make a simple tomato sauce by combining 2 tablespoons extra-virgin olive oil, 1 minced onion, and 1 can (14½ ounces) crushed tomatoes, with the juice, in a saucepan over medium heat. Simmering until the onion is soft and the sauce slightly thick, 15 to 20 minutes. Season to taste, then pour into a shallow baking dish. Place the cabbage rolls on top, seam sides down, and cover the dish with foil. Bake in an oven preheated until piping hot, about 25 minutes.

Lemon-Mackerel Pâté

Whether you are planning a family meal or a dinner party, this fresh-tasting fish pâté makes a perfect appetizer, served with mixed-grain toast. For an elegant presentation, spoon it into scooped-out lemon shells, which also enhance the tangy lemon flavor.

Serves 4

2 smoked mackerel fillets, about 4 ounces each, skinned

¾ cup plus 2 tablespoons quark

Finely grated zest and fresh juice of 1 small lemon

2 teaspoons bottled soft green peppercorns, rinsed and chopped, or 1 teaspoon dried green peppercorns, coarsely crushed

1 tablespoon finely snipped fresh chives

1 tablespoon finely chopped parsley

To serve

Parsley sprigs

lemon wedges

Preparation time: 10 to 15 minutes, plus 30 minutes chilling

1 Using a fork, break up the mackerel fillets into large pieces and place in a bowl. Add the quark, lemon zest, half of the lemon juice, the peppercorns, chives, and parsley. Mash all the ingredients together with a fork: This will make a coarse-textured pâté. (For a smooth version, combine the ingredients in a food processor and process.) Taste the pâté and stir in more lemon juice, if necessary.

2 Spoon the pâté into 4 ramekins, cover with plastic wrap, and chill at least 30 minutes. Just before serving, top each with a parsley sprig. Serve with lemon wedges.

Some More Ideas

• For a Smoked Trout Pâté, substitute smoked trout fillets for the mackerel and add 1 tablespoon creamed horseradish instead of the green peppercorns.

• Add a crushed garlic clove and use fresh dill instead of chives.

• Toast ⅓ cup shelled walnuts or hazelnuts. Chop coarsely and fold into the finished pâté. Season with freshly ground black pepper or a small pinch of cayenne.

• Chill the pâté in a bowl, then scoop out using an ice-cream scoop or a spoon and serve in cup-shaped lettuce leaves. Offer crudités for dipping into the pâté, such as celery, fennel, and carrot sticks, strips of red bell pepper, and whole radishes.

• To make lemon shells to use as serving containers, cut a sliver off the stem end of 4 lemons so they stand upright. Cut a lid from each lemon, about ½ inch from the top. Using a grapefruit knife or pointed teaspoon, remove all the flesh from the lemons (keep it for another recipe). Fill the lemon shells with the mackerel pâté and top with the lids. Alternatively, cut the lemons in half horizontally, from the stem end to the tip. Scoop out the flesh from the halves and fill with the pâté. Serve 2 halves per person.

Each serving provides

cals 250, **protein** 16 g, **fat** 19 g (of which saturated fat 4 g), **carbohydrate** 3.5 g (of which sugars 3.5 g), **fiber** 0 g

✓✓✓	B₁, B₆, B₁₂, niacin
✓✓	selenium
✓	B₂, iron

Plus Points

• Mackerel is an excellent source of vitamin D. Most people obtain all the vitamin D they need from the action of sunlight on skin, but those who remain indoors a lot will benefit from including this fish in their diet on a regular basis.

• Lemons, like other citrus fruits, contain excellent levels of vitamin C. Toward the end of the 18th century, lemon juice was used as a means of protecting sailors against scurvy, the disease caused by vitamin C deficiency.

Soups and Appetizers

Pears Broiled with Pecorino

Many cuisines have traditions of combining fruit with cheese. This recipe stems from the Tuscan combination of juicy pears with salty pecorino. With some cheese melted over the pears and the rest combined with grapes and salad leaves, this is a very attractive dish.

Serves 4

2 ounces pecorino cheese

1 bunch watercress, about 2 ounces, leaves removed from stems

4 ounces arugula leaves

½ cup seedless green grapes, halved

2 not-too-firm pears

Balsamic Vinaigrette

2 tablespoons extra-virgin olive oil

1 tablespoon best-quality balsamic vinegar

½ teaspoon Dijon mustard

Pinch sugar

Salt and fresh-ground black pepper

Preparation time: 15 minutes

Cooking time: about 2 minutes

Each serving provides Ⓥ

cals 150, protein 6 g, fat 10 g (of which saturated fat 3 g), carbohydrate 10 g (of which sugars 10 g), fiber 0.8 g

✓✓ C

✓ A, B$_{12}$, folate, calcium

1 First make the dressing. Put the olive oil, balsamic vinegar, mustard, sugar, and salt and pepper to taste into a small screw-top jar. Screw on the lid and shake all the ingredients together until blended. Keep the dressing in the refrigerator until required.

2 Preheat the broiler to high. Place a strip of foil onto a cookie tray; set aside.

3 Using a vegetable peeler, peel the pecorino cheese into fine shavings. Reserve half of these and finely chop the remainder. Put the watercress, arugula leaves, and grapes into a salad bowl and toss together.

4 Peel, halve, and core the pears. Arrange the pear halves, cut sides down, on the foil strip. Top the pears with the shavings of cheese, slightly overlapping them. Broil about 6 inches from the heat until the cheese just starts to bubble and turn golden, about 2 minutes.

5 Meanwhile, shake the dressing well, pour it over the salad leaves and toss to coat. Add the chopped pecorino. Divide the salad equally between 4 plates.

6 Using a metal spatula, carefully transfer one pear half to each plate, placing it on top of the dressed salad.

Some More Ideas

• Use diced kiwi fruit instead of grapes.

• Parmesan cheese, another Italian firm cheese, is suitable for this recipe and it has less fat.

• If you are in a hurry, just chop the pears and toss them in the salad with all the cheese.

• Substitute baby spinach leaves for the arugula.

• Broil the pear halves cut sides up, then sprinkle a blue cheese, such as Stilton, into the cavities and continue broiling until it melts.

• A creamy goat cheese can be used in a fruit and cheese salad instead of high-fat pecorino. Goat cheese has a natural affinity with fresh raspberries, so for a delicious first course, omit the pears and pecorino cheese from the recipe above and replace the balsamic vinegar in the vinaigrette with raspberry vinegar. Toss 7 ounces raspberries with the salad. Toast 8 thin slices of baguette on one side under the broiler, then turn over and top with slices of goat cheese. Broil until the cheese is bubbling. Transfer 2 slices to each plate. Dress the salad and arrange next to the cheese-topped toasts.

Plus Points

• This salad is a useful source of calcium, needed for healthy bones and teeth. The pecorino cheese, watercress, and arugula all provide this vital mineral.

Soups and Appetizers

Parmesan-Topped Mussels

Make this stylish appetizer when you can buy large mussels, such as the green-lipped mussels from New Zealand, because small ones can become tough when broiled. Although you need only 24, buy at least 30 because some might have to be discarded.

Serves 4

7 tablespoons white wine or fish stock, preferably homemade

1 large onion, minced

3 large garlic cloves, crushed

About 30 large mussels, scrubbed and beards removed

1¾ ounces (1 thick slice) fresh wholewheat bread

½ cup chopped parsley

¼ cup freshly grated Parmesan cheese

½ tbsp finely grated lemon zest

Pinch cayenne

1 tablespoon extra-virgin olive oil

Lemon wedges

Preparation and cooking time: 30 minutes

Each serving provides

cals 167, **protein** 12 g, **fat** 7 g (of which saturated fat 2 g), **carbohydrate** 12 g (of which sugars 4 g), **fiber** 2.5 g

✓✓✓	B$_1$, B$_6$, B$_{12}$, niacin, iron
✓✓	selenium
✓	A, C, folate, calcium, copper, potassium, zinc

1 Pour the wine or stock into a large saucepan over high heat. Add the onion and garlic, and bring to a boil. Boil rapidly 1 minute. Add the mussels, cover the pan tightly, and cook, shaking the pan occasionally, 2 to 3 minutes. Uncover the pan and give the mussels a good stir. Using tongs, remove the mussels from the pan as soon as they open and set them aside: Discard any mussels that remain shut.

2 When the mussels are cool enough to handle, remove and discard the top shells. Place 24 mussels on the half shell in a single layer in a shallow flameproof dish, loosening the mussels from the shells, but leaving them in place; set the dish aside.

3 Preheat the broiler to high. Put the bread in a food processor or blender and process to fine crumbs. Add the parsley, Parmesan, lemon zest, cayenne, and olive oil. Process again until well blended.

4 Using your fingers, put a mound of the cheese-and-crumb mixture on each mussel, packing it firmly so the mussel is completely covered. Put the dish under the broiler until the crumb topping is crisp and lightly brown, 2 to 3 minutes. Divide the mussels between individual plates and serve with lemon wedges.

Another Idea

• Rather than broiling the mussels with the crumb-and-Parmesan topping, serve them French-style, cooked in cider. Put 4¼ cups hard cider in the pan with the onion and garlic and boil until reduced to about half. Stir in the parsley, lemon zest, and cayenne. Add the mussels and steam them open. Transfer the mussels to serving bowls. Season the cooking liquid to taste and ladle it over the mussels.

Plus Points

• Mussels are a good source of iron, an essential component of haemoglobin in red blood cells responsible for transporting oxygen around the body.

• Parmesan cheese is a very hard cheese made from skimmed or partically skimmed cow's milk. Although Parmesan has a high fat content, it also has a strong flavor and a little goes a long way in a recipe.

• Cayenne pepper, made from one of the smallest and hottest chiles, is often used in herbal medicine to stimulate the circulation.

Main Meals

Fish, poultry, meat and vegetarian dishes—here are main meals to suit all tastes and occasions. The selection includes delicate Thai-Style Crab Cakes, Summer Salmon and Asparagus, Basil-Stuffed Chicken Breasts, attractive Tomato and Pecorino Clafoutis, Herb and Saffron Risotto, Perfect Pot Roast, Fragrant Lamb with Spinach, and Sticky Ribs. Packed with protein, many of the dishes are also quick and simple to prepare.

Bulgur Wheat and Shrimp Salad

A coarsely ground wheat grain, Bulgur has already been parboiled, so it's quick to prepare and makes an ideal standby to use in salads, as well as in hot dishes. This nutty-textured, colorful salad is full of goodness, and is very attractive to the eye.

Serves 4

1¼ cups bulgur wheat

1 small red onion, very thinly sliced

1 carrot, coarsely grated

1 tomato, diced

6 baby corn cobs, sliced into rounds

½ cucumber, diced

7 ounces shelled cooked shrimps

Lime and Chile Dressing

4 tablespoons extra-virgin olive oil

2 tablespoons lime juice

1 garlic clove, crushed

¼ teaspoon dry chile flakes

Salt and fresh-ground black pepper

Preparation and cooking time: 20 to 25 minutes

1 Put the bulgur wheat in a saucepan over medium heat and pour over 2¾ cups water. Bring to a boil. Reduce the heat and simmer until the bulgur wheat is tender and all the water is absorbed, about 10 minutes. Tip the bulgur wheat into a flat dish, spread out, and leave to cool slightly.

2 Combine the onion, carrot, tomato, corn, cucumber, and shrimp in a large salad bowl. Add the bulgur wheat and stir together.

3 To make the dressing, put the oil, lime juice, garlic, chile flakes, and salt and pepper to taste in a small bowl. Whisk with a fork until combined. Stir the dressing into the salad, tossing to coat all the ingredients evenly. If not serving the salad immediately, cover and keep in the refrigerator.

Some More Ideas

• For a Bulgur Wheat and Feta Salad, replace the shrimp with 7 ounces diced feta cheese. Another alternative to the shrimp is diced tofu.

• To make a Bulgur Wheat and Ham Salad, combine the cooked bulgur wheat with 5½ ounces thinly sliced Parma or serrano ham, trimmed of all fat and cut into strips, 3 chopped scallions, 1 seeded and diced yellow bell pepper, 7 ounces halved cherry tomatoes, and 3 tablespoons capers. Make the dressing by whisking together 4 tablespoons extra-virgin olive oil, 2 tablespoons red-wine vinegar, 1 teaspoon honey, and 6 finely crushed allspice berries. Season to taste and toss with the salad.

Plus Points

• Bulgur wheat is a good source of starchy carbohydrate, dietary fiber, and B vitamins, as it contains all the particularly nutritious outer layers of the grain except the bran itself.

• The inclusion of raw vegetables in this salad not only adds texture and color, but also vitamins, particularly those with antioxidant properties.

• Shrimp, like all seafish, contain iodine, which is needed for the formation of the thyroid hormones and the functioning of the thyroid gland itself.

Each serving provides

cals 366, **protein** 18 g, **fat** 13 g (of which saturated fat 2 g), **carbohydrate** 44 g (of which sugars 5 g), **fiber** 1.6 g

✓✓✓	B$_{12}$
✓✓	A, niacin, copper, iron
✓	B$_1$, C, E, calcium, potassium, selenium, zinc

Main Meals

Tuna and Bell Pepper Salad

This bright, attractive salad is full of varied flavors and textures. Chunks of tuna, wedges of new potato, crisp beans, and fleshy tomatoes re-create the original dish from the heart of Provence and are packed with healthy nutrients. Serve with crusty baguettes.

Serves 4

12 ounces new potatoes

2 ounces thin green beans

4 small eggs

8 ounces mixed salad leaves

1 tablespoon chopped parsley

1 tablespoon snipped fresh chives

1 small red onion, thinly sliced

1 tablespoon tapenade (black olive paste)

2 garlic cloves, chopped

2 tablespoons extra-virgin olive oil

1 tablespoon red-wine vinegar

1 teaspoon balsamic vinegar

10 to 15 radishes, thinly sliced

1 can (7 ounces) water-packed tuna, drained

3 ounces cherry tomatoes

1 red bell pepper, seeded and thinly sliced

1 yellow bell pepper, seeded and thinly sliced

1 green bell pepper, seeded and thinly sliced

8 black olives

Salt and fresh-ground black pepper

Fresh basil leaves

Preparation time: 45 minutes

Each serving provides

cals 295, **protein** 21 g, **fat** 13 g (of which saturated fat 3 g), **carbohydrate** 24 g (of which sugars 10 g), **fiber** 4 g

✓✓✓	B₁, B₆, B₁₂, C, niacin, selenium
✓✓	A, folate, iron, potassium
✓	B₂, E, calcium, copper, zinc

1 Place the potatoes in a saucepan and cover with boiling water. Boil over medium heat 10 minutes. Add the beans and continue boiling until the potatoes are tender and the beans are just cooked, about 5 minutes longer. Drain well; set aside to cool.

2 Bring a medium saucepan of water to a boil over high heat. Reduce the heat to medium, add the eggs, and from the time the water starts to simmer cook 10 minutes. Rinse the eggs in cold water, peel, and place in cold water.

3 Toss the salad leaves with the parsley, chives, and red onion in a large shallow bowl.

4 To make the dressing, beat the tapenade with the garlic, olive oil, red-wine vinegar, and balsamic vinegar, in a small bowl, and season with salt and pepper to taste. Pour two-thirds of the dressing over the salad leaves and toss together.

5 Halve the potatoes and arrange them on top of the leaves with the green beans, radishes, tuna chunks, tomatoes, bell peppers, and olives. Halve the eggs and add them to the salad. Pour the remaining dressing over, and sprinkle with basil leaves.

Some More Ideas

● For a classic Italian Cannellini Bean and Tuna Salad, omit the potatoes and eggs and add 1 can (15 ounces) cannellini beans, well rinsed, to the salad leaves. Use the fresh juice of ½ lemon in the dressing instead of balsamic vinegar.

● Try this salad using different varieties of tomatoes, such as yellow cherry tomatoes, baby plum tomatoes, or quartered vine-ripened plum tomatoes.

Plus Points

● Canned tuna retains a high vitamin content, particularly vitamins B₁₂ and D.

● In common with many other salad ingredients, radishes are a useful source of vitamin C and are very low in calories. The radish has a hot flavor due to an enzyme in the skin that reacts with another substance to form a mustard-like oil.

● Green beans are a good source of dietary fiber and provide valuable amounts of folate.

Main Meals

Thai-Style Crab Cakes

Made from crabmeat and white fish, together with classic Thai flavorings, these are light, but packed with protein. Serve these with a piquant dipping sauce and crunchy salad, as well as fragrant Thai rice.

Serves 4

2 cans (6 ounces) white crabmeat, drained and patted dry with paper towels

2 skinless white fish fillets, such as cod or haddock, about 8 ounces in total, chopped

1 tablespoon bottled Thai red curry paste

1 fresh lime leaf

2 tablespoons chopped fresh cilantro

½ teaspoon sugar

1 large egg, beaten

2 carrots, finely chopped

½ cucumber, finely chopped

4 scallions, minced

2 tablespoons peanut or sunflower oil

Salt

Sweet-and-Sour Dipping Sauce

3 tablespoons white-wine vinegar

¼ cup sugar

1 tablespoon bottled Thai fish sauce

1 fresh red chile, seeded, deveined, minced

To garnish

Lime wedges

Fresh cilantro sprigs

Preparation and cooking time: 30 minutes

Each serving provides

cals 330, **protein** 30 g, **fat** 13 g (of which saturated fat 2 g), **carbohydrate** 23 g (of which sugars 22 g), **fiber** 2 g

✓✓✓	A, copper
✓✓	B₆, B₁₂, E, selenium, zinc
✓	B₁, folate, calcium, potassium

1 Place the crab and white fish in a food processor or blender and process until mixed. Add the red curry paste, lime leaf, chopped cilantro, sugar, a pinch of salt, and the egg. Process again to mix. Divide the mixture into 12 even-size pieces. Roll each one into a ball, then flatten to make a small cake. Chill while making the dipping sauce.

2 Put the vinegar, sugar, fish sauce, and 2 tablespoons water in a small pan over medium heat and stir until the sugar dissolves. Increase the heat, bring to a boil, and boil until syrupy, 2 to 3 minutes. Remove the saucepan from the heat and leave to cool. Stir in the chile.

3 Mix together the carrots, cucumber, and scallions in a serving bowl or in 4 small dishes.

4 Heat the oil in a large nonstick frying pan over medium heat. Add the crab cakes and fry until golden and cooked through, for 2 to 3 minutes on each side. Drain on paper towels. Serve garnished with lime wedges and cilantro sprigs, with the dipping sauce and the carrot and cucumber salad.

Some More Ideas

• If you like a really hot dipping sauce, include the chile seeds. Chopped peanuts can also be added to the sauce for extra texture.

• Halve the quantities of carrot, cucumber, and scallions, and add to the dipping sauce.

• For Thai-Style Shrimp Cakes, use 8 ounces shelled cooked shrimp instead of the crab. Or, make fish cakes using all white fish fillet—1 pound in total.

• Try Thai green curry paste instead of red—it is slightly milder and more aromatic.

• If you can't find lime leaves, use the fresh-grated zest of 1 lime instead. Look for lime leaves in Asian food stores.

Plus Points

• Crabmeat is an excellent low-fat source of protein and omega-3 fatty acids as well as a good source of phosphorus, which is important for healthy bones and strong teeth.

• A study that compared the diets of over 5,500 people in Holland, showed that those who ate fish regularly were less likely to develop dementia in later life.

• Some studies suggest that eating chiles might help to prevent gastric ulcers by causing the stomach lining to secrete a coating of mucus that protects it from irritants such as alcohol or aspirin.

Main Meals

Cod with Spicy Puy Lentils

Dark-green Puy lentils, grown in the south of France, have a unique, peppery flavor that is enhanced by chile. They do not disintegrate during cooking and their texture is a perfect complement for the flakiness of fresh cod. Serve this dish with warm crusty bread.

Serves 4

2 tablespoon extra-virgin olive oil

1 onion, chopped

2 celery stalks, chopped

2 medium leeks, chopped

1 or 2 fresh red chiles, seeded and chopped

1 cup Puy lentils, rinsed and drained

3 cups vegetable stock

1 sprig fresh thyme

1 bay leaf

Fresh-squeezed juice of 1 lemon

Pinch cayenne

4 pieces skinless cod fillet or cod steaks,
    about 5 ounces each

Salt and fresh-ground black pepper

To Serve

Lemon wedges

Preparation and cooking time: about 35 minutes

1 Preheat the broiler to medium-high. Heat 1 tablespoon of the olive oil in a medium saucepan over medium heat. Add the onion, celery, leeks, and chiles, and sauté 2 minutes. Stir in the lentils. Add the vegetable stock, thyme, and bay leaf. Bring to a boil, reduce the heat, and simmer until the lentils are tender, about 20 minutes. If the lentils have not absorbed all the stock, drain them (you can use the excess stock to make a soup).

2 Meanwhile, prepare the fish. Stir together the remaining oil, the lemon juice, and cayenne. Lay the cod in the broiler pan, skinned side up. Season with salt and pepper to taste, and brush with the oil mixture. Broil until the flesh flakes easily, 6 to 7 minutes: There is no need to turn the fish over.

3 Divide the lentils between warm plates and arrange the pieces of cod on top. Serve with lemon wedges.

Some More Ideas

• For Cod with Mustard Lentils, cook the lentils as in the main recipe, omitting the chiles. Mix ½ cup quark or sour cream with 1 to 2 tablespoons Dijon mustard and stir into the cooked lentils. Spread a thin layer of Dijon mustard over the seasoned cod, drizzle with olive oil, and broil. Serve the cod on top of the lentils, garnished with broiled cherry tomatoes.

• Hake, halibut, or salmon can be used instead of cod.

Plus Points

• White fish, such as cod, is low in calories. Frying it in batter more than doubles the calorie content, whereas brushing it with a little oil and broiling it keeps the fat and therefore the calories within healthy levels.

• Lentils, which are small seeds from a variety of leguminous plants, are classified as legumes, but unlike other legumes they do not need to be soaked before cooking. Lentils are a good source of protein, starch, dietary fiber, and B vitamins. Iron absorption from lentils is poor, but vitamin C-rich foods, such as the lemon juice in this recipe, can improve this process considerably.

• Thyme has been used as an antiseptic since Greek and Roman times.

Each serving provides

cals 324, **protein** 38 g, **fat** 7.5 g (of which saturated fat 1 g), **carbohydrate** 26 g (of which sugars 6 g), **fiber** 3 g

✓✓✓	B_1, B_6, niacin, selenium
✓✓	B_{12}, C
✓	A, E, folate, iron, potassium

Main Meals

Halibut Steaks with Tomato and Bell Pepper Salsa

Firm-fleshed halibut is suited to quick cooking on a ridged, cast-iron grill pan, that produces attractive markings. A hot salsa adds color and a spicy touch. Serve with a mixed salad and crusty bread for a balanced meal.

Serves 4

4 halibut steaks, about 5 ounces each

4 tablespoons extra-virgin olive oil

Fresh juice of 1 small orange

1 garlic clove, crushed

1 orange, cut into wedges, to garnish

Tomato and Bell Pepper Salsa

2 medium plum tomatoes, seeded and diced

½ red bell pepper, seeded and diced

½ red onion, finely chopped

Fresh juice of 1 small orange

½ cup chopped fresh basil

1 tablespoon balsamic vinegar

1 teaspoon sugar

Salt and fresh-ground pepper

Preparation time: 15 minutes

Cooking time: 4 to 6 minutes

1 Place the halibut steaks in a shallow glass bowl. Mix together the oil, orange juice, garlic, and salt and pepper to taste, and spoon over the fish steaks; set aside.

2 Meanwhile, to make the salsa, put the tomatoes, bell pepper, red onion, orange juice, basil, vinegar, sugar, and salt and pepper to taste in a medium bowl and stir together. Spoon into a serving bowl and chill until required.

3 Heat a lightly oiled ridged, cast-iron grill pan or skillet over high heat. Place the fish steaks on the grill pan or in the skillet and fry, basting from time to time with the oil mixture, until the fish just flakes easily, 2 to 3 minutes on each side

4 Place the fish steaks on warm serving plates and grind black pepper over. Garnish with wedges of orange and serve with the salsa.

Some More Ideas

● Other white fish steaks, such as cod, haddock, swordfish, or monkfish fillets, can be cooked the same way.

● For a Tomato and Olive Salsa, combine the diced tomatoes with ½ diced cucumber, 4 chopped scallions, ⅓ cup chopped pitted green or black olives, and ½ cup chopped fresh basil. Or, use 1 tablespoon rinsed capers instead of olives.

● In summer, cook the fish outdoors on a barbecue. Lay the steaks on a sheet of foil to prevent the delicate flesh slipping through the barbecue grid.

Plus Points

● Halibut is a good source of niacin, which has an important role to play in the release of energy within cells. Niacin is one of the most stable vitamins, and there are little or no losses during preparation or cooking.

● Red bell peppers are an excellent source of vitamin C—½ cup chopped raw red bell pepper provides more than the Recommended Daily Allowance. They also supply beta-carotene and some vitamin E.

Each serving provides

cals 260, **protein** 26 g, **fat** 14 g (of which saturated fat 2 g), **carbohydrate** 8 g (of which sugars 8 g), **fiber** 1.7 g

✓✓✓	B_1, B_6, C, niacin
✓✓	A, B_{12}, E
✓	iron, potassium

Main Meals

Herbed Fish Crumble

This family-style dish is comfort food at its healthiest: Smoked haddock and whiting in a smooth sauce, covered with a crisp herby topping. Baked potatoes, baby carrots, and peas go well with this dish.

Serves 4

7 ounces whiting fillet

7 ounces smoked haddock fillet

1 medium-sized leek, thinly sliced

1¼ cups low-fat (2%) milk

2 bay leaves

3 tablespoons butter, diced

⅔ cup wholewheat flour

3 tablespoons grated Parmesan cheese

2 tablespoons chopped fresh marjoram, or 2 teaspoons dried

4 teaspoons cornstarch

1½ cups thinly sliced white mushrooms

2 tablespoons chopped flat-leaf parsley

Salt and fresh-ground black pepper

Fresh marjoram sprigs

Preparation time: 25 minutes

Cooking time: 35 to 40 minutes

Each serving provides

cals 340, **protein** 29 g, **fat** 14 g (of which saturated fat 9 g), **carbohydrate** 26 g (of which sugars 5 g), **fiber** 3.8 g

✓✓✓	B₁, B₆, niacin, selenium
✓✓	A, B₁₂, calcium, copper
✓	B₂, C, folate, iron, potassium, zinc

1 Preheat the oven to 375°F. Put the fish in a single layer in a large, heavy-bottomed saucepan or skillet over medium heat. Add the leek, milk, bay leaves, and salt and pepper to taste. Bring just to a boil, then reduce the heat and simmer 5 minutes. Take the pan off the heat and leave to stand about 5 minutes.

2 Meanwhile, in a bowl, cut the butter into the flour until the mixture resembles fine crumbs. Stir in the cheese, marjoram, and salt and pepper to taste.

3 Using a pancake turner, lift the fish out of the milk and transfer to a plate. Remove the skin and flake the flesh; discard any bones.

4 Mix the cornstarch to a smooth paste with a little water. Add to the milk in the pan and bring to a boil, stirring until the sauce thickens; discard the bay leaves. Stir in the mushrooms and cook 1 minute. Gently stir in the flaked fish and chopped parsley and season with salt and pepper to taste.

5 Pour the fish mixture into a 5-cup shallow baking dish. Spoon the crumble mixture evenly over the top. Bake until the top is golden, 35 to 40 minutes. Serve garnished with marjoram.

Plus Points

• Milk is an excellent source of calcium, which is essential for healthy, strong bones and forms part of the structure of the teeth. An adult requires a daily intake of 700 mg, although this varies with age and sex. A lack of calcium in childhood and adolescence can lead to osteoporosis in later life.

• Mushrooms contain useful amounts of the B vitamins B₂ and niacin. They are also a good source of iron, which is essential to carry oxygen in your blood.

Some More Ideas

• Some children do not like the taste of wholemeal flour, so it's a good trick to mix it with an equal quantity of white flour. It will reduce the amount of fibre, but encourage them to eat the protein-rich fish.

• Make up a large batch of crumble topping and store it in a plastic box in the freezer. Then simply take out as much as you need and bake from frozen.

• Whiting, also called hake or silver hake, is a firm white fish which can be used in place of cod in this dish.

Main Meals

Summer Salmon and Asparagus

Fresh young vegetables and succulent salmon make this casserole highly nutritious, and it is also quick to prepare. Choose tiny leeks, tender asparagus and sugar-snap peas, all of which add visual appeal to the dish. Serve boiled new potatoes to complete the meal.

Serves 4

4 skinless salmon fillets, about 5 ounces each

7 ounces baby leeks

8 ounces tender asparagus spears

5 ounces sugar-snap peas

4 tablespoons dry white wine

¾ cup fish or vegetable stock, preferably fresh stock

2 tablespoons butter, diced

Salt and fresh-ground black pepper

1 tablespoon snipped fresh chives

Preparation time: 10 minutes
Cooking time: about 20 minutes

1 Run your fingertips over each salmon fillet to check for stray bones, pulling out any that remain between the flakes of fish. Arrange the leeks in a single layer in the bottom of a large, shallow flameproof casserole. Lay the pieces of salmon on top. Surround the fish with the asparagus and sugar-snap peas. Pour in the wine and stock, and dot the butter over the fish. Season with salt and pepper to taste.

2 Bring to a boil, then cover the casserole with a tight-fitting lid and reduce the heat so the liquid simmers gently. Simmer the fish and vegetables until the salmon is pale pink all the way through and the vegetables are fork-tender, 12 to 14 minutes. Sprinkle the chives over the salmon.

Some More Ideas

● Mackerel fillets can be casseroled the same way. Season the mackerel fillets and fold them loosely in half, with the skin outside. Use baby carrots, or large carrots cut into short, thick sticks, instead of the asparagus, and hard cider instead of the wine. Add 2 sprigs fresh rosemary to the vegetables before arranging the mackerel on top and pouring in the cider and stock.

● For a quick Oriental Fish Casserole, use cod or halibut fillet instead of salmon, 4 scallions instead of the leeks, and 4 cups whole white mushrooms instead of the asparagus. Arrange the vegetables and fish as in the main recipe, adding 4 tablespoons Chinese rice wine or dry sherry with the stock instead of the white wine. Omit the butter and sprinkle 1 tablespoon soy sauce, 1 tablespoon grated ginger, and 1 tablespoon sesame oil over the fish. Garnish with chopped fresh cilantro instead of chives and serve with plain boiled rice.

Each serving provides

cals 360, **protein** 33 g, **fat** 22 g (of which saturated fat 7 g), **carbohydrate** 4 g (of which sugars 4 g), **fiber** 2.5 g

✓✓✓	B₁₂
✓✓	B₆, C, folate
✓	B₁, niacin, iron, selenium

Plus Points

● Asparagus contains asparagine, a phytochemical that acts as a diuretic. The ancient Greeks used the plant to treat kidney problems. Today, modern-day naturopaths recommend eating asparagus to relieve bloating associated with premenstrual syndrome (PMS).

● Salmon is a rich source of omega-3 fatty acids, a type of polyunsaturated fat thought to help protect against coronary heart disease and strokes by making blood less "sticky" and therefore less likely to clot. A diet rich in omega-3 fatty acids might also help prevent and treat arthritis.

Main Meals

Shrimp Gumbo

A bowl of steaming gumbo—a thick and spicy cross between a soup and a stew, full of bell peppers, tomatoes, okra, herbs, and shrimp—brings you the good tastes of the Louisiana bayou. Serve with steamed rice or crusty bread so you can enjoy all the sauce.

Serves 4

1 tablespoon extra-virgin olive oil

2 onions, chopped

1 red bell pepper, seeded and chopped

2 celery stalks, chopped

3 garlic cloves, chopped

2 ounces lean smoked Canadian bacon, diced

1 tablespoon all-purpose flour

1 tablespoon paprika

1 quart fish stock, preferably homemade

1 teaspoon chopped fresh thyme

½ can (14 ounces) crushed tomatoes

2 tablespoons chopped parsley

2 bay leaves

2 teaspoons Worcestershire sauce

Hot red pepper sauce to taste

3 ounces okra, sliced crosswise

12 ounces shelled raw large shrimp, with tails left

⅓ cup thin green beans, cut into bite-size pieces

Salt and fresh-ground black pepper

3 scallions, thinly sliced

Preparation time: 25 minutes

Cooking time: 40 minutes

1 Heat the oil in a large saucepan. Add the onions, bell pepper, and celery and sauté until light brown, 5 to 6 minutes. Stir in the garlic and bacon and cook 3 to 4 minutes longer. Stir in the flour, increase the heat slightly, and stir 2 minutes. Stir in the paprika and continue stirring 2 minutes longer. Gradually add the stock, stirring well to dissolve the flour mixture.

2 Add the thyme, tomatoes, parsley, bay leaves, and Worcestershire sauce. Bring to a boil, then reduce the heat to low, and add hot red pepper sauce to taste. Add the okra and simmer until the okra is tender and the gumbo mixture thick, about 15 minutes.

3 Add the shrimp and green beans and cook until the shrimp turn pink and the beans are crisp-tender, about 3 minutes. Remove the bay leaves and season the gumbo with salt and pepper to taste. Serve in bowls, sprinkled with the sliced scallions.

Some More Ideas

• Try a gumbo with a flavor of Trinidad. Instead of lean bacon, use 2 ounces lean smoked sausage, such as kabanos. In Step 2, add 1 teaspoon chopped fresh ginger, ½ teaspoon Angostura bitters, ½ can (15 ounces) red kidney beans, rinsed, and 1 tablespoon dark rum with the tomatoes and other ingredients. Replace half the parsley with fresh cilantro.

• Use a mixture of 6 ounces shrimp and 6 ounces canned crabmeat, adding the crab at the very end, with the final seasoning.

Plus Points

• Okra contains a mucilaginous substance that is useful to thicken the liquid in dishes such as this (the name gumbo comes from the African word for okra). The nutrient content of okra is very similar to other green vegetables in that it provides useful amounts of dietary fiber, potassium, calcium, folate, and vitamin C.

• Bacon is a good source of vitamin B_1, which is essential for maintaining a healthy nervous system.

Each serving provides

cals 206, **protein** 23 g, **fat** 6 g (of which saturated fat 1 g), **carbohydrate** 17 g (of which sugars 10 g), **fiber** 4 g

✓✓✓	B_1, B_6, B_{12}, C, niacin
✓✓	A, E, iron, potassium
✓	folate, calcium, copper, selenium, zinc

Main Meals

Turbot with Sauce Maltaise

To enhance its excellent flavor, this turbot is simply poached and served with a lower-fat version of a classic hollandaise-style sauce flavored with oranges. Serve with steamed new potatoes, snow peas, and baby corn cobs for added taste, color, and texture.

Serves 4

1¼ cups fish stock, preferably homemade

1 shallot, sliced

1 lemon slice

1 bay leaf

6 black peppercorns, crushed

4 turbot fillets, about 5 ounces each

Sauce Maltaise

6 tablespoons unsalted butter

1 tablespoon blood orange juice

1 tablespoon white-wine vinegar

3 black peppercorns, lightly crushed

2 large egg yolks

1 teaspoon lemon juice

1 teaspoon fresh-grated fine orange zest

1 medium tomato, skinned, seeded, and finely diced

Salt and fresh-ground black pepper

Fresh tarragon sprigs

Preparation and cooking time: 30 minutes

Each serving provides

cals 331, **protein** 27 g, **fat** 24 g (of which saturated fat 13 g), **carbohydrate** 2 g (of which sugars 2 g), **fiber** 0.5 g

✓✓✓	B₁, B₁₂, niacin
✓✓	A
✓	B₆, C, E, calcium, iron, potassium

1 Place the stock, shallot, lemon slice, bay leaf, and peppercorns in a pan wide enough to hold the fillets in a single layer over medium heat. Bring to a boil, then remove from the heat and set aside to infuse while you make the sauce.

2 Melt the butter in a small saucepan. Pour the clear, golden liquid into a small bowl, discarding the milky sediment; set aside to cool slightly.

3 Put the orange juice, vinegar, peppercorns, and 1 tablespoon water in a small saucepan over high heat. Bring to a boil and boil until reduced by half, about 2 minutes. Transfer to the top of a double boiler or a heatproof bowl set over a saucepan of simmering water: The bottom of the double-boiler top or bowl should not touch the water.

4 Whisk in the egg yolks and continue whisking until the mixture is thick and pale, 4 to 5 minutes. Gradually whisk in the melted butter, drop by drop. Continue whisking after all the butter has been incorporated, until the sauce is thick enough to hold a ribbon trail on the surface when the whisk is lifted, 4 to 5 minutes.

5 If at any point the sauce begins to curdle, immediately remove it from the heat, add an ice cube, and whisk until it comes together again. Remove

the ice cube, return to the heat, and continue whisking in the butter.

6 Stir in the lemon juice, orange zest, and salt and pepper to taste. Remove the saucepan or double boiler from the heat. Stir in the tomatoes, then cover and set aside.

7 Strain the cool fish stock and return it to the saucepan over medium heat. Add the fish fillets— the liquid should just cover the fillets (if there is too much, spoon it off and reserve to use in fish soups.) Slowly increase the heat so the stock simmers, but does not boil. Poach the fish fillets until they flake easily, about 5 minutes, depending on the thickness.

8 Remove the fillets from the saucepan gently shaking off the excess liquid; set on warm plates. Spoon the sauce over and garnish with tarragon sprigs.

Plus Points

• Turbot is an excellent source of niacin, which is needed to release energy from carbohydrate foods.

• Black pepper has been viewed traditionally as a digestion stimulant, in addition to improving the circulation of the body.

Some More Ideas

• Turbot is an expensive fish. For a more economical version, use 8 skinned sole fillets, about 2 ounces each, poaching them as in the main recipe.

• Instead of the sauce maltaise, serve the fish with Fresh Orange and Tomato Salsa. Halve and finely chop 7 ounces mixed red and yellow cherry tomatoes. Peel and segment 2 oranges, then chop the segments. Toss the oranges and tomatoes together. Season with salt and pepper to taste, and sprinkle 2 tablespoons finely chopped fresh herbs, such as tarragon, parsley or chives over. Stir gently, then cover and chill until required.

• The poaching liquid can be cooled and stored in the refrigerator up to a day to use as the base of a fish soup.

Tuna and Tomato Pizzas

Add canned fish to a tomato sauce, spread it on a pizza crust, and you have a delicious, healthy pizza without a heavy cheese quotient. If you don't want to use a store-bought crust, virtually any type of crusty bread can be used instead.

Serves 4

3 teaspoon extra-virgin olive oil

1 onion, minced

1 can (14½ ounces) crushed tomatoes

½ teaspoon dried oregano

Pinch sugar

2 thick pizza crusts about 10 ounces each

2 tablespoon tomato paste

1 can (7 ounces) water-packed tuna,
   drained and flaked into chunks

4 teaspoon capers, rinsed

8 pitted black olives, sliced

Salt and fresh-ground black pepper

Fresh basil leaves

Preparation time: 15 minutes
Cooking time: 10 minutes

1 Preheat the oven to 425°F. Heat 1 teaspoon of the oil in a small saucepan over medium heat. Add the onion and sauté over medium heat until soft, about 4 minutes. Add the tomatoes, oregano, sugar and salt and pepper to taste. Bring to a boil, then reduce the heat and leave to simmer, uncovered, 10 minutes, stirring occasionally.

2 Put the pizza crusts on 2 baking sheets. Spread 1 tablespoon tomato paste over each crust. Spoon the tomato sauce over the pizzas, then add the tuna. Sprinkle with the capers and olives. Drizzle the remaining 2 teaspoons of olive oil over the tops.

3 Bake the pizzas until the crusts are crisp and golden, about 10 minutes, or following package directions. Sprinkle with torn basil leaves and serve at once.

Some More Ideas

● Instead of using pizza crusts, use a baguette or 4 wholewheat English muffins, split in half. The muffins will provide more fiber.

● Any canned fish will work well on these pizzas. Oil-rich fish such as sardines, anchovies, salmon, and mackerel are particularly good because they are excellent sources of omega-3 essential fatty acids.

● For Clam and Tomato Pizzas, use 1 can (8 ounces) baby clams, rinsed. Make the sauce by heating 1 teaspoon extra-virgin olive oil in a saucepan over medium heat. Add 1 cup sliced cremini mushrooms and sauté 3 minutes. Add 4 chopped scallions, 1 can (14½ oz) crushed tomatoes, and 1 teaspoon bottled chile. Simmer uncovered, until the sauce is reduced, about 10 minutes. Stir in the clams, 2 tablespoons chopped parsley, and salt and pepper to taste. Spread the tomato paste over the pizza crusts and spoon the clam filling on top, spreading it almost to the edges. Add 8 sliced green olives. Bake as in the main recipe.

● For a meaty pizza, cut 4 ounces wafer-thin slices cooked ham or turkey into fine shreds and arrange them on the tomato sauce, pushing them under the sauce a little. Sprinkle ⅓ cup diced mozzarella cheese over the top. Bake as in the main recipe.

Each serving provides

cals 300, **protein** 28 g, **fat** 9 g (of which saturated fat 3 g), **carbohydrate** 37 g (of which sugars 9 g), **fiber** 3.7 g

✓✓	B₆, B₁₂, C, selenium
✓	E, niacin, copper

Plus Point

● Canned tomatoes and tomato paste are healthy cupboard ingredients—they are both rich sources of the phytochemical lycopene (other good sources include pink grapefruit, watermelon, and guava), which can help to protect against several types of cancer and heart disease.

Main Meals

Basil-Stuffed Chicken Breasts

This stylish main course is, surprisingly, not laden with fat. The chicken breast halves can be prepared in advance, covered and refrigerated. Tagliatelle tossed with a little grated lemon zest makes a good accompaniment, plus ciabatta with olives or sun-dried tomatoes.

Serves 4

4 skinless boneless chicken breast halves, about 5 ounces each

3 ounces mozzarella cheese, thinly sliced

1 tomato, thinly sliced

1 garlic clove, crushed

1 bunch fresh basil, about ¾ ounce

4 slices prosciutto, about 2 ounces in total

1 tablespoon extra-virgin olive oil

Salt and fresh-ground black pepper

Green salad

2 tablespoons extra-virgin olive oil

Fresh juice of ½ lemon

4 ounces gourmet mixed salad leaves

1 bunch fresh watercress, large stems discarded

Preparation time: 25 to 30 minutes
Cooking time: about 15 minutes

Each serving provides

cals 339, **protein** 40 g, **fat** 19 g (of which saturated fat 6 g), **carbohydrate** 1.5 g (of which sugars 1 g), **fiber** 1 g

✓✓✓	B₆
✓✓	A, B₁₂, C, niacin, calcium, iron
✓	B₁, B₂, E, folate, copper, potassium, zinc

1 Preheat the oven to 425°F. Make a slit along the length of each chicken breast half and enlarge to form a "pocket".

2 Divide the mozzarella cheese between the chicken breast halves, sliding the slices into the pockets. Top the cheese with the tomato slices and crushed garlic. Roughly chop a little of the basil and add a sprinkling to each pocket.

3 Season each chicken breast. Place a large sprig of basil on each, then wrap in a slice of prosciutto, making sure the ham covers the slit in the chicken. Tie the ham securely with 3 or 4 pieces of string on each breast.

4 Heat the oil in a large frying pan (preferably one with an ovenproof handle) over medium heat. Add the chicken breasts and sauté over high heat until brown on both sides, 3 to 4 minutes. Transfer the skillet to the oven or transfer the chicken to a baking dish. Bake until the chicken is cooked through and the juices run clear when the thickest part is pierced with a knife, 10 to 12 minutes.

5 Meanwhile, make the salad. Put the oil and lemon juice in a bowl, season with salt and pepper to taste, and whisk together. Add the lettuce and watercress, and toss together. Divide between 4 serving plates.

6 Remove the string from the chicken breasts. Cut each piece crosswise into slices, holding it together so it keeps its shape. Arrange on the salad and garnish with the remaining basil.

Another Idea

● As an alternative to the mozzarella filling, use feta cheese and watercress. Melt 1 tablespoon butter in a skillet over medium heat. Sauté ½ minced red onion, until soft, 3 to 5 minutes. Add 2½ ounces watercress sprigs and sauté until the watercress just wilts, about 1 minute longer. Crumble in 3 ounces feta cheese, and season with nutmeg and black pepper.

Plus Points

● Mozzarella contains less fat than many cheeses. For example, a 1 ounce serving of whole-milk mozzarella has 79 calories and 6.1g fat, while the same amount of cheddar cheese has 113 calories and 9.3g fat.

● The Greeks and Romans believed eating watercress could cure madness. We, too, attribute healing powers to this green leaf, because it contains powerful phytochemicals that help to protect against cancer. It is also a good source of many B vitamins, plus vitamins C and E, and beta-carotene, which the body converts into vitamin A.

Main Meals

Chicken with Apricots and Cumin

Tender, flavorful chicken thighs are excellent in a casserole. Fresh apricots and fennel make good partners, especially when spiced with ground cumin and cilantro. Plain boiled or saffron rice, boiled new potatoes, or baked potatoes go well with this dish.

Serves 4

2 tablespoons sunflower oil

8 chicken thighs, about 1 pound in total

1 onion, sliced

2 garlic cloves, chopped

2 teaspoons ground cumin

2 teaspoons ground cilantro

1¼ cups chicken stock

3 carrots, halved crosswise, then each half cut into 6 to 8 thick pieces

1 bulb fennel, halved lengthwise, then cut crosswise into slices

5 ripe but firm apricots, pitted and quartered

Salt and fresh-ground black pepper

Chopped fennel leaves from the bulb, or herb fennel

Preparation time: 15 minutes

Cooking time: 50 minutes

1 Heat the oil in a large Dutch oven over medium heat. Add the chicken thighs and sauté until golden brown all over, 5 to 10 minutes. Remove from the pan. Add the onion and garlic to the Dutch oven and sauté until soft and golden, about 5 minutes.

2 Stir in all the cumin and cilantro and sauté 1 minute. Pour in the stock, and return the chicken to the Dutch oven together with the carrots and fennel. Bring to a boil and stir well. Reduce the heat, cover, and simmer until the chicken is tender and the juices run clear when the thickest part is pierced with a knife, about 30 minutes. Uncover and, if there is too much liquid, boil to reduce slightly.

3 Add the apricots to the Dutch oven and stir gently to mix. Simmer over low heat 5 minutes longer.

4 Season to taste with salt and pepper, sprinkle with the fennel leaves, and serve with rice or potatoes.

Plus Points

- Chicken is a good source of protein.
- Both apricots and carrots provide some vitamin A in the form of beta-carotene, which gives them their distinctive color, but carrots are by far the better source, providing about 20 times more of this nutrient per 3 ounce serving than apricots. Vitamin A is essential for proper vision and increasingly valued for its role as an antioxidant, helping to prevent cancer and coronary heart disease.

Some More Ideas

- Most of the fat in chicken is contained in the skin, so removing the skin before cooking reduces the calories and fat per serving.
- For a different flavor, omit the ground cumin and coriander, and add 8 tablespoons bottled black bean sauce at the end of Step 3 and heat through.
- Replace the apricots with 1 fresh mango, cut into slices or chunks. Sprinkle with chopped fresh cilantro instead of fennel leaves.
- Use 1 can of apricot halves in natural juice, about 400 g, drained and cut in half, instead of fresh apricots.

Each serving provides

cals 360, **protein** 22 g, **fat** 24 g (of which saturated fat 6 g), **carbohydrate** 12 g (of which sugars 11 g), **fiber** 3.3 g

✓✓✓	A
✓✓	B₆, C
✓	B₁, B₂, folate, copper, iron, potassium, selenium, zinc

Main Meals

Indian-Style Broiled Chicken

Tandoori dishes are often the healthiest option in Indian restaurants because they are cooked without fat added. At home, a hot broiler gives a similar result. These lean chicken pieces are served with creamy low-fat raita. All that is needed to complete the meal is rice or warm bread.

Serves 4

4 skinless boneless chicken breast halves, about 5 ounces each

Sunflower oil for brushing

Lemon or lime wedges, to serve

Fresh cilantro sprigs

Yogurt Marinade

1 garlic clove, crushed

1 tablespooon minced fresh ginger

1½ teaspoon tomato paste

1½ teaspoon garam masala or curry powder

1½ teaspoon ground coriander

1½ teaspoon ground cumin

¼ teaspoon ground turmeric

Pinch cayenne pepper, or to taste

7 tablespoons plain low-fat yogurt

Raita

1½ cups plain low-fat yogurt

1 cucumber, about 10 ounces, cut into quarters lengthwise and seeded

1 small tomato, seeded and finely chopped

½ teaspoon ground coriander

½ teaspoon ground cumin

Pinch cayenne pepper

Pinch salt

Preparation time: about 15 minutes
Cooking time: 15 minutes

1 Preheat the broiler to high. To make the marinade, put garlic, ginger, tomato paste, garam masala, cilantro, cumin, turmeric, cayenne and yogurt into a bowl and whisk. If you prefer, process the ingredients in a blender or food processor. Transfer to a bowl large enough to hold all the chicken pieces.

2 Score 2 slits on each side of the chicken breasts. Place them in the marinade, turning to coat and rubbing the marinade into the slits. (If you have time, leave the chicken to marinate in the refrigerator overnight.)

3 Brush the broiler rack with oil, then place the chicken pieces on top. Broil, turning and basting with the remaining marinade, until the chicken is tender, and the juices run clear when the chicken is pierced with a knife, and the marinade looks lightly charred, 12 to 15 minutes.

4 Meanwhile, make the raita. Place the yogurt in a bowl. Coarsely grate the cucumber, then squeeze to remove as much moisture as possible. Stir the cucumber, tomato, ground coriander, cumin, cayenne, and salt into the yogurt. Spoon the raita into a serving bowl.

5 Transfer the chicken pieces to a serving plate. Add lemon or lime wedges and garnish with cilantro sprigs. Serve with the raita on the side.

Plus Points

● Chicken is a low-fat source of protein and this marinade adds very little extra fat.

● Yogurt is an excellent source of protein and calcium, needed for healthy bones and teeth, and it provides useful amounts of phosphorus and vitamins B_2 and B_{12}, as well as beneficial bacteria.

Each serving provides

cals 267, **protein** 37 g, **fat** 8 g (of which saturated fat 3 g), **carbohydrate** 11 g (of which sugars 11 g), **fiber** 0.8 g

✓✓✓	B_6, niacin
✓✓	B_2, calcium, potassium, selenium
✓	B_1, B_{12}, C, E, folate, copper, iron, zinc

Main Meals

Some More Ideas

- For a crisper texture on the broiled chicken, omit the yogurt from the marinade, double the other ingredients, and stir in 1 tablespoon white distilled vinegar.
- Try this Onion and Herb Raita with either version of the broiled chicken: Very finely chop 1 large sweet onion, such as Vidalia, or 7 ounces scallions. Place in a medium bowl. Stir in 4 to 6 tablespoons minced fresh mint, 2 tablespoons minced fresh cilantro, 1 seeded and minced fresh green chile, or to taste, and 1½ cups plain low-fat yogurt. Heat a dry skillet over high heat. Add 2 teaspoons cumin seeds and sauté, stirring constantly, until they give off their aroma and start to jump: Immediately tip them on top of the raita.
- For Indian-style kabobs, cut the chicken into cubes before you put it in the marinade. While preheating the broiler, soak 8 bamboo skewers in water. Thread the cubes onto the skewers, alternating with chunks of zucchini and red and yellow bell pepper cubes. Broil, basting with the marinade and turning the skewers over several times, until the chicken is tender and the juices run clear, 12 to 15 minutes.
- A quick alternative to raita is to serve the chicken with a simple salad of chopped tomatoes and onions on lettuce leaves with minced cilantro sprinkled over.

Main Meals

123

French-Style Chicken in Wine

This up-dated and low-fat version of a classic bistro dish contains shallots, mushrooms, and carrots, all you need to add is potatoes—and, of course, lots of fresh French bread—for a truly satisfying meal.

Serves 4

12 shallots or pear onions

1½ tablespoons garlic-flavored olive oil

2 ounces Canadian bacon, cut into thin strips

12 cremini or white mushrooms

4 chicken pieces such as breast halves, about 6 ounces

Several sprigs parsley, stems bruised

Several sprigs fresh thyme

1 bay leaf

⅔ cup chicken stock, preferably homemade

1½ cups full-bodied red wine, such as shiraz

2 carrots, about 10 ounces, cut into chunks

Pinch sugar

1 tablespoon cornstarch

Salt and fresh-ground black pepper

Chopped parsley

Preparation time: 15 minutes

Cooking time: about 1¼ hours

Each serving provides

cals 398, **protein** 40 g, **fat** 16 g (of which saturated fat 4 g), **carbohydrate** 15 g (of which sugars 10 g), **fiber** 3.8 g

✓✓✓	A, B₆, niacin, copper
✓✓	B₁, B₂, iron, potassium, selenium, zinc
✓	E, folate

1 Put the shallots or onions in a heatproof bowl and pour enough boiling water to cover over. Leave for 30 seconds, then drain. When cool enough to handle, peel and set aside.

2 Heat 1 tablespoon of the oil in a Dutch oven over medium heat. Add the bacon and sauté, stirring often, until crisp, about 3 minutes. Remove the bacon with a draining spoon and set aside.

3 Add the shallots to the Dutch oven and sauté until brown all over, 5 to 8 minutes. Remove with a draining spoon and set aside.

4 Add the mushrooms to the Dutch oven, with the remaining ½ tablespoon oil, if needed, and sauté until golden, 3 to 4 minutes.

5 Return half of the bacon and shallots to the Dutch oven. Place the chicken pieces on top and sprinkle with the remaining bacon and shallots. Tie the herbs into a bouquet garni and add to the Dutch oven with the stock and wine. Season generously with pepper.

6 Bring to a boil, then reduce the heat to very low, cover, and simmer 15 minutes. Add the carrots and continue simmering over low heat until the chicken is cooked tender and the juices run clear when pierced, and the carrots are fork-tender.

7 Remove the chicken and arrange on a warm serving platter. Strain the liquid into a saucepan. Add the bacon, mushrooms, shallots, and carrots to the chicken and keep warm.

8 Put the bouquet garni back in the strained liquid, add the sugar, and bring to a boil. Boil until the sauce is reduced to about 1½ cups. Meanwhile, mix the cornstarch with a little water until a smooth paste forms. Stir into the sauce, and simmer until thicker. Adjust the seasoning to taste and discard the bouquet garni. Spoon the sauce over the chicken and vegetables and sprinkle with the parsley.

Plus Points

• Unlike most vegetables, which are most nutritious when eaten raw, cooking carrots increases their nutritional value. Because raw carrots have tough cell walls, the body can convert only about 25 percent of the beta-carotene present into vitamin A. Cooking breaks down the cell membrane, making it easier for the body to absorb and convert the beta-carotene.

• Red wine contains flavonoid compounds, which might help to protect against heart disease.

Some More Ideas

● If you do not have garlic-flavored olive oil, use extra-virgin olive oil and fry 1 crushed garlic clove with the mushrooms.

● For Chicken with Riesling, typical of the Alsace region of northeastern France, take 1¼ pounds skinless boneless chicken breast halves or thighs, cut into large chunks. Use Riesling instead of red wine. Add the carrots with the chicken and simmer 30 minutes, then add 1 cup frozen peas, straight from the freezer, and continue simmering about 5 minutes. Strain and reduce the cooking liquid as above, then thicken and enrich with 4 tablespoons whipping cream or sour cream. Serve the chicken with egg noodles, boiled and tossed with minced parsley or poppy seeds.

Marsala Chicken with Fennel

Cooking with a little wine gives depth to a sauce: Almost all the alcohol and calories burn away, leaving only great flavor behind. This sauce is thickened with a mixture of egg and lemon juice, which is typically Mediterranean and less rich than beurre manié or cream.

Serves 4

1 chicken, about 3 pounds, jointed

2 tablespoon all-purpose flour

2 tablespoons extra-virgin olive oil

1 large leek, coarsely chopped

1 tablespoon chopped parsley

1 teaspoon fennel seeds

6 tablespoons Marsala

2¼ cups chicken stock, preferably homemade

2 medium fennel bulbs, trimmed and cut into chunks

2 cups shelled fresh or frozen peas

Fresh juice of 1 lemon

1 large egg, lightly beaten

Salt and fresh-ground black pepper

To garnish

Chopped parsley

Lemon zest shreds

Preparation time: 15 minutes

Cooking time: 45 minutes

Each serving provides

cals 392, **protein** 43 g, **fat** 16 g (of which saturated fat 4 g), **carbohydrate** 14 g (of which sugars 3 g), **fiber** 3.3 g

✓✓✓	B₆, niacin
✓✓	B₁, B₂, C, folate, iron, potassium, selenium, zinc
✓	A, B₁₂, E, calcium, copper

1 Remove the skin from the chicken pieces, except for any small pieces, such as the wings, which are too difficult to skin. Season the flour with salt and pepper to taste. Dust the flour over the joints.

2 Heat 1 tablespoon of the oil in a large skillet over medium heat. Add the leek, parsley, and fennel seeds and sauté until the leek is soft, stirring frequently, about 5 minutes. Remove from the pan with a draining spoon; set aside.

3 Heat the remaining 1 tablespoon oil in the skillet. Add the chicken and sauté until just golden all over, 6 to 7 minutes. Remove the chicken from the pan; set aside. Pour in the Marsala and boil until it is reduced to about 2 tablespoons of glaze. Pour in the stock, and return the leek mixture and dark meat chicken pieces and wings to the skillet. (Wait to add the breasts so they don't overcook.) Add the fennel chunks. Cover and simmer over low heat 10 to 15 minutes. Add the chicken breasts and continue to simmer, covered, until all the chicken joints are tender and the juices run clear when pierced in the thickest part, about 15 minutes. Add the peas for the last 5 minutes of cooking.

4 Using a draining spoon, transfer the chicken pieces and vegetables to a serving bowl; keep warm.

5 In a small bowl, mix the lemon juice into the egg. Slowly add about 4 tablespoons of the hot cooking liquid to the lemon and egg mixture, stirring. Slowly stir this mixture back into the liquid in the skillet. Return the chicken and vegetables to the pan and gently warm it all through, taking care that the heat is very low so the sauce does not curdle. Season to taste and return to the serving bowl. Serve, garnished with parsley and shreds of lemon zest.

Plus Points

● Fennel bulbs contain more phytoestrogen than most vegetables. This naturally occurring plant hormone encourages the body to excrete excess estrogen (a high level of estrogen is linked with greater risk of breast cancer).

● Peas provide good amounts of the B vitamins B₁, B₆, and niacin. They also offer dietary fiber, particularly the soluble variety, plus some folate and vitamin C.

● The dark meat of chicken contains twice as much iron and zinc as the light meat.

Main Meals

Some More Ideas

● Use 8 skinless boneless chicken thighs, about 1 pound 2 ounces in total, instead of a jointed chicken.

● Replace the leek with 2 chopped onions.

● For Chicken with Asparagus and Fennel Seeds, omit the peas and fennel bulb. Cut 8 ounces of asparagus into bite-size pieces and add to the simmering chicken at the end of Step 3, just before you remove the chicken pieces and leeks. Thicken with the egg and lemon mixture, as in the main recipe. Do not overcook the asparagus: 1 to 2 minutes should be enough. Asparagus is an excellent source of folate, and a good source of beta-carotene.

Pan-Fried Turkey Scallops with Citrus-Honey Sauce

Here, tangy orange and lemon, with honey and shallots, create a flavorsome, low-calorie sauce to complement the mild flavor of turkey. Serve on a stack of green beans and steamed new potatoes that have been scrubbed, but not peeled.

Serves 4

4 small skinless turkey breast steaks, about 4 ounces each

2 tablespoons butter

4 large shallots, thinly sliced

1 garlic clove, crushed

14 ounces thin green beans, trimmed

2 tablespoons honey

Fresh-grated zest and juice of 1 orange

Fresh-grated zest and juice of 1 lemon

Salt and fresh-ground black pepper

Preparation time: 15 minutes

Cooking time: about 15 minutes

Each serving provides

cals 245, **protein** 27 g, **fat** 9 g (of which saturated fat 5 g), **carbohydrate** 14 g (of which sugars 13 g), **fiber** 3.8 g

✓✓✓	B$_{12}$
✓✓	B$_6$, C, folate, niacin, iron, zinc
✓	A, copper, potassium

1 Put the turkey steaks between sheets of plastic and pound them to flatten to about ¼ inch thick; set aside.

2 Melt the butter in a large skillet over medium heat. Add the shallots and garlic, and sauté until soft, but not brown, 2 to 3 minutes. Using a draining spoon, remove the shallots; set aside.

3 Put the turkey scallops in the pan, in one layer, and fry them 2 to 3 minutes on each side.

4 Meanwhile, bring a large saucepan of salted water to a boil. Add the green beans and boil until crisp-tender, 3 to 4 minutes. Drain and rinse briefly in cold water to stop the cooking; set aside and keep warm.

5 Mix the honey with the orange and lemon zests and juices. Remove the turkey scallops from the skillet; keep hot. Pour the honey mixture into the skillet, return the shallots, garlic, and salt and pepper to taste. Bring to a boil and boil about 2 minutes, stirring constantly.

6 Arrange a mound of beans on 4 plates. Place a turkey scallop on top of each mound. Spoon the sliced shallots and pan juices over.

Some More Ideas

• Use 4 skinless boneless turkey breast halves, about 4 ounces each. Being a bit thicker than scallops, they will need to be sautéed 5 minutes on each side.

• Replace the turkey steaks with 4 small boneless duck breast halves, about 1¼ pounds in total. Remove the skin and all fat from the duck pieces. Pan-fry 3 minutes on each side, if you like duck pink, or a little longer for well-done duck. For the sauce, use the fresh-grated zest and juice from a pink grapefruit, instead of the orange and lemon. Also add a piece preserved ginger, cut into fine slivers, and 1 tablespoon ginger syrup.

• Replace the beans with 3 finely shredded leeks, stir-fried in 1 tablespoon sunflower oil.

Plus Points

• Turkey contains even less fat than chicken, making it one of the lowest fat meats available.

• All citrus fruits are an excellent source of vitamin C. Studies have shown a correlation between a regular intake of vitamin C and the maintenance of intellectual function in elderly people.

Main Meals

129

Turkey Kabobs with Fennel and Red Bell Pepper Relish

Lean bites of turkey are marinated with wine and herbs, and then threaded onto skewers to be broiled or barbecued. A colorful, raw-vegetable relish provides vitamin C, as well as a refreshing taste contrast. A carbohydrate such as couscous is an ideal accompaniment.

Serves 4

1 pound boneless skinless turkey breast meat, ideally in 1 piece

3 garlic cloves, chopped

1½ tablespoons lemon juice

2 tablespoons dry white wine

1 tablespoon chopped fresh sage, or 2 teaspoons dried sage, crumbled

1 tablespoon chopped fresh rosemary needles

1½ teaspoon fresh thyme leaves, or ½ teaspoon dried thyme

1 teaspoon fennel seeds, lightly crushed

2½ tablespoons extra-virgin olive oil

1 red bell pepper, seeded and finely diced

1 fennel bulb, finely diced

1 tablespoon black olive paste (tapenade), or 10 black kalamata olives, pitted and finely diced

8 fresh rosemary sprigs (optional)

8 shallots or pearl onions

Salt and fresh-ground black pepper

Preparation time: 20 minutes, plus at least 10 minutes marinating

Cooking time: 15 minutes

1 Cut the turkey into 24 pieces, each about 2 x ¾ inch. Combine the turkey pieces with 2 of the garlic cloves, 1 tablespoon lemon juice, the wine, sage, rosemary, thyme, fennel seeds, 2 tablespoons of the olive oil, and salt and pepper to taste. Toss so all the turkey pieces are coated with the herb mixture. Leave to marinate for at least 10 minutes, or up to an hour if you have the time.

2 Meanwhile, make the relish. Put the red bell pepper, fennel, and olive paste or diced olives, the remaining garlic, ½ tablespoon lemon juice, and ½ tablespoon olive oil in a medium bowl and stir together. Add salt and pepper to taste; set aside.

3 Preheat the broiler to high, or prepare a charcoal fire in the barbecue. Thread the marinated turkey pieces onto the rosemary sprigs, if using, or onto skewers. Add a shallot or pearl onion to each.

4 Broil or barbecue the kabobs, turning them over and basting with the marinade, until the turkey is cooked through and lightly charred in spots, about 15 minutes. Serve the kabobs hot with the pepper relish.

Plus Points

• Red bell peppers are an excellent source of vitamin C and they are also rich in beta-carotene. Both of these nutrients are powerful antioxidants that can help to counteract the damaging effects of free radicals and protect against many diseases, including cancer and heart disease.

• Fennel provides useful amounts of potassium and the B vitamin folate, which is needed for blood formation. It is also low in calories.

Each serving provides

cals 224, **protein** 28 g, **fat** 9.5 g (of which saturated fat 1.5 g), **carbohydrate** 7 g (of which sugars 6 g), **fiber** 1.6 g

✓✓✓	B$_6$, B$_{12}$, C
✓✓	A, niacin
✓	E, folate, copper, iron, potassium, zinc

Main Meals

Some More Ideas

• Instead of making a vegetable relish, add the red bell pepper and fennel to the kabobs. Cut the pepper and fennel into 1 inch chunks. Alternate the vegetable chunks with pieces of turkey on the skewers, and brush all over with the turkey marinade. Broil or barbecue as above, then serve the turkey and vegetable kabobs drizzled with the remaining extra-virgin olive oil and lemon juice.

• Another delicious relish, without any oil, can be made with roasted red bell pepper and tomatoes. Cut a large red pepper in half and broil the skin side until it is blistered and charred. Put into a bag and leave until cool enough to handle, then peel. Finely dice the flesh and mix with 1 seeded and diced tomato, 1 finely chopped shallot, 2 chopped garlic cloves, 2 tablespoon chopped fresh basil or parsley, a splash of balsamic vinegar, and salt and pepper to taste.

Spiced Stir-Fried Duck

In this dish, strips of duck are stir-fried with onions, water chestnuts, bok choy and—for sweetness—fresh pear. Little oil is needed to stir-fry, and including lots of vegetables keeps the quantity of meat down. Serve with Chinese noodles or boiled or steamed rice.

Serves 4

14 ounces boneless duck breasts

2 teaspoons Chinese five-spice powder

2 tablespoons sunflower oil

⅔ cup thinly sliced pearl onions

4 small celery stalks, thinly sliced, plus a few
leaves to garnish

1 large firm pear, peeled, cored, and diced

1 can (8 ounces) sliced water chestnuts,
drained

1 tablespoon honey

3 tablespoons rice vinegar or sherry vinegar

1 tablespoon soy sauce

3 cups shredded bok choy

5 ounces bean sprouts

Preparation time: about 15 minutes

Cooking time: about 10 minutes

1 Remove the skin and all fat from the duck breasts, then cut them crosswise into thin strips. Sprinkle with the Chinese five-spice powder and toss to coat; set aside for a few minutes while the vegetables are prepared.

2 Place a wok or large skillet over high heat until really hot. Add the oil and swirl to coat the wok. Add the duck pieces and stir-fry 2 minutes. Add the onions and celery and continue stir-frying until soft, about 3 minutes. Add the pear and water chestnuts and stir to mix.

3 Stir in the honey, rice vinegar, and soy sauce. When the liquid is bubbling, reduce the heat to low and simmer 2 minutes, stirring occasionally.

4 Increase the heat to high again. Add the bok choy and bean sprouts and stir-fry until the bok choy just wilts and the bean sprouts are heated through, about 1 minute.

5 Transfer to a warm serving dish and garnish with celery leaves.

Plus Points

- Removing the skin and fat from duck lowers the fat content substantially. Skinless duck breasts contains only a fraction more fat than skinless chicken breast.
- Dark green, leafy vegetables, such as bok choy, provide good amounts of vitamin C, as well as vitamin B_6, folate, and niacin.
- Bean sprouts are a good source of vitamin C and also offer B vitamins.
- Water chestnuts provide small amounts of potassium, iron, and fiber. They also do not contain any fat and only have a few calories.

Some More Ideas

- For a less piquant sauce, replace the rice vinegar or sherry vinegar with red wine or apple or orange juice.
- If in season, use an Asian pear instead of an ordinary pear. Or, substitute 3 or 4 ripe but firm plums, sliced, for the pear.
- For a duck stir-fry with a citrus flavour, use ground star anise instead of Chinese five-spice powder, and 6 ounces sliced and seeded kumquats instead of the pear. Replace the bok choy with ½ head Chinese leaves, shredded. Instead of rice vinegar, use orange juice or red wine.
- Use skinless boneless chicken or turkey breasts, cut into strips, instead of the duck.

Each serving provides

cals 200, protein 13 g, fat 9 g (of which saturated fat 2 g), carbohydrate 17 g (of which sugars 13 g), fiber 5.6 g

✓✓✓	B_{12}
✓✓	B_6, C, E, folate, copper, iron
✓	B_1, B_2, niacin, calcium, potassium, zinc

Main Meals

Pheasant Casseroled with Ginger

Casseroling is an excellent way to cook pheasant, as it produces succulent pieces of both breast and dark meat, and the goodness from both creates a rich sauce. Herby mashed potatoes, baby carrots, and broccoli are good accompaniments for this aromatic dish.

Serves 4

1 large fennel bulb, about 10 ounces

1 tablespoon sunflower oil

1 pheasant, about 2¼ pounds, jointed into 4 or 8 pieces

⅔ cup halved shallots or pearl onions

4 pieces preserved ginger, about 4 ounces in total, cut into thin strips

4 tablespoons white zinfandel

1¼ cups chicken stock, preferably homemade

Salt and fresh-ground black pepper

Preparation time: 15 minutes
Cooking time: about 1¼ hours

1 Preheat the oven to 375°F. Trim the fennel, retaining any feathery leaves for the garnish, then cut the bulb lengthwise into 8 wedges; set aside.

2 Heat the oil in a large Dutch oven over medium-high heat. Add the pheasant pieces and shallots or button onions and fry to brown on all sides.

3 Add the fennel wedges. Turn the pheasant pieces skin side up and sprinkle the ginger strips over. Add the wine and enough stock to come halfway up the pheasant pieces, but not cover them completely. Season with salt and pepper to taste.

4 Bring to a boil, then cover the Dutch oven and transfer to the oven. Cook until the pheasant is tender, 1 to 1¼ hours. Serve garnished with the reserved fennel leaves.

Plus Points

● Pheasant is an excellent source of protein, as well as iron and B vitamins. Although it is higher in fat than other game birds, most of this fat is monounsaturated.

● There is evidence to suggest onions help to prevent circulatory diseases such as thrombosis and many conditions associated with strokes, because they appear to contain a substance that stops blood clotting.

Some More Ideas

● Try Pheasant Casserole with Chestnuts and Cabbage. Brown the pheasant pieces and shallots as in the main recipe. Add 7 ounces shelled and skinned chestnuts and 1 small head red cabbage, cut into 4 wedges, instead of the fennel wedges. Replace the ginger with 2 tablespoons orange marmalade and use red wine instead of white wine.

● Other game birds can be jointed and casseroled in the same way.

● When game is out of season, use duck or chicken joints.

Each serving provides

cals 238, **protein** 32 g, **fat** 11 g (of which saturated fat 2 g), **carbohydrate** 3.5 g (of which sugars 3 g), **fiber** 0.5 g

✓✓✓	B_6, B_{12}, niacin, iron
✓✓	B_2, potassium, zinc
✓	E, folate, calcium, copper

Main Meals

135

Pot-Roasted Partridge with Sage

Naturally low in calories, partridge is perfect for pot roasting. Cooking in hard cider, or apple juice, and stock keeps the meat moist, and sage, walnuts, and apple add wonderful flavors. Carrot and celery-root puree is an ideal extra, or try mashed potato with scallions.

Serves 4

4 partridges
½ ounce fresh sage
1 tablespoon butter
1 tablespoon extra-virgin olive oil
1 onion, finely chopped
1 tablespoon all-purpose flour
1¼ cups hard cider or apple juice
⅔ cup chicken stock, preferably homemade
2 teaspoons German or whole-grain mustard
3 walnut halves, thinly sliced
1 red-skinned dessert apple, cored and cut into thick slices
Salt and fresh-ground black pepper

Preparation time: 10 minutes
Cooking time: about 1¼ hours

Each serving provides

cals 371, **protein** 40 g, **fat** 19 g (of which saturated fat 4.8 g), **carbohydrate** 9 g (of which sugars 7 g), **fiber** 1.7 g

✓✓✓	iron
✓	potassium

1 Preheat the oven to 325°F. Tuck some sage sprigs into the body cavity of each partridge, reserving a few sprigs for garnish.

2 Melt the butter with the oil in a Dutch oven just large enough to hold the birds over medium heat. Add the partridges and fry over a moderately high heat, turning until evenly brown, 3 to 4 minutes. Lift the birds out of the Dutch oven; set aside.

3 Add the onion to the Dutch oven and sauté until light brown, about 3 minutes. Sprinkle in the flour and stir into the onion. Add the cider, or apple juice, stock, mustard, and salt and pepper to taste. Bring to a boil, stirring constantly. Add the walnuts.

4 Return the partridges to the Dutch oven, breasts side down. Cover and transfer to the oven. Cook until the partridges are tender, about 1 hour.

5 Lift the partridges out of the Dutch oven and place on a warm serving plate; cover and keep hot.

6 Set the Dutch oven on the stovetop over high heat. Bring to a boil and boil the cooking liquid until reduced by a third, about 5 minutes. Add the apple slices for the last 2 minutes of cooking.

7 Spoon the apple slices around the birds and garnish with the reserved sage sprigs. Serve with the sauce.

Some More Ideas

• To make a Carrot and Celery-root Puree, cook 2 cups each peeled and diced celery-root and carrots in boiling water until very tender, about 20 minutes. Drain and mash, or puree in a food processor, with 3 tablespoons low-fat (2%) milk and salt and pepper to taste. Spoon into a serving dish and sprinkle a little fresh-grated nutmeg over.

• For partridge pot-roasted with mushrooms, soak ½ ounce dried porcini mushrooms in 1¼ cups boiling water 30 minutes. Drain, reserving the soaking liquid. Make the liquid up to 2 cups with the fresh juice of 1 orange and chicken stock. Add 2 teaspoons tomato paste and 1¼ cups dry red wine. Use this as the cooking liquid. Replace the sage with fresh thyme, and add the mushrooms instead of walnuts. Omit the apple, and garnish the dish with orange slices and a sprinkling of fresh thyme leaves.

Plus Points

• Walnuts, like most nuts, are high in fat, however, this is not all a bad thing as it is mostly the healthy form of unsaturated fatty acids. Recent tests have shown that a daily consumption of ⅔ cup of walnuts—when used in place of saturated fats as part of a low-fat diet—lowers blood cholesterol.

Main Meals

Tagliatelle with Green Sauce

This simple, creamy vegetable sauce is bursting with fresh flavors, and it is much lighter than any of the classic cream sauces for pasta. A mixed-leaf salad with crisp radicchio completes the meal.

Serves 4

1 bag (10 ounces) baby spinach, thick stems discarded
3 ounces watercress, thick stems discarded
1 cup frozen peas
1 pound fresh tagliatelle
2 teaspoons cornstarch
1 cup nonfat sour cream
4 tablespoons chopped parsley
6 sprigs fresh basil, torn into pieces
Salt and fresh-ground black pepper

Preparation time: 5 minutes
Cooking time: 7 to 8 minutes

Each serving provides Ⓥ
cals 215, **protein** 11 g, **fat** 6 g (of which saturated fat 3 g), **carbohydrate** 30 g (of which sugars 3 g), **fiber** 4.7 g

✓✓✓	A
✓✓	C, E, folate, calcium
✓	B$_2$, niacin, copper, iron, zinc

1 Rinse the spinach and watercress and place in a large saucepan with just the water clinging to the leaves. Cover and cook over medium heat, stirring and turning the vegetables occasionally, until they wilt, about 2 minutes.

2 Add the peas and heat through, uncovered, 2 minutes; there should be enough liquid in the saucepan to cook the peas. Tip the greens and their liquid into a bowl; set aside.

3 Cook the pasta in a large saucepan of boiling water over high heat until al dente, 3 minutes, or according to package directions.

4 Meanwhile, blend the cornstarch to a smooth paste with the sour cream. Put into the saucepan used for cooking the vegetables and stir over medium heat until just bubbling. Stir in the vegetables, parsley, basil, and salt and pepper to taste. Heat the sauce through, then remove the saucepan from the heat.

5 Drain the pasta and add to the sauce. Toss to mix with the sauce.

Some More Ideas

• When fresh peas are in season, use them instead of frozen. Add to the spinach and watercress in Step 1 and cook 4 minutes.
• For a Creamy Broccoli and Pea Sauce, replace the spinach and watercress with

1 small head broccoli, broken into flowerets. Cook the broccoli in a little boiling water until fork-tender, 5 to 8 minutes. Drain, refresh in cold water, drain well again, and return to the pan. Mash the broccoli with a potato masher, then add the nonfat sour cream mixed with the cornstarch and 5 tablespoons low-fat (2%) milk. Stir in 1 cup frozen peas and 2 minced scallions. Bring to a boil, stirring, and boil until thick, 1 to 2 minutes. Season to taste and add a dash of lemon juice, if you like. Toss with the freshly cooked pasta, then sprinkle with plenty of chopped parsley.

Plus Points

• Spinach and watercress are high on the list of foods that assist in the fight against cancer. They are also full of calcium and carotenoids and contain good amounts of vitamins C and E, and some B vitamins.
• Heat can destroy vitamin C. The best way to cook leafy green vegetables, such as spinach and watercress, and still retain the maximum vitamin C, is to wilt them quickly.
• Peas provide protein. They are also rich in fiber, some of it soluble, and this helps to keep blood sugar levels and cholesterol under control.

Main Meals

139

Pea Curry with Indian Paneer

Paneer is a low-fat Indian cheese, similar to ricotta, but drier. It's often combined with peas in a curry. This flavorsome recipe uses homemade paneer, which is surprisingly simple to make. Serve with basmati rice for a well-balanced Indian-style meal.

Serves 4

Paneer

2½ cups whole milk

6 tablespoons lemon juice

Pea and tomato curry

3 tablespoons sunflower oil

1 large onion, chopped

2 garlic cloves, minced

2 inch piece fresh ginger, minced

1 fresh green chile, seeded, deveined and
   thinly sliced

1 tablespoon coriander seeds, crushed

1 tablespoon cumin seeds, crushed

1 teaspoon ground turmeric

1 tablespoon garam masala or curry powder

2 large, firm tomatoes, quartered

2 cups frozen peas

½ bag (10 ounces) spinach leaves

½ cup roughly chopped fresh cilantro

Salt

Preparation time: 15 minutes, plus about
   45 minutes draining and 3 hours pressing
Cooking time: about 20 minutes

Each serving provides Ⓥ

cals 298, **protein** 20 g, **fat** 15 g (of which saturated fat 5 g), **carbohydrate** 22 g (of which sugars 14 g), **fiber** 6.5 g

✓✓✓	A, C, E
✓✓	B₁, B₁₂, folate, niacin, calcium, zinc
✓	B₂, B₆, copper, iron, potassium

1 First make the paneer. Put the milk into a large saucepan over high heat and bring to a boil. Immediately reduce the heat to low and add the lemon juice. Stir until the milk separates into curds and whey, 1 to 2 minutes. Remove the saucepan from the heat.

2 Line a large sieve or colander with cheesecloth, and set over a large bowl. Pour the milk mixture into the lined sieve or colander. Leave to drain until cool, about 15 minutes.

3 Bring together the corners of the cheesecloth to make a bundle around the drained curds. Squeeze them, then leave to drain until all the whey has dripped though the sieve into the bowl, about 30 minutes. Reserve 1 cup of the whey.

4 Keep the curds wrapped in the cheesecloth and place on a board. Set another board on top and press down to flatten the ball shape into an oblong block. Place cans or weights on top and leave in a cool place until firm, about 3 hours.

5 Carefully peel off the cheesecloth. Cut the cheese into ¾ inch squares. Heat 1 tablespoon of the oil in a large, nonstick skillet over medium heat. Fry the paneer until golden, 1 to 2 minutes on each side. As the pieces brown, remove from the pan with a draining spoon; set aside.

6 To make the curry, heat the remaining oil in the skillet over medium heat. Add the onion and sauté until soft, about 5 minutes. Stir in the garlic and ginger, and continue sautéing 1 minute. Stir in the chile, coriander and cumin seeds, turmeric, and garam masala. Cook 1 minute longer, stirring constantly.

7 Stir in the tomatoes, the reserved whey, and a pinch of salt. Reduce the heat to low, cover the saucepan, and simmer 5 minutes.

8 Add the peas and return the curry to a boil. Reduce the heat, cover again, and simmer 5 minutes longer. Add the spinach, stirring it in gently so you do not breakup the tomatoes too much. Simmer until the spinach wilts and the peas are hot and tender, 3 to 4 minutes.

9 Stir in most of the cilantro. Transfer the curry to a serving dish and scatter the paneer on top. Spoon the curry over the paneer to warm it, then sprinkle with the rest of the cilantro.

Plus Point

• Paneer is low in fat and very nutritious, providing protein, calcium, and vitamins, including vitamins A and D.

Some More Ideas

- Use frozen minted peas.
- For a cottage cheese and vegetable curry, which is similar, but much quicker to make, boil 1 pound 5 ounces peeled potatoes, cut into large chunks, in a large saucepan of boiling water 5 minutes. Add 1 small head cauliflower, cut into flowerets, to the pan and boil 5 minutes longer. Finally, add 1½ cups halved fine green beans and continue boiling until all the vegetables are fork-tender, 3 to 4 minutes. While the vegetables are cooking, place 1½ cups cottage cheese in a sifter and leave to drain. Cook the onion and spices as in Step 6 of the main recipe, then add 1¼ cups vegetable stock and simmer 5 minutes longer. Add the drained potatoes, cauliflower, and beans to the spiced sauce and stir to coat. Season with salt to taste. Fold in the cottage cheese and heat through gently. Serve hot, with wholewheat parathas or naan bread.

Tomato and Pecorino Clafoutis

This savory version of the classic French batter dessert features sweet cherry tomatoes baked in a light, fluffy batter flavored with pecorino cheese. Crusty bread or boiled new potatoes and green beans go well with this dish.

Serves 4

2 teaspoons extra-virgin olive oil

1 pound cherry tomatoes

4 tablespoons snipped fresh chives

¾ cup g (3 oz) coarsely grated sharp pecorino cheese

6 extra large eggs

⅓ cup all-purpose flour

3 tablespoons sour cream

1¼ cup low-fat (2%) milk

Preparation time: 20 minutes
Cooking time: 30 to 35 minutes

1 Preheat the oven to 375°F. Lightly grease 4 shallow ovenproof dishes, each 5 to 6 inches in diameter. Divide the cherry tomatoes among the dishes, spreading them out. Sprinkle with the chives and all but 1 tablespoon of the cheese.

2 Break the eggs into a bowl and whisk them together. Slowly whisk in the flour until smooth. Add the sour cream, then gradually whisk in the milk to make a thin, smooth batter. Season with salt and pepper to taste.

3 Pour the batter over the tomatoes, dividing it evenly between the dishes. Sprinkle the remaining cheese and an extra grinding of pepper over. Bake until set, puffed, and lightly golden, 30 to 35 minutes.

4 Remove the clafoutis from the oven and leave to cool for a few minutes before serving, because the tomatoes are very hot inside.

Some More Ideas

● Bake one large clafoutis, using a lightly greased 9 inch round baking dish that is about 2 inches deep. Increase the baking time to 35 to 40 minutes.

● Use torn fresh basil leaves or chopped fresh oregano instead of chives.

● For a Cheddar and Onion Clafoutis, cut 1 large red onion into thin wedges. Heat 1 tablespoon extra-virgin olive oil in a skillet over medium heat until golden, about 5 minutes. Stir in 1 tablespoon fresh thyme leaves toward the end of the cooking. Scatter the onions over the bottom of a lightly greased 9 inch round baking dish that is about 2 inches deep. Coarsely grate 3 ounces Cheddar cheese and sprinkle all but 1 tablespoon over the onions. Make the batter as in the main recipe and pour over the onions. Give the mixture a stir, then sprinkle the remaining cheese and a few sprigs of fresh thyme over. Bake until set, puffed, and golden, 35 to 40 minutes.

Plus Points

● Pecorino is a hard Italian cheese made from sheep milk. Like Parmesan, it is very high in fat, but only needs be used in small quantities because it has a strong flavour.

● Both sour cream and light cream—the fresh version of sour cream—contain considerably more calcium than other creams.

● Tomatoes contain lycopene, a valuable antioxidant that might help to protect against prostate, bladder, and pancreatic cancers if tomatoes are included in the diet regularly.

Each serving provides Ⓥ

cals 392, **protein** 26 g, **fat** 26 g (of which saturated fat 11 g), **carbohydrate** 17 g (of which sugars 8 g), **fiber** 1.9 g

✓✓✓	B₁₂, calcium
✓✓	A, B₂, C, E, niacin, zinc
✓	B₁, B₆, folate, copper, iron, potassium, selenium

Main Meals

Leek and Mustard Green Pie

Spring vegetables, lively herbs, and zesty lemon make a refreshing filling for a crisp phyllo crust that is easy to prepare and healthy, too. Add baby carrots and new potatoes boiled in their skins to create a well-balanced meal.

Serves 4

Fresh finely grated zest of 1 lemon

2 tablespoons extra-virgin olive oil

1 medium leek, thinly sliced

4 ounces mustard greens, thinly sliced

1 cup frozen peas

2 tablespoons chopped fresh tarragon

1 tablespoon chopped fresh mint

2 extra large eggs

4 tablespoon plain low-fat yogurt

¾ cup diced Gruyère cheese

4 ounces phyllo pastry dough, thawed if frozen

Salt and fresh-ground black pepper

Preparation time: 20 minutes
Cooking time: 20 to 25 minutes

Each serving provides Ⓥ

cals 321, **protein** 16.5 g, **fat** 18 g (of which saturated fat 6 g), **carbohydrate** 23 g (of which sugars 3 g), **fiber** 3.3 g

✓✓✓	B_{12}, C, folate, calcium
✓✓	A, B_1, B_2, B_6, E, niacin, iron
✓	zinc

1 Preheat the oven to 425°F. Mix the lemon zest with the oil; set aside to infuse for about 5 minutes. Heat half the lemon-infused oil in a large saucepan over medium heat. Add the leeks, mustard greens, peas, tarragon, and mint, stirring to coat the vegetables with the oil. Reduce the heat, cover and cook, stirring occasionally, until the greens are lightly cooked and wilted, about 5 minutes.

2 Season the vegetables to taste. Transfer them to an 8 inch pie plate or quiche dish.

3 Beat the eggs with the yogurt. Add a little seasoning and the Gruyère cheese. Pour the mixture evenly over the vegetables and mix lightly.

4 Brush a sheet of phyllo pastry dough very sparingly with a little of the remaining lemon-infused oil. Lay it over the vegetables, tucking the edges neatly inside the rim of the dish. Brush the remaining sheets of phyllo dough with oil and place them on top, greased side up, pinching and pleating them into folds to cover the top evenly.

5 Lay a piece of foil loosely over the top of the pie. Bake 10 minutes. Remove the foil and continue baking until the pastry is crisp and golden brown, 10 to 15 minutes longer. Serve immediately.

Some More Ideas

● Replace the mustard greens and peas with mushrooms and spinach. Sauté 1½ cups sliced white mushrooms with the leeks and herbs, adding 2 crushed garlic cloves, and 1 bunch scallions, sliced. Place in the bottom of the pie plate. Rinse 1 bag (10 ounces) spinach and place in a saucepan over high heat. Cover and cook until the leaves wilt, about 2 minutes (the water remaining on the leaves will provide sufficient moisture). Drain well, pressing out excess liquid, then coarsely chop the spinach and place on top of the mushrooms. Sprinkle evenly with 3 ounces crumbled feta cheese. Pour the egg and yogurt mixture over (omit the Gruyère). Top with the phyllo dough and bake.

● Curly kale and chickpeas are another good combination. Use 1½ cups shredded kale, and 1 can (15 ounces) rinsed chickpeas instead of the mustard greens and peas.

Plus Points

● Phyllo pastry dough can be cooked with just a little fat to give light and crisp results. It is an ideal alternative to rich pastries.

● The leek, a most useful member of the onion family, provides vitamin C, carotenoids and folic acid, as well as the beneficial phytochemicals quercetin and allicin.

Baked Eggplants with Yogurt

In this delicious, low-calorie dish, broiled eggplant and zucchini slices are layered with a rich tomato sauce and cumin-flavored yogurt, before baking. Thick slices of Greek sesame bread, or a sliced baguette, and a crisp green salad are perfect accompaniments.

Serves 4

3 tablespoons extra-virgin olive oil
1 red onion, minced
2 garlic cloves, minced
1 can (14 ounces) crushed tomatoes
2 teaspoons sun-dried tomato paste
6 tablespoons dry red wine
1 bay leaf
2 tablespoons chopped parsley
3 large eggplants, cut into ½ inch slices
3 zucchini, thinly sliced
½ teaspoon ground cumin
¾ cups plain low-fat yogurt
2 large eggs, beaten
2 tablespoons fresh-grated Parmesan cheese
Salt and fresh-ground black pepper

Preparation time: about 50 minutes
Cooking time: 40 to 45 minutes

Each serving provides Ⓥ

cals 304, **protein** 17 g, **fat** 16 g (of which saturated fat 4 g), **carbohydrate** 20 g (of which sugars 18.5 g), **fiber** 5 g

✓✓✓	C, calcium
✓✓	A, B$_6$, B$_{12}$, folate, copper, potassium, zinc
✓	B$_1$, B$_2$, E, niacin, iron, selenium

1 Heat 1 tablespoon of the oil in a large saucepan over medium heat. Add the onion, and cook until soft, about 8 minutes. Add the garlic and cook, stirring, 1 minute longer. Stir in the tomatoes, the tomato paste, wine, and bay leaf. Cover and simmer 10 minutes.

2 Uncover the pan and leave the sauce to bubble until thick, stirring occasionally, about 10 minutes longer. Remove the bay leaf from the sauce. Stir in the parsley and season with salt and pepper to taste.

3 Meanwhile, the sauce is simmering, preheat the broiler to medium. Lightly brush the eggplant and zucchini slices with the remaining oil. Broil, in batches until brown and very tender, 3-4 minutes on each side.

4 Preheat the oven to 350°F. Stir the cumin into half of the yogurt.

5 Arrange a third of the eggplant slices, in one layer, in a 2½-quart baking dish. Spoon half of the tomato sauce over. Arrange half of the zucchini slices on top, in one layer, then drizzle with half of the cumin-flavored yogurt. Repeat the layers, finishing with a layer of eggplant slices.

6 Mix the remaining yogurt with the eggs and half of the Parmesan. Spoon the yogurt mixture over the eggplant, spreading with the back of the spoon to cover evenly. Sprinkle with the remaining Parmesan.

7 Bake until the top is lightly brown and set, and the sauce is bubbling, 40 to 45 minutes. Serve hot, from the baking dish.

Plus Points

• Your normal gut flora can be upset by antibiotics, stress, and a poor diet. Including yogurt in the diet helps to maintain the "good" bacteria in the gut and prevent the growth of less desirable bacteria.

• Eggplants are a useful vegetable to include in dishes, because they add bulk and dietary fiber without adding calories—½ cup boiled cubed eggplant has just 15 calories.

• Flavonoids are compounds found in onions, which can help to protect against heart disease. Although they occur in both red and white onions, red onions have been shown to have higher levels of flavonoids.

Another Idea

• For Chicken, Spinach, and Yogurt Layered Bake, cook 2 large sliced leeks in lightly boiling water until just tender, 4 to 5 minutes. Drain and spread half over the bottom of a 1¾ quart baking dish. Cut 10 ounces cooked skinless, boneless chicken breast into thick slices and arrange on top of the leeks; set aside. Pack 1½ bags (10 ounces) rinsed spinach into a large saucepan, cover, and simmer, stirring occasionally, until the spinach wilts, 2 to 3 minutes. Drain, but do not squeeze dry. Soften 2 finely chopped shallots in 1 tablespoon butter in the wiped-out saucepan. Add 1 crushed garlic clove and sauté a minute longer. Stir in ¾ cup large-curd cottage cheese, 3 tablespoons low-fat (2%) milk, 1 teaspoon wholegrain mustard, a pinch fresh-grated nutmeg, and salt and pepper to taste. Heat gently, stirring, until smooth and blended, then stir in the spinach. Spoon the mixture over the chicken in the baking dish and spread the remaining leeks on top. Mix ⅔ cup plain low-fat yogurt with 1 tablespoon grated Gruyère cheese, 1 beaten egg, and salt and pepper to taste. Spoon over the leeks and sprinkle with another tablespoon grated Gruyère cheese. Bake in a preheated 350ºF oven 35 minutes. Leave to stand 5 minutes, then serve with baked potatoes.

Herb and Saffron Risotto

This fragrant, fresh-tasting risotto should be eaten as soon as it is cooked—if it is left to stand, the starch in the rice will begin to set, resulting in a heavy texture. Lemon zest and juice and fresh herbs stirred in at the end add a wonderful burst of flavor.

Serves 6

1 tablespoon butter

1 tablespoon extra-virgin olive oil

1 small onion, chopped

1¾ cups risotto rice

⅔ cup dry white wine

Small pinch saffron strands

1¾ quarts vegetable stock, hot

Fresh-grated zest of 1 lemon

2 tablespoons lemon juice

2 tablespoons snipped fresh chives

2 tablespoons chopped parsley

Salt and fresh-ground black pepper

To serve

½ ounce piece Parmesan cheese

Snipped fresh chives

Preparation time: 10 minutes

Cooking time: about 25 minutes

1 Melt the butter with the oil in a large saucepan over medium heat. Add the onion and sauté until soft, stirring occasionally, 4 to 5 minutes.

2 Add the rice and stir 1 minute, to coat all the grains with the butter and oil. Stir in the wine and boil until almost evaporated.

3 Stir the saffron into the hot stock. Add a ladleful of the stock to the saucepan and slowly boil until it is absorbed, stirring frequently. Continue adding stock a ladleful at a time, letting each be almost absorbed before adding the next, and stirring frequently: Total cooking time will be 15 to 20 minutes. The risotto is ready when the rice is tender, but the grains are still whole and firm, and the overall texture is moist and creamy.

4 Remove the saucepan from the heat and stir in the lemon zest and juice, chives, and parsley. Season with salt and pepper to taste.

5 Using a swivel-bladed vegetable peeler, pare thin shavings from the Parmesan and scatter them over the risotto together with the chives.

Some More Ideas

● Stir 3 ounces lightly cooked asparagus tips or ⅔ cup thawed frozen peas into the risotto toward the end of cooking.

● To make an Artichoke Risotto, omit the onion and cook the rice as in the main recipe, adding 2 tablespoons lemon juice with the wine. A few minutes before the end of cooking, stir in 12 ounces artichoke hearts in water, drained. Add mint instead of parsley, and sprinkle with 2 tablespoons chopped walnuts instead of the Parmesan shavings.

Plus Points

● Vitamin loss from rice is reduced when it is cooked by the absorption method, as in making a risotto—the vitamins remain in the liquid, which is then absorbed into the dish.

● Parsley is one of the most nutritious of herb garnishes and it also contains useful amounts of vitamin C and iron. Fresh parsley is also a great breath freshener, and if chewed after a meal can neutralize the aftertaste of ingredients such as garlic.

Each serving provides Ⓥ

cals 285, **protein** 6 g, **fat** 6.5 g (of which saturated fat 2 g), **carbohydrate** 50 g (of which sugars 1 g), **fiber** 1.8 g

✓ niacin, copper, zinc

Main Meals

Broccoli and Bell Pepper Tart

This vegetable-packed quiche is cooked in a deep pan and the dough is rolled out thinly to give a generous amount of filling and small proportion of crust in each slice. Serve warm, rather than piping hot or chilled, with a lightly dressed, crisp salad.

Serves 8

1 tablespoon butter
1 tablespoon extra-virgin olive oil
1 medium onion, thinly sliced
1 red bell pepper, seeded and finely chopped
½ head broccoli, cut into small flowerets
3 extra large eggs, beaten
1 cup low-fat (2%) milk
3 tablespoons minced parsley or snipped
   fresh chives
1½ cups sliced shiitake mushrooms or small
   white mushrooms
½ bag (10 ounces) frozen whole corn kernels,
   thawed and drained
Salt and fresh-ground black pepper

Crust

1 cup all-purpose flour
1 cup wholewheat flour
Pinch cayenne pepper (optional)
½ cup (1 stick) butter, chilled and diced

Preparation time: 1¼ hours, plus at least
   30 minutes chilling
Cooking time: 40 to 45 minutes

Each serving provides ⓥ

cals 330, **protein** 9 g, **fat** 20 g (of which
saturated fat 11 g), **carbohydrate** 32 g (of
which sugars 5 g), **fiber** 4.6 g

✓✓✓	C
✓✓	A, B₁₂, E, folate
✓	B₁, niacin, calcium, iron, selenium

1 To make the dough, sift both flour and the cayenne, if using, into a large bowl, adding the bran left in the sifter. Cut in the butter until the mixture resembles fine crumbs. Sprinkle with 2 tablespoons of ice-cold water and mix to form a dough, adding an extra 1 tablespoon water, if necessary.

2 Gather the dough into a ball. Roll out the dough on a lightly floured surface into an 11 inch circle, about ⅛ inch thick. Line a loose-bottomed 9 inch fluted tart pan with the dough, about 1¼ inches deep. Prick the dough all over with a fork. Cover with plastic wrap and chill at least 30 minutes.

3 Place a baking sheet in the oven and preheat it to 400°F. Melt the butter with the olive oil in a skillet over medium heat. Stir in the onions, reduce the heat to very low, cover, and cook until very tender, about 30 minutes.

4 Meanwhile, bring a saucepan of water to a boil over high heat. Add the red bell pepper and blanch, 1 minute. Remove the pepper with a slotted spoon, place in a colander and refresh under cold water; drain well. Add the broccoli to the same water and blanch 30 seconds, then remove, refresh, and drain well.

5 Line the tart shell with a piece of wax paper and cover with baking beans or rice. Place on the hot baking sheet and bake 20 minutes. Remove the paper and beans, then continue baking 5 minutes longer. Brush the bottom of the crust with a little of the beaten egg and bake 2 minutes longer. Remove the tart shell from the oven, leaving the baking sheet inside. Reduce the oven to 375°F.

6 Beat the milk with the eggs. Add the herbs and salt and pepper to taste. Spread the onions in the tart shell, then add the bell pepper, broccoli, mushrooms, and corn. Pour the egg mixture over the vegetables.

7 Place the tart on the hot baking sheet. Bake until the filling is set, 40 to 45 minutes. Leave to cool at least 10 minutes before serving.

Plus Points

● Eggs have received a "bad press" in recent years because of their cholesterol content, but they are an excellent source of many nutrients, including protein, iron, and vitamins A, B group, and E.

Main Meals

Some More Ideas

• For a crisp Mediterranean-Style Pastry, low in saturated fat, replace the butter with ½ cup olive oil. Use 2 to 4 tablespoons lukewarm water rather than ice-cold. Gather the dough into a soft ball, then press it over the bottom and up the side of the tart pan, trimming any excess dough: This delicate dough must be handled with care or it will tear. Cover and chill at least 30 minutes. Do not prebake the crust. Add the filling to the unbaked tart shell. Bake 350ºF for 55 to 60 minutes. Leave the tart to set and cool before serving. Cut it with a serrated knife.

• Other suitable vegetables to include are finely chopped and seeded tomatoes, shelled peas, and sliced zucchini. For an anise-like flavor, soften a thinly sliced fennel bulb with the onions. Chopped, well-drained cooked spinach can also be added, spread in a thin layer over the onions.

Feta and Couscous Salad

Couscous makes a great background for raw and lightly steamed vegetables, together with toasted almonds, fresh mint, and creamy feta cheese in this Mediterranean-style salad. A touch of chile gives extra bite to the dressing.

Serves 4

1⅓ cups couscous

1¼ cups vegetable stock, hot

6 ounces slim asparagus spears, halved

2 zucchini, cut into thin sticks

1 red bell pepper, seeded and cut into thin strips

2 tablespoons slivered almonds, toasted

Handful of fresh mint leaves, finely chopped

6 ounces feta cheese, drained

Chile Dressing

3 tablespoons extra-virgin olive oil

Grated zest of 1 lemon

1 tablespoon lemon juice

1 garlic clove, minced

½ teaspoon crushed dried chiles

Salt and fresh-ground black pepper

Preparation and cooking time: 30 to 35 minutes

1 Put the couscous into a large heatproof bowl and pour the hot stock over. Leave to soak until all the liquid is absorbed, 15 to 20 minutes.

2 Meanwhile, bring a saucepan of water to a boil and place a steamer on top. Add the asparagus and steam 3 minute. Add the zucchini and continue steaming until both vegetables are crisp-tender, about 2 minutes longer. Tip the vegetables into a colander and run under cold running water; drain well.

3 For the dressing, combine the oil, lemon zest and juice, garlic, chiles, and salt and pepper to taste in a screw-top jar. Secure the top and shake.

4 Fluff up the couscous with a fork. Fold in the pepper strips, almonds, mint, asparagus and zucchini. Pour the dressing over and stir gently together. Crumble the feta over the top just before serving.

Some More Ideas

● Use 1 yellow and 1 green zucchini for some extra color.

● Instead of, or as well as, mint, use other herbs, such as chopped fresh cilantro.

● For Halloumi and Lentil Salad, cook ½ cup Puy or other green lentils in plenty of boiling water until just tender, 15 to 20 minutes. At the same time, cook ½ cup long-grain rice in boiling water until tender, 10 to 15 minutes, or according to package directions. Add 6 ounces fresh or frozen shelled lima beans or peas to the lentils for the last 4 minutes of the cooking time. Drain the rice and lentils well. Stir in 3 finely chopped scallions, 1 seeded and diced red bell pepper, and 2 tablespoons toasted slivered almonds. Make the chile dressing as in the main recipe, and toss with the rice and lentil salad. Cut 6 ounces halloumi cheese into 8 slices. Brush each slice with a little extra-virgin olive oil, using about 1 tablespoon oil in total. Broil or griddle for a few minutes or until golden on both sides. Serve the salad topped with the cheese and an extra grinding of black pepper.

Each serving provides (V)

cals 388, protein 14 g, fat 22 g (of which saturated fat 7.5 g), carbohydrate 35 g (of which sugars 5 g), fiber 2.2 g

✓✓✓	A, C
✓✓	E, folate, calcium, iron
✓	B₁, B₆, B₁₂, niacin, copper, potassium, zinc

Plus Points

● Feta cheese is very salty. If you are concerned about your sodium intake, you can reduce the salt content of the cheese by soaking it in milk 30 minutes before use; discard the milk.

● Couscous, made from semolina, is low in fat and high in starchy carbohydrate.

● Zucchini belong to the same family as melons, cucumbers, and pumpkins. Their skin is a rich source of beta-carotene, which the body converts into vitamin A. This vitamin helps to maintain healthy eyesight and skin, and a properly functioning immune system.

Main Meals

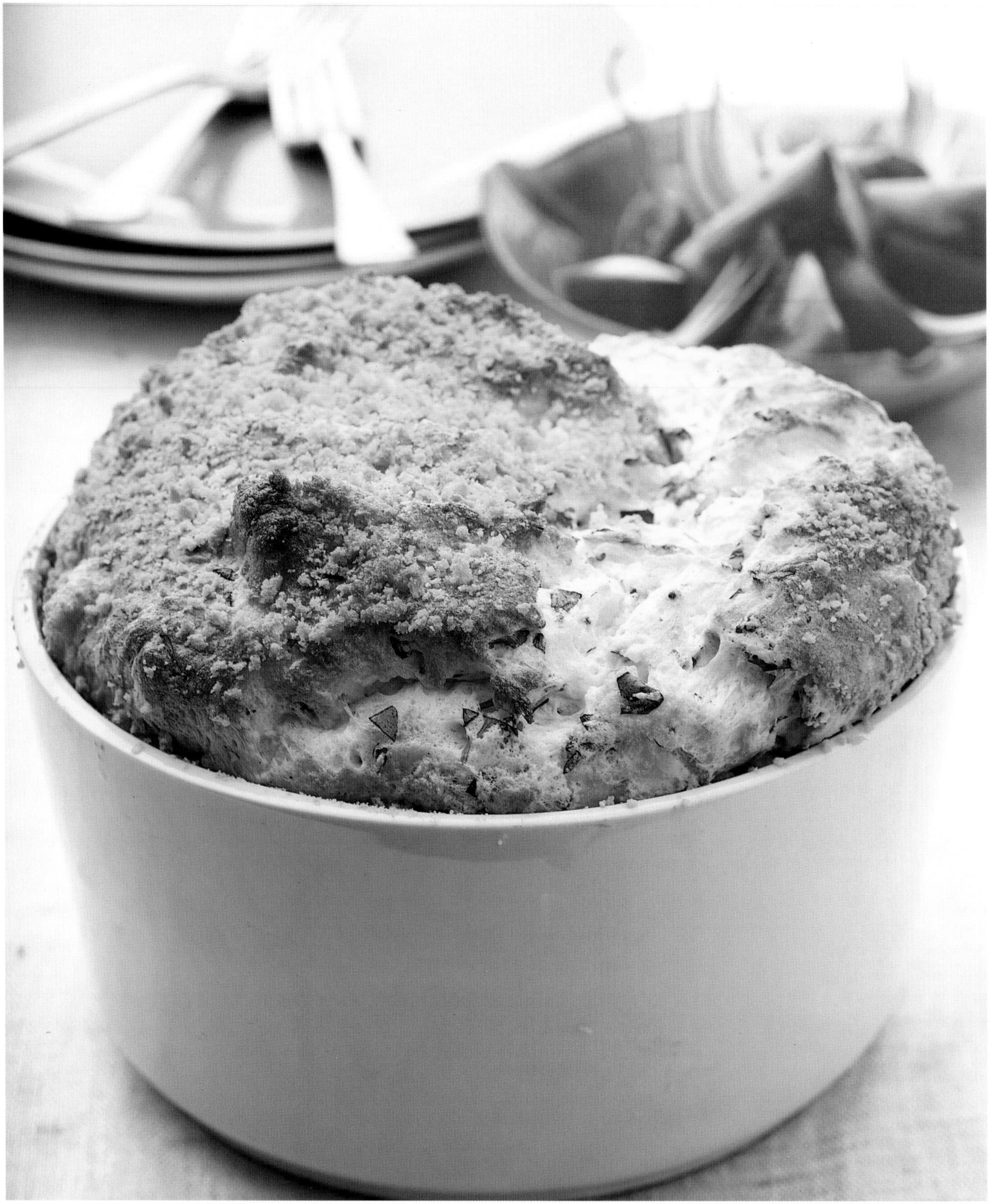

Cheese and Watercress Soufflé

Soufflés have a undeserved reputation for being difficult to make. This flavorsome soufflé is, in fact, quick and easy to prepare and makes a satisfying lunch with crusty bread and a side salad. Using low-fat (2%) and cornstarch keeps it lower in calories than other soufflés.

Serves 4

1 teaspoon butter
1 tablespoon fresh-grated Parmesan cheese
2 tablespoons fine dry bread crumbs
3 ounces fresh watercress
3 tablespoons cornstarch
1¼ cups low-fat (2%) milk
4 large eggs, separated
1 tablespoon wholegrain mustard
¾ cup grated Gruyère cheese
Salt and fresh-ground black pepper

Preparation time: 20 minutes
Cooking time: 30 to 35 minutes

Each serving provides Ⓥ

cals 293, **protein** 19 g, **fat** 18 g (of which saturated fat 8 g), **carbohydrate** 16 g (of which sugars 4 g), **fiber** 0.8 g

✓✓✓	A, B$_{12}$, niacin, calcium
✓✓	E, niacin, zinc
✓	B$_2$, C, folate, copper, iron, selenium

1 Preheat the oven to 400°F. Lightly butter the inside of a 1¾ quart soufflé dish. Mix together the Parmesan and bread crumbs, and sprinkle half of the mixture over the bottom and side of the dish, turning and tilting the dish to coat evenly; set aside.

2 Remove the thick stems from the watercress and discard. Finely chop the rest of the watercress; set aside.

3 Put the cornstarch in a large bowl and stir in a little of the milk to make a smooth paste. Pour the rest of the milk into a medium, heavy-bottomed saucepan over high heat and bring almost to a boil, then pour onto the cornstarch mixture, stirring constantly. Return to the pan and stir until the sauce is thick and smooth.

4 Remove from the heat and add the egg yolks, beating them thoroughly into the sauce. Stir in the chopped watercress, mustard, Gruyère cheese, and salt and pepper to taste.

5 In a clean, dry bowl, whisk the egg whites until soft peaks form. Fold a quarter of the whites into the sauce, then gently fold in the rest of the whites.

6 Spoon the mixture into the soufflé dish and sprinkle the top with the remaining Parmesan-and-bread crumb mixture. Bake the soufflé until well risen and golden brown, 30 to 35 minutes. Serve immediately.

Some More Ideas

• Instead of Gruyère, use a blue cheese such as Gorgonzola, Stilton, or Danish blue.
• Try Greek-Style Feta and Watercress Soufflé, replacing the Gruyère cheese with ½ cup crumbled feta. Sprinkle the soufflé with a pinch of fresh-grated nutmeg before serving.
• For a Smoked Haddock and Spinach Soufflé, use 3 ounces smoked haddock fillet and 3 ounces fresh spinach leaves. Simmer the haddock in the milk 5 to 6 minutes; drain, reserving the milk for the sauce. Flake the haddock, discarding any skin and bones. Rinse the spinach, with just the water clinging to the leaves, until wilted, 2 to 3 minutes. Drain well, squeezing out excess moisture. Chop the spinach. Add the haddock and spinach to the sauce in Step 4, in place of the Gruyère and watercress.

Plus Points

• Gruyère cheese has a distinctive flavor and creamy, melting texture. It contributes to the protein and calcium content of this soufflé, as well as providing zinc, a mineral that has an important role to play in wound healing.
• Most soufflés are based on a mixture of butter and flour called a roux. This version uses cornstarch instead, which works just as well and keeps the total fat content much lower than traditional soufflés.

Main Meals

Moroccan-Style Pumpkin and Lima Beans

Middle Eastern spices flavor this low-fat vegetarian casserole, which is full of fiber-rich ingredients. It is a great recipe for a cook-ahead meal as the flavors improve when the casserole is chilled overnight, then reheated for serving. Try it with couscous.

Serves 4

2½ cups water, boiling

2 vegetable bouillon cubes, crumbled, or 2 teaspoons vegetable bouillon granules

½ teaspoon ground turmeric

½ teaspoon ground coriander

Pinch ground cumin

2 small leeks, halved lengthwise and sliced

1 parsnip, peeled and cut into ½ inch cubes

1 pound 5 ounces pumpkin, peeled, seeded, and cut into ½ inch cubes

1 large yellow or green zucchini, sliced

1 red bell pepper, seeded and chopped

⅔ cup chopped dried apricots

1 can (15 ounces) lima beans, drained and rinsed

Pinch dried red chile flakes, or to taste (optional)

Salt and fresh-ground black pepper

To garnish

2 tablespoons pine nuts

Chopped parsley or fresh cilantro

Preparation time: about 10 minutes
Cooking time: about 20 minutes

1 Pour the boiling water into a Dutch oven over medium heat. Stir in the bouillon cube or powder, the turmeric, coriander, and cumin. Add the leeks and parsnips and bring to a boil. Reduce the heat, cover the pan, and simmer 5 minutes.

2 Add the pumpkin, zucchini, and red bell pepper to the pot. Return the broth to a boil. Stir in the apricots, lima beans, and chile flakes, if using, adding more to taste for a spicier result. Season with salt and pepper to taste. Reduce the heat, cover, and simmer until all the vegetables are tender, about 10 minutes.

3 Meanwhile, put the pine nuts in a nonstick skillet over medium heat and toast, stirring constantly, until just beginning to brown and giving off their nutty aroma. Tip the pine nuts onto a board and chop them coarsely.

4 Taste the casserole and adjust the seasoning, if necessary. Ladle the broth and vegetables into deep bowls. Sprinkle with the pine nuts and parsley or cilantro and serve.

Plus Points

• Pumpkin is a rich source of beta-carotene and other carotenoid compounds. Save the seeds, and roast or toast them to enjoy as a snack, as they provide good amounts of protein and zinc.

• Dried apricots are an excellent source of beta-carotene and a useful source of the mineral calcium.

• Parsnips provide useful amounts of potassium, folate, and vitamin B_1.

Each serving provides

cals 250, **protein** 12 g, **fat** 7 g (of which saturated fat 1 g), **carbohydrate** 35 g (of which sugars 21 g), **fiber** 10 g

✓✓✓	A, C, iron
✓✓	B_1, B_6, folate
✓	calcium

Some More Ideas

● This casserole is delicious ladled over couscous. Place 2 cups quick-cook couscous in a heatproof bowl. Add salt to taste and pour in 2½ cups boiling water to cover. Cover the bowl and leave to stand until all the water is absorbed and the couscous is plumped up and tender, about 5 minutes. Stir in 1 tablespoon butter and fluff up the couscous with a fork to separate the grains.

● Try other vegetables with the pumpkin—for example, broccoli flowerets can be added with the pumpkin instead of the zucchini. The distinctive flavor of turnips is also good with the other vegetables.

● For a fresh, peppery flavor, garnish the casserole with ½ cup grated red radishes or large white radish (mooli).

Beef and Mushroom Stroganoff

This version of the classic East European dish of quick-fried steak with mushrooms shows how vegetables can be used to enhance and "stretch" a modest portion of meat. The result is every bit as special and delicious as true Stroganoff, but much lower in fat.

Serves 4

2 tablespoons extra-virgin olive oil

3 cups halved cremini mushrooms

1 red bell pepper, seeded and cut into fine strips

1½ cups small brocolli flowerets

⅔ cup beef stock, preferably homemade

1 onion, sliced

10 ounces beef tenderloin, cut into thin strips

2 tablespoons brandy

3 tablespoons bottled grated horseradish (optional)

⅔ cup sour cream

Salt and fresh-ground black pepper

Preparation time: 10 minutes
Cooking time: about 12 minutes

Each serving provides

cals 300, **protein** 20 g, **fat** 18 g (of which saturated fat 7 g), **carbohydrate** 6 g (of which sugars 5 g), **fiber** 1.6 g

✓✓✓	A, B₁₂, C
✓✓	B₂, B₆, E, folate, copper, iron, zinc
✓	B₁, niacin, potassium, selenium

1 Heat half of the oil in a large saucepan over medium heat. Add the mushrooms and sauté until beginning to soften, about 2 minutes. Stir in the red bell pepper and broccoli flowerets and continue to sauté, stirring, 3 to 4 minutes.

2 Pour in the stock and bring to a boil. Reduce the heat, cover the saucepan, and simmer until the broccoli is just tender, about 5 minutes.

3 Meanwhile, heat the remaining 1 tablespoon oil in a large skillet over high heat. Add the onion and sauté until soft and beginning to brown, about 5 minutes.

4 Add the beef strips to the onions and sauté until the beef begins to change color, about 1 minute. Stand back from the pan, pour in the brandy, and set light to it.

5 As soon as the flames subside, stir in the horseradish, if using, and the sour cream. Add the vegetables with their cooking liquid. Stir well and season to taste. A rice pilaf is the traditional Russian accompaniment for Stroganoff; tagliatelle is very popular today. Boiled new potatoes are also delicious with this vegetable-rich version.

Plus Points

• Broccoli is a good source of vitamin C, which helps to increase the absorption of iron from the beef in this recipe.

• Mushrooms are low in fat and calories and they provide useful amounts of copper, as well as many B vitamins.

• Although not eaten in large quantities, horseradish contributes some fiber, B-group vitamins, and vitamin C.

Some More Ideas

• Try lean ham, cut into fine strips, instead of the beef tenderloin and replace the mushrooms and broccoli with 3 cups shredded white or green cabbage and 1 cup frozen peas. Use vegetable stock instead of beef stock and hard cider instead of brandy (cider will not flame). Stir in 2 tablespoons Dijon mustard (or your favorite mustard) instead of the horseradish.

• Lean pork tenderloin or boneless chicken or turkey breast meat are good alternatives to the beef.

• For a vegetarian Stroganoff, omit the steak and use vegetable stock. Increase the quantity of mushrooms to 7 cups, including a variety such as white, shiitake, and cremini, and use 2 bell peppers of colors of your choice.

Main Meals

Perfect Pot Roast

This long-simmered, one-pot meal is wonderfully satisfying, with its mixture of beef and chunky vegetables. The dish can be prepared ahead of time, so it's perfect for family dinners, as well as for informal entertaining. Serve with a crunchy mixed salad and bread.

Serves 6

1 teaspoon extra-virgin olive oil

2¼ pounds boneless beef chuck, in one piece, about 3 inches thick, trimmed of fat and tied

2 large onions, minced

1 celery stalk, minced

3 garlic cloves, crushed

1 cup dry red or white wine

½ can (14 ounces) crushed tomatoes

1 large carrot, grated

1 teaspoon chopped fresh thyme

2 cups beef stock, preferably homemade

1 pound 5 ounces new potatoes, scrubbed and quartered

1 medium celery root, peeled and cut into 1 inch cubes

1 medium rutabaga, peeled and cut into 1 inch cubes

4 medium carrots, sliced

Salt and fresh-ground black pepper

3 tablespoons chopped parsley

Preparation and cooking time: 4 hours

Each serving provides

cals 399, protein 43 g, fat 12 g (of which saturated fat 4 g), carbohydrate 33 g (of which sugars 15 g), fiber 8 g

✓✓✓	A, B₁, B₆, B₁₂, C, folate, niacin, zinc
✓✓	B₂, iron
✓	selenium

1 Preheat the oven to 325°F. Heat the oil in a large Dutch oven over medium-high heat. Add the beef and fry it until colored on all sides, 6 to 8 minutes. Transfer the meat to a plate.

2 Reduce the heat to medium. Add the onions, celery, and garlic and sauté, until the onions begin to soften, about 3 minutes. Add the wine and let it bubble about 1 minute. Add the tomatoes and the grated carrot and cook 2 minutes longer.

3 Return the beef to the Dutch oven with any juices that have collected on the plate and the chopped thyme. Tuck a piece of wax paper or foil around the top of the meat, turning back the corners so it doesn't touch the liquid, then cover with a tight-fitting lid. Transfer the Dutch oven to the oven and cook 2½ hours.

4 About 20 minutes before the end of the cooking time, bring the stock to a boil in a deep saucepan with a lid. Add the potatoes, celery root, rutabaga, and carrots. Cover and simmer until the vegetables begin to become tender, 12 to 15 minutes.

5 Meanwhile, remove the beef from the Dutch oven; set aside. Remove any fat from the cooking liquid, either by spooning it off or by using a bulb baster. Put the casseroled vegetables and liquid in a blender or food processor and blend until smooth. Season to taste.

6 Drain the potatoes and other root vegetables, reserving the liquid. Make a layer of the vegetables in the Dutch oven, put the beef on top, and add the remaining root vegetables and their cooking liquid. Pour the smooth vegetable sauce over. Cover the Dutch oven and return to the oven until the root vegetables are fork-tender, about 20 minutes longer.

7 Transfer the beef to a chopping board, cover, and leave to rest for 10 minutes. Keep the vegetables and sauce in a very low oven.

8 Carve the beef and arrange on warm plates with the vegetables and sauce. Sprinkle with the parsley.

Plus Points

• Rutabaga is a member of the cruciferous family of vegetables. It is a useful source of vitamin C and beta-carotene and is rich in phytochemicals that are believed to help protect against cancer.

• A freshly dug potato might contain as much as 10 times more vitamin C than one that has been stored.

Main Meals

Some More Ideas

• Brisket can be used instead of chuck, as can topside.

• Any leftover beef can be chopped or shredded and mixed with the sauce and/or a freshly made tomato sauce, then served over spaghetti or other pasta.

• Substitute a boneless ham joint, soaked if necessary, for the beef. Soften 1 chopped onion in 1 teaspoon extra-virgin olive oil with 2 chopped garlic cloves (omit the celery). Add the wine (use white) and ham (there is no need to brown it first). Omit the tomatoes, grated carrot, and thyme, and add 3 cups unsalted vegetable stock, 3 cloves, 1½ teaspoons dry mustard, and 1 strip orange zest. Cover and simmer 1¼ hours, adding the root vegetables after 25 minutes. When the meat is cooked, transfer it to a chopping board as in Step 7. Strain the cooking liquid and remove the fat, then boil rapidly until reduced to 2½ cups. Stir in 2 tablespoons cornstarch mixed with 1½ tablespoons cold water. Boil until the liquid is thick. Finish as in the main recipe.

Ground Beef Curry

With just a hint of chile, this mellow curry is ideal for those who like to experiment with new tastes, without too much spice. Team with steamed basmati rice for a meal that is packed full of protein and vitamins.

Serves 4

1 pound 2 ounces lean ground beef

1 onion, minced

4 medium potatoes, peeled and diced

3 garlic cloves, chopped

1 inch piece fresh ginger, peeled and minced

1 cinnamon stick, halved

1 teaspoon ground turmeric

1 teaspoon cumin seeds, roughly crushed

1 teaspoon coriander seeds, roughly crushed

½ teaspoon dried red chile flakes

1 can (14 ounces) crushed tomatoes

1¼ cups beef or lamb stock, preferably homemade

½ bag (10 ounces) baby leaf spinach

Salt and fresh-ground black pepper

Fresh mint leaves

Raita

⅔ cup plain low-fat yogurt

¼ cucumber, finely diced

4 teaspoons chopped fresh mint

Preparation time: 10 to 15 minutes

Cooking time: 35 minutes

Each serving provides

cals 369, **protein** 35 g, **fat** 14 g (of which saturated fat 6 g), **carbohydrate** 30 g (of which sugars 10 g), **fiber** 3 g

✓✓✓	B₁, B₆, B₁₂, C, E, folate, iron, zinc
✓✓	A, B₂

1 Put the beef and onion in a large saucepan over medium heat and sauté until evenly brown, stirring to break up the meat, about 5 minutes. Add the potatoes, garlic, ginger, and spices and sauté 2 minutes longer. Add the tomatoes and the stock and season with salt and pepper to taste. Bring to a boil, cover, reduce the heat, and simmer, stirring occasionally, 20 minutes.

2 Meanwhile, make the raita. Mix the yogurt, cucumber, and mint together with a little seasoning. Spoon into a bowl and chill until required.

3 Stir the spinach into the curry and heat through 1 minute. Taste and adjust the seasoning, if necessary. Spoon the curry onto warm plates and sprinkle with fresh mint leaves. Serve immediately, with the chilled raita.

Some More Ideas

● If you prefer, cook the curry in the oven. Brown the beef and onion in a Dutch oven. Add the other ingredients and bring to a boil. Cover and cook in a preheated 350°F oven 1 hour. Add the spinach and toss with the beef and vegetable mixture. Cover and return to the oven 10 minutes longer.

● If you don't have the individual dried spices, use 2 tablespoons mild curry paste instead.

● Use chard or mustard greens in place of the spinach. Tear into bite-size pieces before adding to the meat.

● For Fruity Curry, add ⅓ cup golden raisins and 1 sliced apple with the potatoes. Omit the spinach. Garnish the curry with 1 diced banana tossed with the juice of ½ lemon, 2 tablespoons chopped fresh cilantro, and 2 tablespoons toasted shredded coconut.

● Any leftover curry is delicious reheated and served in warm pita bread pockets.

● To vary the raita, add ½ grated carrot, 2 chopped scallions or a sprinkling of toasted cumin seeds to the basic mixture.

Plus Points

● A raita, or sauce, of yogurt, cucumber, and mint is often served with curries to act as a cooling agent against the heat of the chiles and spices. Banana can also be used.

● Yogurt contains vitamin B₂, which is needed to release energy from food. Yogurts with active cultures are claimed to be particularly beneficial to the digestive tract.

Main Meals

Slowly Braised Beef and Barley

Here, beef is simmered until meltingly tender while nourishing pot barley thickens the gravy to make a hearty casserole and juniper berries add a distinctive flavor. Serve with mashed potatoes and a green vegetable, such as green beans or spinach.

Serves 4

1 pound 2 ounces beef chuck or lean braising steak, trimmed and cut into 2 inch cubes

2 garlic cloves, halved

3 bay leaves

6 juniper berries, lightly crushed

1 sprig fresh thyme

1 cup full-bodied red wine

12 pearl onions

1 tablespoon extra-virgin olive oil

¼ cup pot barley

1¾ cups beef stock

3 large carrots, cut into large chunks

2 celery stalks, sliced

1 medium rutabaga, peeled and cut into 1½ inch chunks

Salt and fresh-ground black pepper

Preparation time: 20 minutes, plus 8 hours marinating

Cooking time: 2 to 2¼ hours

Each serving provides

cals 367, **protein** 31 g, **fat** 10 g (of which saturated fat 3 g), **carbohydrate** 29 g (of which sugars 18 g), **fiber** 5 g

✓✓✓	A
✓✓	C
✓	B₁, B₆, E, folate, niacin, calcium, copper, iron, potassium, zinc

1 Put the beef in a mixing bowl with the garlic, bay leaves, juniper berries and thyme. Pour the red wine over, then cover and leave to marinate in the refrigerator at least 8 hours or overnight.

2 The next day, preheat the oven to 325°F. Put the pearl onions in a bowl and pour enough boiling water over to cover. Leave 2 minutes, then drain. When cool enough to handle, peel off the skins; set aside.

3 Remove the beef from the marinade and pat dry with paper towels. Heat the oil in a large Dutch oven over medium-high heat. Add the beef and brown on all sides: Do this in batches, if necessary, so the Dutch oven is not overcrowded. Remove the beef from the Dutch oven as it is brown; set aside on a plate.

4 Add the pearl onions to the Dutch oven and sauté until lightly colored, 3 to 4 minutes. Add the pot barley and cook 1 minute, stirring. Return the beef and any beefy juices to the Dutch oven. Pour in the stock and bring to a simmer.

5 Strain the marinade into the Dutch oven, and add the bay leaves and sprig of thyme. Season with salt and pepper to taste. Cover with a tight-fitting lid, transfer to the oven, and braise 45 minutes.

6 Stir in the carrots, celery, and rutabaga. Cover again and braise until the beef, barley, and vegetables are tender, 1 to 1¼ hours longer. Remove the bay leaves and thyme sprig before serving.

Plus Points

• Pot barley, also called Scotch barley, retains the outer layers of the grain (these are removed in the milling of pearl barley), so it contains the nutrients of the whole grain.

• The barley grain contains gummy fibers called beta-glucans, which appear to have significant cholesterol-lowering properties.

• Beef is an excellent source of iron in a form that can be efficiently absorbed and used by the body.

Main Meals

Some More Ideas

• The gravy is thick. If you prefer it slightly thinner, stir in an extra ½ cup beef stock 20 minutes before the end of the cooking time.

• For Slowly Braised Lamb and Barley, use lean boneless stewing lamb, such as from the shoulder, instead of beef. Marinate the lamb overnight in 1 cup hard cider mixed with 2 teaspoons Dijon mustard, 1 teaspoon light molasses, and 1 teaspoon soft dark brown sugar. Dry and fry the lamb as for the beef in the main recipe. Add 1 sliced onion to the Dutch oven and cook until beginning to color, 4 to 5 minutes. Add the barley and stir 1 minute. Pour in 1 cup lamb or vegetable stock, ⅔ cup tomato juice, and the marinade, with 1 sprig fresh rosemary. Cover and braise 45 minutes. Stir in 8 ounces baby carrots and 8 ounces halved or quartered, peeled small turnips. Braise until all the ingredients are tender, 1 to 1¼ hours.

Stir-Fried Beef with Mango

This colorful dish is bursting with fresh flavors and contrasting textures. The dressing is oil-free, so although a little oil is used to stir fry the beef, the dish is still very light in fat. No extra salt is needed because of the spicy dressing and the saltiness of soy sauce.

Serves 4

14 ounces lean steak, such as sirloin, trimmed of all excess fat

3 garlic cloves, minced

1 teaspoon sugar

2 teaspoons soy sauce

1½ tablespoons sunflower oil

Ginger and Honey Dressing

2 teaspoons paprika

½ teaspoon cayenne, or to taste

1½ tablespoons honey

1 inch piece fresh ginger, peeled and grated

4 tablespoons rice vinegar or apple cider vinegar

Fresh juice of 1 lime or lemon

Salad

1 ripe but firm mango, peeled and cut into strips

2 ripe but firm plums, sliced

¼ medium head red cabbage, shredded

2 ounces watercress leaves

½ cucumber, cut into matchsticks

½ red bell pepper, seeded and cut into thin strips

3 or 4 scallions, cut into diagonal pieces

1½ ounces mixed fresh mint and cilantro

2 tablespoons coarsely chopped roasted unsalted peanuts

Preparation time: 30 minutes
Cooking time: about 10 minutes

1 To make the dressing, put the paprika, cayenne, honey, ginger, and vinegar in a saucepan over medium heat. Slowly add 1 cup water, stirring, and bring to a boil. Reduce the heat and simmer 5 minutes. Remove from the heat and stir in the lime or lemon juice; set aside.

2 Combine all the salad ingredients, except the peanuts, in a large, shallow serving dish and toss gently together until evenly mixed; set aside.

3 Cut the steak into thin strips for stir-frying. Put the steak in a bowl with the garlic, sugar, and soy sauce and mix together so the strips of steak are seasoned. Heat a wok or nonstick skillet over high heat. Add the oil and the beef and stir-fry until the strips are evenly brown and cooked to taste, about 3 minutes.

4 Spoon the stir-fried beef over the top of the salad. Drizzle the dressing over the top and sprinkle with the peanuts.

Some More Ideas

• Add cubes of fresh or canned pineapple (canned in juice rather than syrup) or kiwi fruit to the salad, to increase the fruit content.

• Spice up the salad with very thin strips of fresh red chile—particularly if you have a cold, because scientists have suggested that eating chiles can help to alleviate nasal congestion.

• Replace the mango with 2 unpeeled and sliced nectarines.

• For a vegetarian version, omit the stir-fried beef and increase the quantity of shelled peanuts to 1 cup. Peanuts are an excellent source of protein and contain much less saturated fat than meat.

Plus Points

• All orange and red fruit and vegetables, such as mango, red cabbage, and red bell peppers, are excellent sources of beta-carotene and vitamin C—both antioxidants that help to protect against heart disease and cancer. The vitamin C aids the absorption of iron from the steak.

• Apart from adding delicious spiciness to the dressing, ginger also aids digestion.

Each serving provides

cals 265, **protein** 27 g, **fat** 8 g (of which saturated fat 3 g), **carbohydrate** 20 g (of which sugars 18 g), **fiber** 4 g

✓✓✓	B$_{12}$, C
✓✓	A, B$_6$, iron, zinc
✓	B$_1$, B$_2$, E, folate, niacin, copper

Fragrant Lamb with Spinach

Warmly spiced rather than fiery hot, thanks to the cooling effect of the yogurt, this curry has a wonderful flavor. The lamb is infused with spices, and basmati rice, and a tomato and cucumber chutney make this an irresistible meal that is also low in calories.

Serves 4

2 tablespoons sunflower oil

2 onions, minced

4 garlic cloves, crushed

2 inch piece fresh ginger, peeled and chopped

1 red chile, seeded, deveined, and sliced

2 teaspoons paprika

2 teaspoons ground cumin

2 teaspoons ground coriander

1 teaspoon ground white pepper

½ teaspoon cinnamon

Seeds from 8 green cardamom pods, crushed

2 bay leaves

½ teaspoon salt

½ cup plain yogurt

¼ cup nonfat sour cream

1 pound 2 ounces lean boneless lamb, cubed

2 large tomatoes, chopped

1 bag (10 ounces) fresh baby spinach

4 tablespoons chopped fresh cilantro

Fresh cilantro sprigs

Preparation time: 20 to 25 minutes

Cooking time: 1 hour 20 minutes

Each serving provides

cals 329, **protein** 32 g, **fat** 18 g (of which saturated fat 6 g), **carbohydrate** 11 g (of which sugars 9 g), **fiber** 4 g

✓✓✓	B₁₂
✓✓	A, B₆, C, folate, phosphorus, iron, zinc
✓	B₁, B₂, E, niacin, calcium, copper, potassium, selenium

1 Heat the oil in a large saucepan or Dutch oven over medium heat. Add the onions, garlic, and ginger, and sauté, stirring frequently, until the onions are golden, about 10 minutes.

2 Stir in the chile, paprika, cumin, coriander, white pepper, cinnamon, cardamom seeds, bay leaves, and salt. Stir briefly over a medium heat. Stir the yogurt and nonfat sour cream together, then stir into the saucepan with ⅔ cup water. Add the lamb, mix well, and cover the pan. Simmer until the lamb is tender, about 1¼ hours.

3 Add the tomatoes, spinach, and cilantro. Cook, stirring, until the tomatoes are soft and the spinach wilts, 2 to 3 minutes. Taste for seasoning and remove the bay leaf. Serve garnished with fresh cilantro.

Some More Ideas

● The basic curry sauce in this recipe can be used to cook other meats or vegetables. Cubes of skinless boneless chicken or turkey breast meat are delicious, as are lean boneless pork chops. All of these need only 40 minutes simmering in the sauce to cook. A mixture of vegetables—halved new potatoes, cauliflower flowerets, sliced carrots, and chunks of parsnip—is good, too. Use 18 ounces total weight and cook 30 minutes.

● To make a refreshing fresh chutney to serve with the curry, finely chop and mix together 4 plum tomatoes, ½ cucumber, 1 small onion, 1 seeded and deveined fresh green chile, and 4 tablespoons chopped fresh cilantro.

Plus Points

● Onions contain a type of dietary fiber called fructoligosaccarides (FOS), which is also found in Belgian endive, leeks, garlic, Jerusalem artichokes, asparagus, barley, and bananas. It is thought to stimulate the growth of friendly bacteria in the gut while inhibiting bad bacteria.

● Cardamom is believed to help relieve digestive problems such as indigestion, flatulence, and stomach cramps, and it can help prevent acid regurgitation and belching.

Main Meals

169

Lamb Burgers with Fruity Relish

The advantage of making your own burgers is that you know exactly what's in them—and with good lean meat they can make a healthy meal. A fruity relish, full of vitamin C, adds a fresh flavor to these juicy burgers. Serve with a tossed green or mixed salad.

Serves 4

14 ounces lean ground lamb

1 carrot, grated

1 small onion, minced

1 cup fresh wholewheat bread crumbs

Pinch fresh-grated nutmeg

2 teaspoons fresh thyme leaves, or 1 teaspoon dried thyme

1 extra large egg, beaten

2 teaspoons extra-virgin olive oil

4 wholewheat buns, weighing about 2 ounces

Salt and fresh-ground black pepper

Shredded lettuce

Orange and Raspberry Relish

1 orange

¾ cup fresh or thawed frozen raspberries

2 teaspoons soft light brown sugar

Preparation and cooking time: 30 minutes

Each serving provides

cals 390, **protein** 29 g, **fat** 13 g (of which saturated fat 5 g), **carbohydrate** 40 g (of which sugars 12 g), **fiber** 8 g

✓✓✓	A, B₁₂
✓✓	B₁, B₆, C, niacin, copper, iron, selenium, zinc
✓	B₂, folate, calcium, potassium

1 Preheat the broiler. Put the lamb into a large bowl. Add the carrot, onion, bread crumbs, nutmeg, and thyme. Season with salt and pepper to taste and mix with a spoon. Add the egg and use your hands to mix the ingredients together thoroughly.

2 Divide the mixture into 4 portions and shape each into a burger 4 to 5 inches in diameter, or about 1 inch wider than the diameter of the buns. Brush both sides of the burgers with oil, and put them on the broiler pan. Broil 4 inches from the heat, 4 to 5 minutes on each side, depending on thickness.

3 Meanwhile, make the relish. Using a sharp knife, cut the peel and pith from the orange, holding it over a bowl to catch the juice; cut between the membrane to release the segments. Roughly chop the segments and add them to the juice. Add the raspberries and sugar, lightly crushing the fruit with a fork to mix it together.

4 Split the buns and toast briefly under the broiler. Put a lamb burger in each bun and add some lettuce to garnish and a good spoonful of relish. Serve with the remaining relish.

Another Idea

• Make Turkey Burgers with Orange and Summer Fruit Relish. Use ground turkey instead of lamb, and flavor with the zest of ½ lemon and 4 tablespoons chopped parsley in place of the nutmeg and thyme; omit the bread crumbs. Serve in toasted sesame buns, with arugula leaves and a relish made by simmering ¾ cup frozen summer fruits until thawed, about 3 minutes. Stir in 1 tablespoon sugar and the chopped orange.

Plus Points

• Although lamb still tends to contain more fat than other meats, changes in breeding, feeding, and butchery techniques mean lean cuts only contain about one-third of the fat that similar cuts contained 20 years ago. More of the fat is monounsaturated, which is good news for healthy hearts.

• Using wholewheat buns instead of white ones doubles the amount of fiber intake. The bread also provides B-complex vitamins, iron, and calcium.

• A fruity relish gives a huge bonus of protective antioxidants. It also provides useful amounts of potassium and fiber, especially from the raspberries.

Main Meals

Hotchpotch with Golden Parsnips

The influence of the Middle East brings beans, eggplants, apricots, garlic, and warm spices to this lamb casserole. The topping is in traditional British style—a golden layer of parsnip slices—which is low in calories and supplies more vitamins.

Serves 6

1 cup dried black-eyed peas, soaked
   overnight
2 tablespoons extra-virgin olive oil
2 onions, sliced
1 garlic clove, chopped
1 pound 2 ounces boneless leg of lamb, cut
   into 1 inch cubes
1 large eggplant, cubed
1 cup quartered dried apricots
2 carrots, diced
2 turnips, peeled and diced
½ teaspoon cinnamon
1 teaspoon ground cumin
1 teaspoon ground coriander
1½ pounds parsnips, peeled and thinly sliced
About 1 quart vegetable stock, preferably
   homemade
Salt and fresh-ground black pepper
Flat-leaf parsley sprigs

Preparation time: 30 minutes, plus overnight
   soaking
Cooking time: 1½ hours

Each serving provides

cals 375, **protein** 25 g, **fat** 15 g (of which
saturated fat 5 g), **carbohydrate** 38 g (of
which sugars 19 g), **fiber** 16 g

✓✓✓	B$_{12}$
✓✓	A, B$_1$, C, E, folate, copper, iron, zinc
✓	B$_6$, niacin, calcium, potassium

1 Preheat the oven to 325°F. Drain the black-eyed peas and place them in a saucepan. Add cold water to cover, bring to a boil, and boil rapidly 10 minutes. Drain well and set aside.

2 Reserve 1 teaspoon of the oil and heat the remainder in a large Dutch oven over medium heat. Add the onions and garlic, and sauté until soft, 2 to 3 minutes. Add the lamb and fry, stirring frequently, until brown, about 5 minutes. (If you do not have a suitable Dutch oven, cook the onions and lamb in a skillet, then transfer to a baking dish. Bring the stock to a boil in the pan before pouring it into the dish.)

3 Stir in the egg plant, apricots, carrots, turnips, cinnamon, cumin, and coriander, with seasoning to taste. Add the black-eyed peas and stir well.

4 Arrange the parsnip slices in a thick layer on top of the hotpot, slightly overlapping them, then pour in sufficient stock to come just below the surface of the parsnips. Bring to a boil, cover the Dutch oven, and transfer to the oven and cook 1½ hours.

5 Preheat the broiler. Brush the reserved 1 teaspoon oil over the parsnips. Broil about 4 inches from the heat to crisp the top. Serve garnished with parsley sprigs.

Plus Points

• A high proportion of vegetables, legumes and additional flavoring ingredients can extend a modest portion of lean meat into a heart-healthy dish.

• Dried apricots are a valuable source of many minerals—phosphorus, potassium, and iron—as well as fiber.

• Eaten in moderation, red meat, such as lamb or beef, makes a valuable contribution in a well-balanced diet. As well as being high in protein, meat provides zinc and iron in a form that is readily absorbed by the body. Red meat also provides most of the B vitamins.

Some More Ideas

• Use other varieties of dried beans, such as red kidney beans, borlotti beans, or pinto beans, instead of the black-eyed peas.

• Add the grated zest and juice of 1 large orange with the spices.

• Replace the eggplant with 2 cups pumpkin or butternut squash flesh, cut into large cubes.

Main Meals

Mediterranean Stuffed Vegetables

An array of colorful stuffed vegetables make an appetizing and satisfying main dish. The mixture of lean lamb, fresh vegetables, and rice makes this a very balanced and healthy main course. Lots of French bread and a mixed leaf salad complete the meal.

Serves 4

½ cup long-grain rice

8 ounces lean ground lamb

1 onion, chopped

4 bell peppers

4 large tomatoes, ripe but firm

2 large zucchini, about 8 ounces each

1 tablespoon extra-virgin olive oil

3 garlic cloves, coarsely chopped

½ bag (10 ounces) baby spinach leaves

2 tablespoons shredded fresh basil

1 large egg, lightly beaten

Salt and fresh-ground black pepper

To serve

2 to 3 tablespoons shredded fresh basil

Preparation time: 45 minutes

Cooking time: 45 to 50 minutes

Each serving provides

cals 324, **protein** 21 g, **fat** 15 g (of which saturated fat 5 g), **carbohydrate** 27 g (of which sugars 18 g), **fiber** 7 g

✓✓✓	A, B$_1$, B$_6$, B$_{12}$, C, E, folate, niacin, zinc
✓✓	B$_2$, iron, potassium
✓	calcium

1 Cook the rice in a saucepan of boiling water until tender, 10 to 12 minutes, or according to the package directions; drain.

2 While the rice is cooking, put the lamb and onion in a nonstick skillet over medium heat. Sauté until the lamb is lightly brown and cooked through and the onion is soft. Turn and break up the meat as it cooks so it browns evenly. Place a sieve over a bowl and tip the meat into it: The fat will drip through and can be discarded.

3 Cut each pepper in half lengthwise through the stem and remove the core and seed. Cut the tops (stem end) off the tomatoes and hollow out the insides. Chop the tops and hollowed-out flesh and place in a bowl with any tomato juices. Cut the zucchini in half lengthwise and hollow to make shells ¼ inch thick. Chop the hollowed-out zucchini flesh and add it to the chopped tomatoes.

4 Preheat the oven to 350°F. Heat the olive oil in a nonstick skillet over medium heat. Add the garlic and chopped vegetables, and sauté, stirring, until slightly soft, about 5 minutes. Add the spinach and sauté until it wilts, about 1 minute. Remove from the heat and stir in the basil, rice, and lamb. Add the egg, season with salt and pepper to taste, and mix together.

5 Spoon the stuffing into the pepper, tomato, and zucchini shells. Arrange the peppers and zucchini in a single layer in 1 or 2 roasting pans: The vegetables should not be too crowded together. Cover with foil and roast 15 minutes. Add the tomatoes and continue roasting until the vegetables are almost tender, about 15 minutes longer.

6 Uncover the vegetables and continue roasting until they are tender and the tops lightly brown, 15 to 20 minutes longer. Serve either warm or cool, sprinkled with the shredded fresh basil.

Plus Points

• Peppers, tomatoes, zucchini, and spinach are high in phytochemicals and antioxidant vitamins. They all contain beta-carotene, whose antioxidant properties help to protect cells from damage by free radicals produced in the body in response to stress.

• Zucchini belong to the same family as melons, pumpkins, and cucumbers. Their skin is particularly rich in beta-carotene, and they also provide niacin and vitamin B$_6$.

Main Meals

Another Idea

● Make Middle Eastern-Style Stuffed Vegetables. Use brown rice instead of white rice and combine it with the fried lamb and onion. Add 3 thinly sliced scallions, 3 chopped garlic cloves, 2 tablespoons each chopped fresh dill and mint, ½ teaspoon ground cumin, a good pinch cinnamon, 3 tablespoons plain low-fat yogurt, 2 tablespoons raisins, the juice of ½ lemon, and salt and pepper to taste. Cut 2 eggplants in half lengthwise and steam until just tender, about 5 minutes. Leave until cool enough to handle, then hollow them out, leaving shells about ¼ inch thick. Dice the flesh and add it to the rice-and-lamb mixture. Blanch 4 large savoy cabbage leaves until pliable, 30 to 60 seconds. Arrange the eggplant shells in a roasting pan and spoon in some of the filling. Roll the rest of the filling in the cabbage leaves and place in the pan. Mix ½ can (14 ounces) crushed tomatoes with ½ cup lamb or vegetable stock and spoon around the vegetables. Cover the pan with foil. Roast 30 minutes. Uncover and continue roasting until the tops of the vegetables are tinged light brown, 15 to 20 minutes. Serve hot or cool, garnished with chopped fresh mint.

Roast Pork with Applesauce

Roast pork with applesauce, an all-time favorite, is given a new twist in this dish inspired by German cuisine, and is kept healthy by using stock instead of fat to make the gravy. It is delicious served with roast or baked potatoes and seasonal green vegetables.

Serves 8

2 pounds boned loin of pork without skin, in one piece, trimmed of fat
3 cooking apples
1 small onion, minced
½ cup pitted chopped prunes
8 gingersnap cookies, crushed
1 large egg yolk
1¼ cups chicken stock
1 cup dry white wine
2 tablespoons extra-virgin olive oil
8 medium parsnips, peeled and quartered
1 tablespoon honey
1 pound 2 ounces shallots
Salt and fresh-ground black pepper

Applesauce

2 large cooking apples, peeled, cored, and chopped
1 inch piece fresh ginger, peeled and finely chopped
2 tablespoons sugar

Preparation time: 1¼ hours
Cooking time: 2 hours

Each serving provides

cals 395, **protein** 27 g, **fat** 13 g (of which saturated fat 4 g), **carbohydrate** 41 g (of which sugars 30 g), **fiber** 9 g

✓✓✓	B_1, B_2, B_6, C, E, folate, niacin
✓✓	potassium
✓	B_2, calcium, iron, zinc

1 Preheat the oven to 350°F. Place the pork on a chopping board, skinned side down. Slit the joint lengthwise, cutting two-thirds of the way through the meat, then open it out like a book.

2 Peel, core, and finely chop 1 of the dessert apples. Mix the chopped apple with the onion, prunes, cookies, egg yolk, and seasoning to taste. Spoon onto the pork, spreading evenly, then press the joint back together. Tie into a neat shape with fine string.

3 Put the joint, skinned side up, into a roasting pan and pour in the stock and wine. Cover the pan with foil, twisting the ends tightly over the edges. Put into the oven and roast 2 hours.

4 After 45 minutes, heat the oil in a second roasting pan on the shelf above the pork 5 minutes. Add the parsnips to the pan to roast, turning them once or twice.

5 Meanwhile, make the applesauce. Put the apples, ginger, sugar, and 2 tablespoons water into a small saucepan over medium-low heat. Cover and simmer, stirring occasionally, until pulpy, about 10 minutes. Remove from the heat and set aside.

6 When the pork has been roasting for 1¼ hours, remove the foil and drizzle with the honey. Add the shallots to the parsnips, toss together, and continue roasting.

7 About 20 minutes before the end of the roasting time, peel, core and thickly slice the remaining 2 apples, then add them to the vegetables.

8 Transfer the pork to a chopping board, cover with foil, and keep warm. Strain the cooking liquid into a saucepan, then skim off any fat. Boil the cooking liquid, stirring constantly, 2 minutes. Pour into a sauceboat. Carve the pork and serve immediately, with the roasted vegetables, applesauce, and gravy.

Plus Points

- Prunes supply useful amounts of iron, potassium, and vitamin B_6, and they also contain fiber, which helps to prevent constipation. Prune juice contains an ingredient that has an additional laxative effect, which is why some people drink the juice rather than eat the fruit itself.
- Apples are relatively low in calories and contain a high proportion of fructose, a simple sugar that is sweeter than sucrose (table sugar) and metabolized more slowly, helping to control blood sugar levels.

Some More Ideas

● Instead of fresh pork use smoked pork loin, which is slightly milder and sweeter than smoked ham. Look for it in the cooked meats section of large supermarkets, or ask the butcher if he can source it for you.

● Spice the dish with cardamom rather than ginger. In the stuffing, substitute ¼ cups fresh bread crumbs for the gingersnap cookies and ⅔ cup chopped dried apricots for the diced apple,

and add the seeds of 4 crushed cardamom pods. In the applesauce, replace the ginger with the seeds of 6 to 8 crushed cardamom pods. Serve the pork with spiced roast vegetables: add 5 medium potatoes, peeled and cut in chunks, to the parsnips. Toss in the hot oil, then sprinkle with 1 teaspoon each crushed coriander and cumin seeds and turmeric.

● For an alternative accompaniment, stir-fry 7 cups finely shredded red cabbage in

1 tablespoon sunflower oil 5 minutes. Add 2 diced apples, 3 tablespoons wine vinegar, 3 tablespoons water, 2 tablespoons honey, and salt and pepper to taste. Mix together, cover, and simmer 4 to 5 minutes.

● As an alternative to roast vegetables, serve with pureed celery root. Cook 1 large head peeled and diced celery root in boiling water 15 minutes, then mash or purée with 4 tablespoons milk and seasoning.

Goulash in a Hurry

This rich, short-cut version of classic Hungarian goulash keeps the calories low. Lean pork, red cabbage, and green bell pepper taste excellent with the traditional flavorings of paprika and caraway seeds. Serve rice or noodles and a green tossed salad alongside.

Serves 4

2 tablespoons extra-virgin olive oil

1 large onion, minced

2 garlic cloves, crushed

3 thick lean, boneless pork loin chops, cut into thin strips

1 tablespoon all-purpose flour

2 cans (14 ounces) crushed tomatoes

½ cup extra-dry vermouth

2 tablespoons paprika

1 teaspoon caraway seeds

1 teaspoon sugar

2 chicken bouillon cubes, crumbled

1 large green bell pepper, seeded and chopped

3 cups finely shredded red cabbage

Salt and fresh-ground black pepper

To serve

4 tablespoons nonfat sour cream

Paprika

Fresh chives

Preparation time: 10 minutes
Cooking time: about 20 minutes

Each serving provides

cals 284, **protein** 21 g, **fat** 11 g (of which saturated fat 3 g), **carbohydrate** 19 g (of which sugars 14 g), **fiber** 4.5 g

✓✓✓	B$_{12}$, C
✓✓	B$_1$, B$_6$
✓	folate, niacin, iron, selenium, zinc

1 Heat the oil in a large skillet or saucepan over high heat. Add the onion, garlic, and pork and sauté until the meat changes color and becomes firm and the onion is slightly soft, about 3 minutes. Meanwhile, blend the flour with 4 tablespoons juice from the canned tomatoes to make a smooth paste; set aside.

2 Stir the vermouth, paprika, caraway seeds, and sugar into the skillet. Add the tomatoes, breaking them up as you mix them in. Stir in the bouillon cubes, and the flour-and-tomato-juice mixture. Bring to a boil, stirring, and boil until the juices thicken.

3 Stir in the green bell pepper and red cabbage until both are coated in the cooking juices. Reduce the heat, cover the skillet, and simmer until the meat is cooked and the vegetables are crisp-tender, about 15 minutes.

4 Taste the goulash and season with salt and pepper, if necessary. Ladle the goulash into bowls and top each portion with a spoonful of nonfat sour cream and a sprinkle of paprika. Garnish with chives and serve.

Some More Ideas

● To make a vegetarian goulash, omit the pork and red cabbage. Cut 1 eggplant into large chunks and add to the onion and garlic in Step 1 with 6 halved sun-dried tomatoes, 2 thickly sliced celery stalks, and 2 thickly sliced zucchini. Follow the main recipe, using 2 vegetable bouillon cubes or 2 teaspoons bouillon granules. Simmer until the vegetables are crisp-tender, about 25 minutes. Stir in 1 can (15 ounces) chickpeas, and 1 can (15 ounces) red kidney beans, both well drained. Cook 5 minutes longer. Serve the goulash topped with plain yogurt or nonfat sour cream.

● Halved small new potatoes are good in the vegetarian version, above. Add them with the other vegetables and leave out the canned red kidney beans.

Plus Points

● Several studies have shown that eating garlic might reduce the risk of heart attack and stroke by making the blood less sticky and likely to clot. Garlic might also help to reduce high blood pressure.

● As the red cabbage is cooked in the dish, the vitamin C from this vegetable is retained in the juice. Cabbage is thought to offer some protection from cancer.

Main Meals

Spiced Pork with Sweet Potatoes

Try this contemporary casserole for a healthy example of fusion cooking, marrying ingredients and flavors from diverse cuisines. Here, Oriental spices, sweet potatoes, and fruit go very well with the pork. A simple tossed salad makes a refreshing accompaniment.

Serves 4

1 tablespoon sunflower oil

4 boneless pork loin chops, about 5 ounces each, trimmed of any excess fat

1 red onion, coarsely chopped

2 celery stalks, chopped

1 large sweet potato, peeled and cut into sticks

⅔ cup cranberry juice

⅔ cup chicken stock, preferably homemade

1 piece preserved ginger, drained and cut into fine sticks

1 tablespoon thick-cut orange marmalade

1 tablespoon dry sherry

1 teaspoon Chinese five-spice powder

2 star anise

4 plum tomatoes, quartered lengthwise

Salt and fresh-ground black pepper

3 scallions, shredded

Preparation time: 30 minutes

Cooking time: about 30 minutes

1 Heat the oil in a large Dutch oven or deep skillet over medium heat. Add the pork chops and brown, 3 to 4 minutes on each side; transfer to a plate and set aside.

2 Add the onion and celery to the oil remaining in the Dutch oven or skillet and sauté 2 to 3 minutes. Add the sweet potato, cover the pan, and sweat the vegetables until soft, 3 to 4 minutes.

3 Stir in the cranberry juice, stock, ginger, marmalade, sherry, five-spice powder, star anise, and a little salt and pepper and bring to a boil. Reduce the heat and return the pork to the Dutch oven. Cover and simmer 15 minutes.

4 Add the tomatoes, re-cover the Dutch oven, and simmer until the tomatoes are lightly cooked, but still hold their shape, about 5 minutes. Taste and add more salt and pepper, if necessary. Serve garnished with scallions.

Some More Ideas

● Add 2 cups cubed pumpkin or butternut squash instead of the sweet potato, and 1 chopped small fennel bulb, instead of the celery stalks.

● Tomato Rice goes well with this casserole. Bring 1 cup water to a boil and add heaped 1 cup rinsed basmati rice, 1 can (14 ounces) crushed tomatoes, and 4 chopped sun-dried tomatoes. Cover and simmer until the rice is tender and all the water is absorbed, about 10 minutes.

● For a fruit-rich casserole, add 1 cup pitted prunes and 2 cored and thickly sliced apples instead of the tomatoes. Omit the sherry.

Plus Points

● Sweet potatoes have a delicious natural sweetness that intensifies during storage and cooking. Although they contain slightly more calories than ordinary white potatoes, they are low in fat and contain good amounts of fiber.

● Sweet potatoes are also an excellent source of beta-carotene and they provide good amounts of vitamins C and E.

● Lean pork has a lower fat content than beef or lamb. It is a good source of zinc and provides useful amounts of iron.

Each serving provides

cals 380, **protein** 32 g, **fat** 13 g (of which saturated fat 4 g), **carbohydrate** 32 g (of which sugars 16 g), **fiber** 4 g

✓✓✓	B₁, C
✓✓	A, B₆, B₁₂, E, iron, phosphorus, zinc
✓	B₂, folate, niacin, selenium

Main Meals

Pork with Mustard Sauce

This delectable dish is surprisingly easy to make. Steam the carrots over the pan of potatoes, with the cabbage added after a few minutes, to keep the nutrional value high. Serve with boiled potatoes sprinkled with chives, carrots, and shredded savoy cabbage.

Serves 4

1 teaspoon extra-virgin olive oil

4 boneless pork loin chops, ⅝ to ¾ inch thick, about 1¼ pounds in total, trimmed of all fat

4 tablespoons dry white wine or vermouth

1 garlic clove, minced

¾ cup chicken or vegetable stock

2 teaspoons cornstarch mixed with 1 tablespoon water

½ cup nonfat sour cream

1 tablespoon Dijon mustard

1 tablespoon chopped fresh tarragon

Salt and fresh-ground black pepper

Fresh chives

Preparation and cooking time: 30 minutes

1 Heat the oil in a large nonstick skillet over medium-high heat. Add the pork chops and fry until brown, about 3 minutes on each side. Transfer to a plate; set aside and keep warm.

2 Add the wine or vermouth to the skillet with the garlic and let it bubble briefly. Pour in the stock and boil 2 minutes. Stir together the cornstarch mixture and sour cream until smooth. Add to the hot cooking liquid, stirring well. Reduce the heat and simmer, stirring constantly, until thick and smooth, about 2 minutes. Stir in the mustard and tarragon and season with salt and pepper to taste.

3 Return the pork chops to the sauce in the skillet. Reduce the heat to low, cover the pan, and simmer until the chops are cooked through, 4 to 5 minutes.

4 Arrange the pork chops on warm plates and spoon the sauce over. Garnish with chives.

Another Idea

• Broil the steaks or chops and serve with a cabbage, apple, and onion braise. Brush the chops with a little extra-virgin olive oil and broil 4 inches from the heat under a preheated medium broiler until tender and brown, about 7 minutes on each side. Meanwhile, heat 1 tablespoon extra-virgin olive oil in a large, deep skillet over medium heat. Add 1 large sliced red onion, 2 cored and sliced apples, and 6 cups shredded savoy cabbage. Toss to mix well, then cover and cook until light brown, stirring occasionally, about 4 minutes. Moisten with 3 to 4 tablespoons apple juice and continue cooking, covered, until the cabbage wilts and is crisp-tender, stirring frequently.

Plus Points

• In the past, pork had a reputation for being rather fatty, but this is no longer the case. Over the last 20 years, in response to consumer demands for leaner meat, farmers have been breeding leaner pigs. While now containing considerably less fat, pork also contains higher levels of the "good" polyunsaturated fats.

• Garlic was first used for a medicinal purpose at least 4,000 years ago—the ancient Egyptians used it to treat infections and headaches, and Roman soldiers who marched across Europe to Britain wedged garlic cloves between their toes to help prevent attacks of athlete's foot. Allicin, the sulphur compound that gives garlic its characteristic smell and taste, acts as a powerful antibiotic and has antiviral and antifungal properties.

Each serving provides

cals 340, **protein** 29 g, **fat** 22 g (of which saturated fat 3.5 g), **carbohydrate** 3 g (of which sugars 1 g), **fiber** 0 g

✓✓✓	B_1
✓✓	B_6, B_{12}, niacin, zinc
✓	B_2, iron, selenium

Main Meals

183

Sticky Ribs

Here pork ribs are simmered to tenderize the meat and remove some of the fat, before being roasted in a delicious orange-and-mustard glaze. Choose the meatiest ribs, such as loin back ribs. Remember to put out finger bowls and napkins for cleaning sticky fingers.

Makes 12 spare ribs

12 meaty pork ribs, about 2 pounds in total, with excess fat trimmed

3 tablespoons red-wine vinegar

2 teaspoons sunflower oil

Large strip pared orange zest

⅔ cup orange juice

1 tablespoon tomato paste

2 tablespoons soft dark brown sugar

2 tablespoons Worcestershire sauce

1 tablespoon French mustard

½ to 1 teaspoon cayenne, or to taste

Preparation time: 30 minutes
Cooking time: 40 to 45 minutes

1 Preheat the oven to 400°F. Put the ribs, trimmed of as much fat as possible, in a saucepan over high heat with enough water to cover. Add 2 tablespoons of the vinegar and bring to a boil. Reduce the heat and simmer, skimming the surface from time to time, 20 minutes.

2 Meanwhile, combine the remaining 1 tablespoon vinegar, the oil, orange zest and juice, tomato paste, brown sugar, Worcestershire sauce, mustard, and cayenne in a small saucepan over high heat. Bring to a boil and simmer until slightly reduced, 4 to 5 minutes.

3 Drain the ribs and arrange them in a single layer in a large roasting pan. Pour the orange mixture over and turn the ribs to coat them evenly. Loosely cover with foil and roast 20 minutes.

4 Remove the foil and continue roasting, turning and basting occasionally, until the ribs are dark brown and sticky, 20 to 25 minutes longer. Transfer to a large serving dish and serve warm.

Some More Ideas

• For Oriental Ribs, make a glaze with 2 teaspoons grated fresh ginger, 3 tablespoons honey, 1 tablespoon tomato paste, 2 tablespoons dark soy sauce, 2 tablespoons rice wine or dry sherry, 2 tablespoons bottled hoisin sauce, 2 teaspoons sherry vinegar, and 1 teaspoon bottled chile sauce.

• Try a Cajun-style dry rub instead of a glaze. Mix together 2 tablespoons paprika, 2 teaspoons ground cumin, 1 teaspoon dried thyme, ¼ teaspoon ground black pepper, ½ teaspoon cayenne and 2 finely chopped garlic cloves. Simmer the ribs as in the main recipe. Drain, cool slightly, and coat in the rub before roasting.

Plus Points

• Pork is an excellent source of the B vitamins, particularly vitamin B_{12}, which is needed for all growth and the division of cells and for red-blood formation.

• Ribs can be one of the fattiest cuts of pork. Trimming off any visible fat and simmering in water before roasting until crisp are clever ways to reduce their fat content.

Each rib provides

cals 90, **protein** 7.5 g, **fat** 4 g (of which saturated fat 1 g), **carbohydrate** 6 g (of which sugars 6 g), **fiber** 0.1 g

✓ B_1, B_6, B_{12}, E, niacin, calcium, zinc

Main Meals

Side Dishes and Breads

Whatever you add to a main course should both complement the food and supply extra nutrients. Vitamin-rich vegetables, which help protect against disease, can be served plain or combined to create delicious side dishes, such as Sesame Greens and Bean Sprouts or Roasted Bell Pepper Salad. Rice and grains also play their part, and warm homemade bread, whether basic or fancy, is sure to win praise.

Basil-Scented Sautéed Vegetables

A large, nonstick skillet is ideal for sautéing, the Western equivalent of stir-frying. Based on quick cooking over high heat, this method preserves color, while bringing out flavor. This vegetable dish goes very well with fish, poultry, meat, and noodles.

Serves 4

1 pound 2 ounces broccoli

1 tablespoon extra-virgin olive oil

3 to 4 large garlic cloves, thinly sliced (optional)

1 large or 2 small red bell peppers, seeded and cut into chunks

1 small turnip, peeled and cut into bite-size chunks

Pinch sugar

Leaves from 8 sprigs fresh basil, finely shredded

Salt

Preparation time: 10 minutes

Cooking time: 7 to 8 minutes

1 Cut the broccoli into small flowerets; trim and thinly slice the stems; set aside. Heat the olive oil in a large, nonstick skillet or wok over high heat. Add the garlic, if using, the red bell pepper, turnip, and the broccoli stems. Sprinkle in the sugar and salt to taste. Sauté, stirring, 2 to 3 minutes.

2 Add the broccoli flowerets and stir. Pour in 6 tablespoons of water to provide a thin covering on the bottom of the skillet or wok. Cover and cook over medium-high heat until the broccoli is crisp-tender and bright green, 3 to 4 minutes.

3 Stir in the basil, re-cover and leave over the heat for a few more seconds. Serve immediately.

Plus Points

• Broccoli, one of the brassicas, is a good source of the phytochemicals called glucosinolates. Red bell peppers are a rich source of the antioxidant beta-carotene that the body can convert into vitamin A. Both of these vegetables can help to fight cancer and prevent heart disease.

• In addition to providing fiber, turnips contain the B vitamins niacin and B_6, and are a surprisingly useful source of vitamin C.

Some More Ideas

• For a Far-Eastern flavor, substitute 8 canned water chestnuts, drained and quartered or halved, for the turnips, and add 1 teaspoon chopped fresh ginger, and ½ fresh green or red chile, seeded, deveined, and minced, with the broccoli flowerets. Increase the quantity of sugar to 1 to 2 teaspoons. At the end of cooking, add 1 tablespoon chopped fresh cilantro with the basil.

• Sugar-snap peas or snow peas can be used instead of the broccoli. They will cook in 1 to 2 minutes and there is no need to add the water. Serve with lemon or lime wedges so the juice can be squeezed over the vegetables.

• As well as replacing the broccoli with sugar-snap peas, use yellow bell peppers in place of red. Omit the garlic. Substitute tiny parboiled new potatoes, halved, for the turnip, and sprinkle generously with fresh tarragon leaves rather than basil. This combination of sautéed vegetables is delicious with fish, especially broiled mackerel or salmon.

Each serving provides Ⓥ

cals 90, **protein** 6 g, **fat** 4 g (of which saturated fat 1 g), **carbohydrate** 7 g (of which sugars 7 g), **fiber** 2 g

✓✓✓	A, C
✓✓	E, folate
✓	niacin, iron

Side Dishes and Breads

New Potatoes with Nori

Nori is a type of Japanese seaweed, sold dried in thin, dark-green sheets, in natural food stores and Oriental grocery stores. It is most frequently used for wrapping around sushi. The flavor is distinctive and savory and goes well with potatoes.

Serves 4

1 pound 2 ounces new potatoes
2 tablespoons butter
Grated zest and juice of ½ small lemon
1 sheet toasted nori, about 8 x 7 inches
2 tablespoons snipped fresh chives
Salt and fresh-ground black pepper

Preparation time: 5 minutes
Cooking time: 15 minutes

1 Put the new potatoes in a saucepan, cover with boiling water, and bring back to a boil, over high heat. Boil until they are just fork-tender, 12 minutes.

2 Reserve 3 tablespoons cooking water from the potatoes, then drain them and return them to the saucepan with the reserved water. Add the butter and lemon zest and juice. Turn the potatoes to coat them with the liquid.

3 Use scissors to snip the nori into fine strips. Scatter the nori over the potatoes and cover the pan. Simmer over low heat until the nori is soft, 1 to 2 minutes. Add seasoning to taste and sprinkle with the chives.

Some more ideas

● Nori is rather like parchment paper in texture. Toasted or roasted nori has been toasted briefly and seasoned. It is shiny and almost black in color—untoasted nori is slightly paler (more green) in color. To toast nori, pass the sheet over a gas flame, once on each side of the sheet, or lay the sheet on a rack in a broiler pan and place under a preheated broiler a few seconds. The sheet will darken and give off its aroma very quickly—take care not to overcook the nori or it will burn.

● Green beans go well with lemon and potatoes, and can be added to the dish, or used to replace the nori. Cut 7 ounces green beans into short pieces and add them to the potatoes about halfway through the cooking:

4 to 5 minutes is sufficient time for cooking the beans. Drain and toss with the butter and lemon zest and juice.

● Look out for Oriental yard-long or asparagus beans, which, as their name suggests, grow to an amazing length. Their flavor is similar to that of runner beans and they are good with the potatoes and nori. Prepare them as for green beans (above).

Each serving provides Ⓥ

cals 160, **protein** 6 g, **fat** 7 g (of which saturated fat 4 g), **carbohydrate** 20 g (of which sugars 2 g), **fiber** 1.6 g

✓✓✓	B₁₂
✓✓	A, B₆, C, E
✓	B₁, B₂, copper, iron, potassium, zinc

Plus Points

● Nori, like other sea vegetables, is rich in vitamin A and minerals, including potassium, which helps to counteract the effects of sodium and keep blood pressure down. Nori also contains iron, zinc, copper, and iodine.

● New potatoes and lemon juice contribute vitamin C, which promotes absorption of iron from the nori.

Roast Root Vegetables with Herbs

Use this recipe as a guide for roasting single vegetables, such as potatoes or parsnips, as well as this superb dish of mixed roots. They are delicious with roast poultry or meat— or with vegetarian main dishes and lightly baked fish.

Serves 4

2¼ pounds mixed root vegetables, such as potatoes, sweet potatoes, carrots, parsnips, rutabaga, and kohlrabi

8 ounces shallots or pearl onions

2 tablespoons extra-virgin olive oil

1 teaspoon coarse sea salt

1 teaspoon cracked black peppercorns

Few sprigs fresh thyme

Few sprigs fresh rosemary

Extra sprigs fresh thyme or rosemary (optional)

Preparation time: 15 to 20 minutes
Cooking time: 30 to 35 minutes

1 Preheat the oven to 425°F. Scrub or peel the vegetables, according to type and your taste. Halve or quarter large potatoes. Cut large carrots or parsnips in half lengthwise, then cut the pieces crosswise in half again. Cut rutabaga or kohlrabi into large chunks (about the same size as the potatoes). Leave shallots or onions whole.

2 Place the vegetables in a large saucepan over high heat and pour in enough boiling water to cover them. Bring back to a boil, then reduce the heat and simmer until the vegetables are lightly cooked, but not yet tender, 5 to 7 minutes.

3 Drain the vegetables and place them in a roasting pan. Brush with the oil and sprinkle with the salt and peppercorns. Add the herb sprigs to the pan and place in the oven.

4 Roast until the vegetables are golden brown, crisp, and tender, 30 to 35 minutes, turning the vegetables over after 15 minutes. Serve hot, garnished with sprigs of thyme or rosemary, if liked.

Some More Ideas

● The vegetables can be roasted at the same time as a joint of meat or poultry. Plan on 45 minutes at 400°F, or longer at a lower temperature, if necessary.

● Baby new vegetables can also be roasted. Try new potatoes, carrots, beets, and turnips. As well as root vegetables, patty-pan squash and asparagus are delicious roasted. Sprinkle with herbs and a little balsamic vinegar or lemon juice, just before serving.

● Quartered acorn squash is good roasted with mixed root vegetables.

Each serving provides Ⓥ

cals 200, **protein** 4 g, **fat** 7 g (of which saturated fat 1 g), **carbohydrate** 33 g (of which sugars 14 g), **fiber** 9 g

✓✓✓	A, C
✓✓	B₁, B₆, E, folate
✓	niacin, potassium

Plus Points

● Combining different root vegetables instead of serving roast potatoes alone, for example, provides a good mix of flavors and nutrients: As well as vitamin C from the potatoes and beta-carotene from the carrots, rutabagas are part of the brassica family, which offer cancer-fighting phytochemicals.

● All these vegetables provide plenty of flavor and satisfying bulk, so portions of meat can be modest. They also contribute dietary fiber.

Side Dishes and Breads

193

Cauliflower with Crisp Crumbs

The crisp, golden topping in this dish is usually made by frying the bread crumbs in a generous quantity of butter. This low-fat version uses a modest portion of olive oil and fresh herbs to flavor a topping that contrasts particularly well with steamed cauliflower.

Serves 4

1 large head cauliflower, trimmed and broken into flowerets

Crispy Crumb Topping

2 tablespoons extra-virgin olive oil

1¾ cups fresh bread crumbs

1 tablespoon chopped fresh thyme

1 tablespoon chopped fresh tarragon

2 tablespoons chopped parsley

Salt and fresh-ground black pepper

Fresh herb sprigs (optional)

Preparation time: 10 minutes
Cooking time: 15 minutes

1 Bring a large saucepan of water with a steamer on top to a boil over high heat. Steam the cauliflower until crisp-tender, about 15 minutes.

2 Meanwhile, heat the oil in a nonstick skillet or saucepan over medium heat. Add the bread crumbs and stir well to coat as evenly as possible with oil. Sauté until the crumbs are brown and crisp, about 10 minutes. As the crumbs cook, the oil will seep out of those that absorbed it initially, leaving the rest to become evenly crisp.

3 Transfer the cauliflower to a warm serving dish. Season the crumbs to taste and mix in the parsley, thyme, and tarragon. Sprinkle the crumb mixture over the cauliflower. Garnish with sprigs of herbs, if using.

Some More Ideas

• The crumb topping also goes well with lightly boiled or steamed Brussels sprouts. Use chopped fresh sage or marjoram instead of the tarragon and add the grated zest of 1 lemon to the crumb mixture. Serve lemon wedges with the sprouts so the juice can be squeezed over.

• The crisp crumbs are delicious with hot beets. Use fresh sage instead of the tarragon and add the grated zest of 1 orange to the crumb mixture. To serve, cut the freshly boiled beets into thick slices, arrange on a serving platter, so they overlap, and sprinkle with the crumb mixture. Garnish with orange slices. This goes well with roast or broiled pork, ham or sausages.

• Celery root is another vegetable that is enhanced by a crisp crumb topping. Cut the celery root into small cubes, fingers, or slices before cooking. For a delicate topping, instead of the herbs listed in the main recipe, use 3 tablespoons finely chopped fresh dill. Celery root garnished in this way is super with broiled, poached, or baked white fish.

Plus Points

• Cauliflower is a member of the brassica family of cruciferous vegetables. It contains sulfurous compounds thought to help protect against cancer. It also provides vitamin C and fiber.

• Extra-virgin olive oil is made from the first pressing of top-grade olives from which the pits have been removed. It can be green in color, has a rich flavor, and is high in monounsaturated fatty acids. These are the kinds of fat that are thought to help lower cholesterol levels in the blood.

Each serving provides Ⓥ

cals 140, **protein** 5 g, **fat** 7 g (of which saturated fat 1 g), **carbohydrate** 14 g (of which sugars 3 g), **fiber** 2.5 g

✓✓✓	C
✓✓	folate
✓	B₁, B₆, niacin

Sesame Greens and Bean Sprouts

With a little inspiration, even the most humble vegetables can be elevated to feature in unusual, well-flavored side dishes. This succulent and healthy stir-fry is full of flavor and crunch. It is equally delicious with plain broiled fish, poultry, or meat.

Serves 4

4 tablespoons sesame seeds
2 tablespoons sunflower oil
1 onion, chopped
2 garlic cloves, chopped
1 small head savoy cabbage, finely shredded
½ head Chinese leaves, finely shredded
1¾ cups bean sprouts
4 tablespoons bottled oyster sauce
Salt and fresh-ground black pepper

Preparation time: 10 minutes
Cooking time: 4 to 6 minutes

1 Heat a small saucepan over high heat. Add the sesame seeds and dry-fry, shaking the pan frequently, until they begin to brown. Tip the seeds out into a small bowl and set aside.

2 Heat the oil in a wok or large skillet over medium heat. Add the onion and garlic and stir-fry until beginning to become soft, 2 to 3 minutes. Add the cabbage and Chinese leaves and continue stir-frying until the vegetables are crisp-tender, 2 to 3 minutes. Add the bean sprouts and continue stir-frying for a few seconds.

3 Make a space in the middle of the pan. Pour in the oyster sauce and 2 tablespoons of water, and stir until hot. Toss the vegetables into the sauce. Taste and add pepper, with salt, if necessary (this will depend on the saltiness of the oyster sauce). Sprinkle with the toasted sesame seeds.

Some More Ideas

• Use 3½ cups finely shredded red cabbage, instead of the savoy cabbage, and add 3 chopped cooked beets, with the bean sprouts. Red cabbage will require 2 minutes additional stir-frying, so add to the wok before the Chinese leaves. Use 1 tablespoon honey with 2 tablespoons soy sauce instead of the oyster sauce.

• Finely shredded Brussels sprouts are crisp and full flavored when stir-fried. Use them instead of the savoy cabbage—slice the sprouts thinly, then shake the slices to loosen the shreds. Or use shredded spinach.

• Toasted flaked almonds can be sprinkled over the vegetables instead of the sesame seeds.

Plus Points

• As well as contributing distinctive flavor, sesame seeds are a good source of calcium and therefore useful for anyone who dislikes or does not eat dairy products, the main source of this mineral in the Western diet. A combination of good supplies of calcium and plenty of physical activity are particularly important for young girls to avoid osteoporosis later in life.

• Bean sprouts, along with other sprouted seeds, are rich in B vitamins and vitamin C. They also provide iron and potassium.

Each serving provides

cals 150, **protein** 5 g, **fat** 11 g (of which saturated fat 1 g), **carbohydrate** 9 g (of which sugars 5 g), **fiber** 6 g

✓✓✓	C, folate
✓✓	B$_{12}$
✓	B$_1$, calcium, iron, potassium

Side Dishes and Breads

197

Fragrant Basmati Rice

Basmati cooks to perfect, separate, fluffy grains and is considered by many to be the finest rice. Here it is subtly scented and colored with saffron, cinnamon, and ginger. The sweet-sharp flavor of pomegranate adds a unique quality to this dish.

Serves 6

1 tablespoon sunflower oil

½ cup slivered blanched almonds, any tiny pieces discarded

1¼ cups basmati rice, rinsed

Pinch saffron strands

1 cinnamon stick

2 cups vegetable stock, boiling

1 ripe pomegranate

1 inch piece fresh ginger, grated

1 teaspoon honey

1 tablespoon chopped fresh mint

2 tablespoons chopped fresh cilantro

Salt and fresh-ground black pepper

Preparation time: 15 minutes, plus standing
Cooking time: 15 to 20 minutes

Each serving provides ⓥ

cals 249, protein 6 g, fat 7 g (of which saturated fat 0.5 g), carbohydrate 40 g (of which sugars 6 g), fiber 1.5 g

✓✓	E
✓	copper

1 Heat the oil in a large saucepan over medium-low heat. Add the almonds and sauté until golden, 2 to 3 minutes. Remove from the pan with a slotted spoon; set aside.

2 Add the rice to the oil and cook, stirring, for 1 minute. Stir in the saffron strands and cinnamon stick, then add the stock and season with salt and pepper to taste. Bring to a boil, stir, and reduce the heat to very low. Cover and simmer until the rice is tender and all of the stock is absorbed, 10 to 15 minutes.

3 Meanwhile, cut the pomegranate in half and remove all the seeds from the membranes: Reserve about one-third of the seeds for garnish. Put the rest of the seeds in a sieve placed over a mixing bowl and crush with a spoon to extract the juice.

4 Put the grated ginger into a garlic crusher, hold over the mixing bowl and squeeze out the ginger juice. Stir the honey into the juices.

5 When the rice is cooked, stir in the pomegranate-juice mixture. Cover again and leave to stand for 2 minutes. Remove the cinnamon stick, fork the mint and cilantro through the rice, and transfer to a warm serving dish. Scatter the almonds and reserved pomegranate seeds over.

Some More Ideas

• For Lemongrass-Scented Basmati Rice, add 1 bruised stem of lemongrass with the cinnamon stick. Instead of pomegranate and ginger juices, mix the juice of ½ lemon with the honey.

• Make Spiced Basmati Pilaf. Toast ½ cup cashew nuts in 1 tablespoon sunflower oil until golden. Remove from the pan with a slotted spoon; set aside. Toast the basmati rice in the oil with 1 teaspoon cumin seeds and the crushed seeds of 3 cardamom pods about 2 minutes. Stir in the stock, 3 tablespoons coconut milk, 1 bay leaf, and 3 cloves. Cover and simmer as in the main recipe. Remove the bay leaf and cloves, then stir in 1 tablespoon lemon juice and 2 tablespoons chopped fresh cilantro. Scatter the cashew nuts over and garnish with a fresh cilantro sprig.

Plus Points

• Pomegranate seeds not only add flavor to this dish, they also contribute vitamin C and some dietary fiber.

• Almonds, like other nuts, provide many of the nutrients usually found in meat, such as protein, many of the B vitamins and essential minerals such as phosphorus, iron, copper, and potassium. They are also a good source of vitamin E, which helps to protect against heart disease.

Millet with Spinach and Pine Nuts

Bright green spinach and golden apricots add rich color and flavor to this easy grain-and-vegetable side dish. It is an ideal alternative to potatoes or rice, and is particularly suitable for serving with stews and casseroles that have plenty of sauce.

Serves 4

1 cup millet

⅓ cup roughly chopped dried apricots

1 quart vegetable stock

4 tablespoons pine nuts

1 bag (10 ounces) baby spinach leaves

Fresh-squeezed juice of ½ lemon

Salt and fresh-ground black pepper

Preparation time: 10 minutes

Cooking time: 20 to 25 minutes

1 Put the millet and dried apricots into a large saucepan and stir in the stock over high heat and bring to a boil. Reduce the heat and simmer until all the stock is absorbed and the millet is tender, 15 to 20 minutes.

2 Meanwhile, toast the pine nuts in a small, dry skillet until they are golden brown and fragrant; set aside.

3 Add the spinach and lemon juice to the millet with salt and pepper to taste. Cover the pan and leave over a very low heat until the spinach wilts, 4 to 5 minutes.

4 Stir the millet and spinach mixture gently, then spoon into a serving bowl. Scatter the toasted pine nuts on top.

Another Idea

• Try Eggplants with Millet and Sesame Seeds. Cut 2 medium eggplants into dice. Heat 2 tablespoons extra-virgin olive oil in a large skillet over high heat. Add the eggplants and brown, stirring constantly. Remove from the heat and stir in 1 cup millet and 1 quart vegetable stock. Return to the heat and bring to a boil. Stir, reduce the heat, and simmer until the stock is absorbed and the millet is tender, 15 to 20 minutes. Season with salt and pepper to taste. Transfer to a serving bowl and scatter with 2 tablespoons chopped fresh cilantro, 1 tablespoon thinly sliced scallions and 2 tablespoons toasted sesame seeds.

Plus Points

• Millet provides useful amounts of iron and B vitamins and, as it is not highly milled, it retains all its nutritional value. Being glutenfree, it can be an additional source of starchy carbohydrate for celiacs.

• Pine nuts are a good source of vitamin E and potassium. They also contribute useful amounts of magnesium, zinc, and iron.

• Dried apricots are one of the richest fruit sources of iron. They also contain beta-carotene, which the body can convert to vitamin A, and other minerals, such as calcium, potassium, and phosphorus.

Each serving provides Ⓥ

cals 307, **protein** 7 g, **fat** 11 g (of which saturated fat 1 g), **carbohydrate** 44 g (of which sugars 6 g), **fiber** 5 g

✓✓✓	A
✓✓	B₁, E
✓	C, folate, niacin, calcium, copper, iron, potassium, zinc

Side Dishes and Breads

Mixed Salad Leaves with Flowers and Blueberries

Combining edible flowers, salad leaves, alfalfa sprouts, and juicy blueberries, this is a pretty summer salad. Some supermarkets sell packages of edible flowers, or you can pick them from your garden—be sure to choose those that have not been sprayed with pesticides.

Serves 4

1 small leaf lettuce, torn into bite-size pieces

3 ounces arugula

3 ounces alfalfa sprouts

⅔ cup blueberries

1 ounce mixed edible flowers, including some or all of the following: nasturtiums, borage, violas or pansies, and herb flowers, such as sage and rosemary

Honey-Mustard Dressing

3 tablespoons grapeseed or sunflower oil

Fresh-squeezed juice of 1 small lemon

1 teaspoon Dijon mustard

1 teaspoon honey

Salt and fresh-ground black pepper

Preparation time: 10 to 15 minutes

Each serving provides

cals 107, **protein** 2 g, **fat** 9 g (of which saturated fat 1 g), **carbohydrate** 5 g (of which sugars 5 g), **fiber** 2.5 g

✓✓✓	B₁, B₆, C, niacin
✓✓	E
✓	A, folate

1 To make the dressing, whisk the oil with the lemon juice, mustard, honey, and salt and pepper to taste in a large shallow salad bowl.

2 Add the lettuce and arugula and toss to coat with the dressing. Sprinkle the salad with the alfalfa sprouts and blueberries. Arrange the flowers on top and serve at once.

Some More Ideas for Flowery Salads

• Make a Flowery Carrot Salad. Tear 1 butterhead or leaf lettuce into bite-size pieces and put into a shallow salad bowl. Cut 2 carrots into long, thin ribbons with a swivel-bladed vegetable peeler and add to the bowl. Peel and divide 2 oranges into segments and add to the bowl with ⅓ cup blueberries. Make the Honey-Mustard Dressing as in the main recipe, but replace the lemon juice with fresh orange juice. Drizzle it over the salad and garnish with mixed orange and yellow nasturtium flowers.

• For a refreshing Lemon and Raspberry Salad, mix ½ ounce lemon balm leaves and a few lemon geranium leaves with 1 small romaine lettuce, torn into pieces. Scatter ¾ cup raspberries over. For the dressing, whisk 2 tablespoons extra-virgin olive oil with the juice of 1 lemon and seasoning to taste. Garnish the salad with 1 ounce mixed edible flowers such as chive, lemon balm, and mint or viola.

• Try Peppery Salad with Pears and Wild Garlic. Separate 1 small romaine lettuce into leaves and mix with 3 ounces arugula in a salad bowl. For the dressing whisk 3 tablespoons extra-virgin olive oil with the juice of 1 lemon and 3 tablespoons snipped fresh chives. Add 1 ripe Williams pear, cored and thinly sliced, and turn to coat with the dressing. Add the pear and dressing to the salad leaves and toss gently. Garnish with 1 ounce edible herb flowers, such as garlic, chive, thyme, or borage.

Plus Points

• Naturally sweet blueberries are rich in vitamin C and also contain antibacterial compounds thought to be effective against some gastrointestinal disorders and urinary infections, such as cystitis.

• The nutritional value of petals and flower heads is very small as they are used in such tiny quantities, but you will get some essential oils and phytochemicals, particularly antioxidants, from some flowers, especially herb flowers.

Side Dishes and Breads

Roasted Bell Pepper Salad

This colorful salad makes a tasty accompaniment to seafood, chicken, or lamb, and the added benefit is that it is low in calories. Peppers are an excellent source of vitamin C, and even when roasted they still retain substantial amounts of this important vitamin.

Serves 6

2 large red bell peppers

2 large yellow or orange bell peppers

2 large green bell peppers

2½ tablespoons extra-virgin olive oil

2 teaspoons balsamic vinegar

1 small garlic clove, minced or crushed

Salt and fresh-ground black pepper

To garnish

12 black olives, pitted

Handful small fresh basil leaves

Preparation time: 45 minutes, plus cooling

1 Preheat the oven to 400ºF. Brush the peppers with 1 tablespoon of the olive oil and arrange in a shallow roasting pan. Roast until the pepper skins are evenly darkened, turning them 3 or 4 times, about 35 minutes. Place the peppers in a paper bag and leave until they are cool enough to handle.

2 Working over a bowl to catch the juice, peel the peppers. Cut them in half and discard the cores and seeds (remove any seeds that fall into the juice), then cut into thick slices.

3 Measure 1½ tablespoons of the pepper juice into a small bowl; discard the remainder. Add the vinegar, garlic, and salt and pepper to taste, and whisk in the remaining 1½ tablespoons olive oil.

4 Arrange the peppers on a serving platter or on individual salad plates. Drizzle the dressing over and garnish with the olives and basil leaves.

Some More Ideas for Pepper Salads

• For Roasted Red Bell Pepper and Onion Salad to serve 4, quarter and seed 4 red bell peppers and put them in a baking dish with 4 small red onions, quartered. Drizzle 1½ tablespoons extra-virgin olive oil over and season to taste. Roast in a preheated 400ºF oven until the vegetables are tender and brown around the edges, turning once, about 35 minutes. Cool, then peel the peppers, if wished, holding them over the baking dish. Whisk 2 teaspoons lemon juice with 1½ tablespoons extra-virgin olive oil in a salad bowl and season to taste. Add 4 ounces arugula or mixed red salad leaves and toss to coat. Pile the peppers and onions on top and drizzle the cooking juices over.

• For Oriental-Style Pepper and Chinese Leaf Salad to serve 4, seed and thinly slice 2 red bell peppers (or 1 red and 1 yellow bell pepper). Seed and devein 1 fresh red chile. Mix the bell peppers and chile in a salad bowl with 2 cups shredded Chinese leaves. For the dressing, whisk together 1 tablespoon rice vinegar, 1 teaspoon toasted sesame oil, 2 teaspoons peanut oil and 1 teaspoon soy sauce. Drizzle over the vegetables and toss to coat. Sprinkle with 2 tablespoons toasted sesame seeds.

Plus Points

• Herbalists recommend basil as a natural tranquilizer. It is also believed to aid digestion, ease stomach cramps, and help relieve the headaches associated with colds.

• Olives are a source of vitamin E, although they are usually not eaten in large enough quantities to make a significant contribution to the diet.

Each serving provides Ⓥ

cals 97, protein 2 g, fat 6 g (of which saturated fat 1 g), carbohydrate 10 g (of which sugars 9 g), fiber 3 g

✓✓✓ A, B₁, B₆, C, E, niacin

✓✓ folate

Side Dishes and Breads

Crunchy Nut Coleslaw

Everyone loves coleslaw, and this fresh-tasting version is sure to appeal. Made with white cabbage, carrot, and radishes, it is flecked with scallions, sweet golden raisins, and roasted peanuts, and tossed with a creamy dressing that is healthily low in fat.

Serves 4

3 cups finely shredded white cabbage

1 large carrot, coarsely grated

⅓ cup golden raisins

4 scallions, minced, with the white and green parts kept separate

2 tablespoons mayonnaise

⅔ cup plain low-fat yogurt

¼ cup sliced radishes

⅓ cup unsalted roasted peanuts

3 tablespoons chopped parsley or snipped fresh chives, or a mixture of the two (optional)

Salt and fresh-ground black pepper

Preparation time: 15 minutes

1 Mix together the cabbage, carrot, golden raisins, and white parts of the scallions in a large salad bowl.

2 Stir the mayonnaise and yogurt together and season with salt and pepper to taste. Stir this dressing into the cabbage mixture and toss to coat all the ingredients.

3 Just before serving, stir in the radishes and peanuts. Sprinkle with the chopped green parts of the scallions and the parsley or chives.

Some More Ideas for Coleslaw

• Toss 1 cored and diced red-skinned apple with 2 tablespoons lemon juice. Stir into the coleslaw with 1 teaspoon caraway seeds.

• Add ⅔ cup either canned or thawed frozen corn kernels.

• Lightly toast 1 tablespoon pumpkin seeds and 2 tablespoons sunflower seeds under a preheated broiler. Use to garnish the coleslaw in place of the herbs.

• For a Celery Root Coleslaw, use 1½ cups peeled celery root, cut into matchstick strips, instead of white cabbage. Flavor the yogurt and mayonnaise dressing with 2 teaspoons wholegrain mustard, or 1 teaspoon Dijon mustard and 1 tablespoon mango chutney.

• For Red Cabbage and Blue Cheese Coleslaw to serve 4 to 6, mix together 3 cups finely shredded red cabbage with 1 cup tiny cauliflower flowerets, 1 cup grated carrot, ½ red onion, minced, and ⅓ cup dried cranberries or cherries. Make the dressing by mashing ⅔ cup plain low-fat yogurt with 4 ounces blue cheese and seasoning to taste. Garnish with 2 slices of lean Canadian bacon, broiled until crisp and cut into thin strips.

Each serving provides Ⓥ

cals 209, **protein** 7 g, **fat** 12 g (of which saturated fat 2 g), **carbohydrate** 19 g (of which sugars 18 g), **fiber** 4 g

✓✓✓	A, B₁, B₆, C, E, niacin
✓✓	folate
✓	calcium, copper, potassium

Plus Points

• Roasted peanuts are a delicious and nutritious addition to this recipe. Research suggests that a daily intake of peanuts, peanut butter, or peanut oil might help to lower total cholesterol, harmful LDL cholesterol, and triglyceride levels to help protect against coronary heart disease.

• Homemade coleslaw not only looks and tastes far superior to store-bought coleslaw, but it can be much lower in fat if a mixture of mayonnaise and low-fat yogurt is used.

Garlic-Tomato Salad

When tomatoes are at their sweetest, this salad is particularly delicious. It can also be eye-catching if you make it with a mixture of different-colored tomatoes—look for yellow cherry tomatoes, as well as small red or yellow pear-shaped plum tomatoes.

Serves 4

1 large butterhead lettuce, large leaves torn into smaller pieces

4 large or 6 small ripe plum tomatoes, sliced

20 cherry tomatoes, halved

16 fresh basil leaves

1½ tablespoons toasted pumpkin seeds

1½ tablespoons toasted sunflower seeds

Garlic Vinaigrette

1 small garlic clove, minced

1½ teaspoons red-wine vinegar

2 tablespoons extra-virgin olive oil

Salt and fresh-ground black pepper

Preparation time: 15 minutes

1 To make the vinaigrette, whisk together the garlic, vinegar, oil, and salt and pepper to taste in a small mixing bowl.

2 Place a layer of lettuce leaves on a serving platter or on 4 plates. Arrange the sliced tomatoes and then the cherry tomatoes on top. Drizzle the vinaigrette over.

3 Scatter the basil leaves and the pumpkin and sunflower seeds over the tomatoes.

Some More Ideas for Tomato Salads

• For Tomato and Black Olive Salad, slice 4 large or 6 small ripe plum tomatoes, and arrange on a serving platter. Top with 1 cup thinly sliced scallions. Drizzle 1 tablespoon extra-virgin olive oil and the juice of ¼ lemon over. Top with 8 black olives, halved and pitted, and 2 tablespoons chopped parsley.

• Make a salad of fresh and sun-dried tomatoes. Cut 6 ripe plum tomatoes into thin wedges and put them in a mixing bowl. Add 3 thinly sliced sun-dried tomatoes to the bowl. Make a vinaigrette by whisking 1½ tablespoons of oil from the jar of sun-dried tomatoes with 1½ teaspoons wine vinegar and seasoning to taste. Drizzle the dressing over the tomatoes and leave to marinate 15 minutes. Arrange 4 ounces arugula leaves on 4 plates and divide the tomatoes between them, or arrange on a serving platter. Sprinkle with 2 tablespoons toasted pine nuts and serve.

• Try a salad of cherry tomatoes and sugar-snap peas. Trim 8 ounces sugarsnap peas and steam until crisp-tender, about 3 minutes. Refresh under cold running water; set aside to cool. Mix with 13 ounces cherry tomatoes, halved if large, and 6 thinly sliced scallions. Make the garlic vinaigrette as in the main recipe and drizzle it over the tomatoes and peas. Add 3 tablespoons chopped fresh mint, or 1 tablespoon each chopped fresh tarragon and parsley, and toss to mix.

Plus Points

• Pumpkin seeds are one of the richest vegetarian sources of zinc, a mineral that is essential for the functioning of the immune system and for growth and wound healing. They are also a good source of protein and unsaturated fat, and a useful source of iron, magnesium, and fiber.

• Tomatoes are a rich source of vitamin C, an important nutrient for maintaining immunity and healthy skin. The vitamin C is concentrated in the jellylike substance surrounding the seeds.

Each serving provides Ⓥ

cals 160, **protein** 5 g, **fat** 12 g (of which saturated fat 2 g), **carbohydrate** 9 g (of which sugars 7 g), **fiber** 2.5 g

✓✓✓	A, B$_1$, B$_6$, C, E, niacin
✓✓	folate, copper
✓	iron, zinc

Basic Loaf of Bread

This recipe makes a delicious basic loaf, and it is infinitely flexible. You can make any number of breads by using different types of flour or adding extra ingredients—you don't even need a loaf pan, because the bread is baked on a baking sheet.

Makes 1 large round loaf (cuts into about 12 slices)

2¾ cups white bread flour

2¾ cups wholewheat bread flour, preferably stoneground, plus a little extra to sprinkle

1 teaspoon salt

1 envelope (¼ ounce) quick-rising yeast

2 cups water (120˚ to 130˚F)

Preparation time: 25 minutes, plus about 2 hours rising

Cooking time: 35 minutes

1 Sift the white and wholewheat flours and salt into a large bowl, tipping in any bran left in the sifter. Stir in the yeast, then make a well in the middle and pour in the water. Using your hands, gradually draw the flour into the water, mixing to make a dough.

2 Gather the dough into a ball that feels firm and leaves the sides of the bowl clean; if necessary, add a little more flour or a little more water.

3 Turn out the dough onto a lightly floured surface and knead until smooth and elastic, about 10 minutes. Put the dough into a large, lightly greased bowl and cover with plastic wrap. Leave to rise in a warm place until the dough doubles in size, about 1 hour, depending on the temperature of the room.

4 Punch down the dough, then turn out onto a floured surface. Gently knead the dough into a neat ball shape, then set it on a large greased baking sheet. Cover with a damp cloth and leave to rise in a warm place until doubled in size again, about 1 hour.

5 Toward the end of the rising time, preheat the oven to 425°F. Uncover the loaf and sprinkle with a little flour. Using a serrated knife, make 4 slashes across the top. Bake until the bread sounds hollow when tapped on the bottom, about 35 minutes.

6 Transfer the loaf to a wire rack and leave to cool completely before slicing. This bread keeps up to 5 days.

Each slice provides

Ⓥ

cals 180, **protein** 6 g, **fat** 1 g (of which saturated fat 0 g), **carbohydrate** 40 g (of which sugars 1 g), **fiber** 3.5 g

✓✓	B₁, B₆, selenium
✓	niacin, copper, iron, zinc

Plus Points

• The positive features of bread are often overlooked, as it has very unfairly gained a reputation for being fattening: It is what you put on the bread, not the bread itself, that can be fattening. Even white bread provides good amounts of dietary fiber, and by law it is fortified with vitamins and minerals, including niacin, reduced iron, riboflavin, and folate.

• This is a fat-free loaf with plenty of fiber from the wholewheat flour. The wholewheat flour also provides B vitamins, magnesium, zinc, iron, copper, and phosphorus.

• Stoneground flour is milled by traditional methods, which keep the wheat grains cool and thus preserve almost all the nutrients in the whole grain.

Side Dishes and Breads

Some More Ideas

- For White Bread, use 5¼ cups strong white bread flour and omit the wholewheat flour. For a loaf with texture, use 5¼ cups wholewheat bread flour and omit the white bread flour.
- For extra calcium, mix the dough with low-fat (2%) milk instead of water, or use a mixture of milk and water.
- To make a tin loaf, after the first rising, knock back the dough, knead it 2-3 minutes, then shape it and place in a greased 9 x 5 inch bread pan. Leave to rise until double in size, then bake as in the main recipe.
- To make rolls, after the first rising divide the dough into 20 equal pieces. For round rolls, shape each piece into a rough ball, then roll it under your cupped hand on the countertop to neaten. For an oval roll, shape each piece into a ball, flatten slightly, then mold to an oval with your hands and make a crease down the middle with the side of your little finger.

Focaccia

This light Italian flat bread is prepared from a soft dough enriched with olive oil. Traditionally, extra olive oil is sprinkled over the dough before baking—sometimes very generously—but this recipe uses just enough to give a good texture and flavour.

Makes 1 round, flat bread (serves 8)

3⅔ cups white bread flour
1 teaspoon salt
1 envelope (¼ ounce) quick-rising yeast
4 tablespoons extra-virgin olive oil
1¼ cups water (120° to 130°F)
½ teaspoon coarse sea salt

Preparation time: 15 minutes, plus about
    45 minutes rising
Cooking time: 15 minutes

1 Put the flour into a large bowl and stir in the salt and yeast. Make a well in the middle and pour in 3 tablespoons of the olive oil and the water. Gradually mix the flour into the oil and water, using a wooden spoon at first, then by hand, to make a soft, slightly sticky dough.

2 Turn out the dough onto a lightly floured surface and knead until smooth and elastic, about 10 minutes. Keep the dough moving by turning, punching and folding it to prevent it from sticking. Sprinkle the surface with a little extra flour, if necessary, but try not to add too much as this will make the dough dry.

3 Shape the dough into a ball and slap it onto a greased cookie sheet. Roll out or push the dough out with your hands into a circle about 8 inches in diameter and ¾ inch thick. Cover loosely with a clean dish towel, tucking the ends under the cookie sheet. Leave in a warm place until the dough doubles in thickness, which can be about 45 minutes, depending on the room temperature.

4 Toward the end of the rising time, preheat the oven to 450°F. Uncover the bread. Pour a little hand-hot water into a cup, then dip your fingers into the water and press into the risen dough to make deep dents all over the top; wet your fingers each time, to leave the top of the loaf moist. Brush the remaining 1 tablespoon olive oil over the bread and sprinkle with the coarse salt.

5 Bake the focaccia until golden brown, about 15 minutes. Transfer to a wire rack to cool 15 minutes, then wrap it in a clean dish towel to soften the crust. Serve warm or leave to cool completely. The bread can be kept in a plastic bag up to 2 days.

Each serving provides

cals 240, protein 5 g, fat 6 g (of which saturated fat 1 g), carbohydrate 44 g (of which sugars 1 g), fiber 2 g

✓   B₁, calcium

Plus Points

• Olive oil is high in monounsaturated fat, which might help to lower blood cholesterol levels.

• Although focaccia has slightly more fat than other types of bread, it has a moist texture, so it can be enjoyed plain, without added butter or other fat.

Some More Ideas

● To make individual focaccias, divide the dough into 8 portions. Press each portion out into a circle about 4 inches in diameter. These small breads will rise in 30 to 45 minutes and bake in 10 to 15 minutes.

● A variety of ingredients can be sprinkled over the focaccia before baking. Try fennel or dill seeds, chopped fresh or dried oregano, finely chopped onion and/or garlic, or chopped black or green olives.

● For Olive Focaccia, pit and chop 8 black olives and add to the dough with the olive oil and water. Sprinkle 1 teaspoon finely chopped fresh rosemary over the focaccia before making the dents on the surface with your fingers.

● For Thyme and Garlic Focaccia, add 1 tablespoon chopped fresh thyme to the dough with the oil, and sprinkle 2 finely chopped garlic cloves over before making the dents.

● For Sun-Dried Tomato Focaccia, add 4 finely chopped sun-dried tomatoes to the dough with the oil and water. Before serving, sprinkle with shredded fresh basil.

Pita Breads

These pita breads are delicious served warm from the oven. They make a good accompaniment to soups and dips, or they can be left to cool, then split and filled: Try goat cheese with roasted vegetables or hummus and a crunchy mixed salad.

Makes 10 breads

3⅔ cups white bread flour

1 teaspoon salt

½ teaspoon sugar

1 envelope (¼ ounce) quick-rise yeast

About 1¼ cups water (120° to 130°F)

Preparation time: 30 minutes, plus 1½ to
  2 hours rising

Cooking time: 8 to 10 minutes

1 Sift the flour and salt into a bowl, then stir in the sugar and yeast. Make a well in the middle and stir in enough water to make a soft dough.

2 Turn the dough out onto a lightly floured surface and knead until smooth and elastic, about 10 minutes. Place in a lightly greased bowl, cover with a dish towel and leave to rise in a warm place until the dough doubles in size, 1 to 1½ hours, depending on the room temperature.

3 Turn out the risen dough onto the lightly floured surface and punch down. Knead 2 to 3 minutes. Divide the dough into 10 pieces and shape each one into a ball. Roll out each ball to an oval about ¼ inch thick. Leave on the floured surface to rise at room temperature, about 30 minutes.

4 Toward the end of the rising time, preheat the oven to 450°F. Place 3 nonstick cookie sheets (or 3 floured cookie sheets) in the oven to heat, about 5 minutes. Place the pita breads on the cookie sheets and bake until firm and golden brown, 8 to 10 minutes.

5 Transfer to a wire rack to cool. Serve warm or reheat under the broiler, or in the toaster, as required. Pita breads are best eaten on the day they are made, but they can be kept, wrapped in foil 1 to 2 days.

Some More Ideas

• Substitute wholewheat flour for half the white flour.

• For Seeded Pita Breads, brush the dough ovals with water, then sprinkle with sesame or other seeds before baking. Alternatively, knead 2 tablespoons seeds into the dough in Step 2.

• For Herb Pita Breads, knead 1 tablespoon chopped fresh rosemary or 2 tablespoons chopped fresh basil into the dough in Step 2.

Plus Points

• White flour provides calcium, a mineral that is essential for healthy bones and teeth. Calcium is also important for normal functioning of nerve impulses and it aids blood clotting.

• These pita breads contain no saturated fat and almost no fat of any kind, making them an excellent healthy choice for a bread to serve with cheese, meat, or other foods that are higher in fat.

Each bread provides

Ⓥ

cals 155, **protein** 4 g, **fat** 0.5 g (of which saturated fat 0 g), **carbohydrate** 35 g (of which sugars 1 g), **fiber** 1.6 g

✓ B₁, folate, calcium

Side Dishes and Breads

Bagels

These little bread rings, Jewish in origin, are delicious teamed with savory fillings.
The double cooking method—first by briefly poaching in boiling water, then baking—gives
bagels their unique texture and slightly chewy crust.

Makes 12 bagels

3⅔ cups white bread flour

1½ teaspoons salt

1 envelope (¼ ounce) quick-rising yeast

3 large eggs

1 teaspoon honey

2 teaspoons sunflower oil

¾ cup plus 2 tablespoons water (120° to
    130°F)

Preparation time: 35 minutes, plus about
    1 hour rising

Cooking time: 15 minutes

1 Put the flour into a large mixing bowl and stir in the salt and yeast. Make a well in the middle.

2 Lightly whisk 2 of the eggs with the honey and oil. Pour this mixture into the well in the middle of the flour. Add the water and mix together until a soft dough forms.

3 Turn out the dough onto a lightly floured surface and knead until smooth and elastic, about 10 minutes. Place the dough in a large greased bowl, cover with a damp dish towel and leave to rise in a warm place until double in volume, which can take 40 minutes, depending on the room temperature.

4 Turn out the dough onto a floured surface and knead lightly. Divide the dough into 12 equal pieces. Form each into an 8-inch-long rope, then shape it into a ring. Dampen the 2 ends with a little water, slightly overlap them, and gently pinch them together to seal.

5 Arrange the bagels on a lightly greased cookie sheet, cover with greased plastic wraps and leave to rise in a warm place until they are slightly puffy, about 20 minutes.

6 Preheat the oven to 400°F. Bring a large pan of lightly salted water to a boil over high heat. Drop the bagels into the water, one at a time, and poach 20 seconds. Lift out with a large slotted spoon and return to the cookie sheet.

7 Lightly beat the remaining egg and brush it over the bagels to glaze. Bake until well risen and golden brown, about 15 minutes. Transfer to a wire rack to cool. The bagels can be kept in an airtight container up to 3 days.

Each bagel provides Ⓥ

cals 160, **protein** 6 g, **fat** 3 g (of which
saturated fat 0.5 g), **carbohydrate** 29 g (of
which sugars 1 g), **fiber** 1 g

✓✓	selenium
✓	B₁, B₁₂

Plus Points

• Enriching the bagel dough with eggs increases the protein, iron, and zinc content, as well as adding vitamins A, D, and E and some of those in the B group.

• Serving the bagels with a vitamin C-rich fruit, or including a vitamin C-rich salad in the bagel filling, will help the body to absorb the iron provided by the bagels.

Some More Ideas

● For Cinnamon and Raisin Bagels, soak ½ cup raisins in 3 tablespoons orange juice until the juice has been absorbed, about 2 hours. Make the dough as in the main recipe, but reduce the salt to 1 teaspoon and add 2 tablespoons sugar and 1 teaspoon cinnamon with the flour. Mix in the raisins with the water.

● For Rye Bagels, substitute 1⅓ cups rye flour for 1⅓ cups of the white flour. Stir in 1 teaspoon caraway seeds with the yeast, and use molasses instead of honey.

● The bagels can be finished with a variety of toppings. After brushing them with the egg glaze, sprinkle with sesame, poppy, or caraway seeds. Or sprinkle them with 1 finely chopped small onion tossed in 1 tablespoon extra-virgin olive oil.

Desserts

The wonderful thing about counting calories while also enjoying a balanced diet is that everything is permitted—in moderation—including luscious desserts. Recipes in this mouthwatering chapter include Fresh Figs with Raspberries and Rose Cream, Pistachio Floating Islands, Blackberry Ripple Frozen Yogurt, Hot Apricot Soufflés, and even Rich Chocolate Tart. Refreshingly fruity, creamy or light, these attractive desserts are a perfect finale to any meal.

Little Custard Pots

Delicately flavored with vanilla, these creamy baked custards are easy to make and sure to be popular. Be careful not to overcook the custards—they should be just set when you take them out of the oven. This dessert can be prepared well ahead of serving.

Serves 6

2½ cups low-fat (2%) milk
½ vanilla bean, split
2 large eggs
2 large egg yolks
3½ tablespoons sugar
½ teaspoon cornstarch
Cherry Compote
2 tablespoons soft light brown sugar
1 pound fresh cherries, pitted
2 teaspoons arrowroot

Preparation time: 15 minutes
Cooking time: 25 to 30 minutes

Each serving provides Ⓥ
cals 188, protein 7 g, fat 6 g (of which saturated fat 2 g), carbohydrate 29 g (of which sugars 26 g), fiber 1 g

✓✓	B₁₂
✓	A, B₂, C, calcium, zinc

1 Heat the milk and vanilla bean in a saucepan over medium-high heat until almost boiling. Remove from the heat, cover, and set aside to infuse 15 minutes.

2 Preheat the oven to 325°F. Put the whole eggs, egg yolks, sugar and cornstarch into a bowl and lightly whisk together.

3 Return the milk to the boiling point. Remove the vanilla bean and pour the hot milk over the egg mixture, whisking constantly. Strain the mixture into a large measuring jug, then divide among 6 lightly buttered ½ cup ramekins.

4 Set the ramekins in a roasting pan and pour in enough hot water to come halfway up the sides of the ramekins. Bake until lightly set—the custards should remain slightly wobbly, because they will continue cooking for a few minutes after being removed from the oven—30 to 35 minutes. Lift them out of the pan and place on a wire rack to cool. Once completely cool, chill until ready to serve.

5 To make the Cherry Compote, put the sugar and 6 tablespoons of water in a saucepan over medium heat. Simmer, stirring, until the sugar dissolves. Bring to a boil, then reduce the heat and add the cherries. Cover and simmer, stirring occasionally, until

tender, 4 to 5 minutes. Lift out the cherries with a slotted spoon and put them into a serving bowl.

6 Mix the arrowroot with 1 tablespoon cold water. Stir into the cherry juices in the saucepan and simmer, stirring, until thick and clear, about 1 minute. Leave to cool a few minutes, then pour over the cherries. (The compote can be served warm or at room temperature.)

7 Spoon a little of the cherry compote over the top of each custard pot, and serve the rest of the compote in a bowl.

Plus Points

● The nutrients found in eggs are concentrated in the yolk, rather than the white. Adding extra egg yolks in this recipe therefore boosts the content of vitamins A and D and most of the B vitamins.
● Cherries are rich in potassium and provide useful amounts of vitamin C.

Desserts

Some More Ideas

• If you want to turn out the custards for serving, line the bottom of each ramekin with a circle of parchment paper, and add an extra egg yolk to the mixture. After baking, chill at least 4 hours or, preferably, overnight. To turn out, lightly press the edge of each custard with your fingertips to pull it away from the dish, then run a knife around the edge. Put an inverted serving plate on top of the ramekin, then turn them both over, holding them firmly together, and lift off the ramekin.

• For Chocolate Custard Pots with Poached Pears, flavor the milk with a thin strip of pared orange zest instead of the vanilla bean. In Step 2, replace the sugar with soft light brown sugar, and add 1 tablespoon sifted unsweetened cocoa powder. Continue making the custards as in the main recipe. For the pears, heat 1¼ cups water with ⅓ cup (3 oz) caster sugar and a split vanilla bean until the sugar dissolves. Bring to a boil, reduce the heat, and simmer 2 to 3 minutes. Add 4 small, firm, peeled, cored, and thickly sliced dessert pears. Cover and simmer until just tender, turning the pear slices in the syrup occasionally, 12 to 15 minutes. Lift out the pears with a slotted spoon and transfer to a serving dish. Simmer the syrup 5 minutes to reduce slightly, then cool 5 minutes. Remove the vanilla bean and pour over the pears.

Fresh Figs with Raspberries and Rose Cream

As well as being a superb end to a meal, this simple fruit dessert is packed with fiber from both the figs and raspberries. Rose water is a popular flavoring in the Middle East and in parts of the Mediterranean. It is made from distilled rose petals and has an intense aroma.

Serves 4

8 small, ripe juicy figs

4 large fresh fig leaves (optional)

1¾ cups fresh raspberries

Fresh mint leaves, to decorate

Rose Cream

7 tablespoons cultured crème fraîche

2 teaspoons raspberry jam

Finely grated zest of 1 lime

1 to 2 tablespoons rose water, or to taste

Preparation time: about 15 minutes

1 To make the rose cream, place the crème fraîche in a bowl and beat in the raspberry jam and lime zest until the jam is well distributed. Add the rose water and stir to mix in. Transfer to a pretty serving bowl.

2 Cut each of the figs vertically into quarters without cutting all the way through, so they each remain whole. Arrange the fig leaves, if using, on 4 plates and place 2 figs on each plate.

3 Spoon a dollop of the rose cream into the middle of each fig; serve the remaining cream separately. Scatter the raspberries over the plates and decorate with the mint leaves.

Some More Ideas

● Stir 1⅓ cups sliced ripe strawberries into the rose cream.

● On the same theme, serve fresh peaches with an orange cream. To make the cream, flavor 7 tablespoons crème fraîche with 2 teaspoons orange-blossom honey, the finely grated zest of ½ orange, and 1 to 2 tablespoons orange-flower water, to taste. For an extra flavor, sprinkle in 1 to 2 teaspoons almond liqueur. Cut 4 large peaches in half and remove the pits. Place 2 halves on each plate and fill with the orange cream. Arrange fresh orange slices on the plates and grate a little nutmeg over both the peaches and the orange slices.

● For a quick dessert that is rich in vitamin C, fold 1 pound 2 ounces raspberries, blackberries, blueberries, or halved strawberries into the rose- or orange-flavored cream and spoon into dessert glasses (omit the figs).

● For a lower-fat dessert use reduced-fat crème fraîche or nonfat sour cream.

Plus Points

● Raspberries provide plenty of vitamin C and also contain vitamin E, an important antioxidant whose effects are enhanced by vitamin C.

● In addition to fiber, fresh figs offer small amounts of vitamins and minerals. Look for them in markets from June through October.

● Crème fraîche—see Plus Points, p32.

Each serving provides Ⓥ

cals 150, **protein** 2 g, **fat** 10 g (of which saturated fat 6 g), **carbohydrate** 12 g (of which sugars 12 g), **fiber** 5 g

✓✓✓	C
✓	B₆

Desserts

Pistachio Floating Islands

In this version of the classic French pudding *îles flottantes*, fluffy poached meringues studded with pistachio nuts float on a creamy vanilla custard. A flourish of fresh blueberry coulis is the finishing touch.

Serves 4

Vanilla Custard

2½ cups low-fat (2%) milk

1 vanilla bean

2 tablespoons sugar

4 extra large egg yolks

1 teaspoon cornstarch

Pistachio Meringues

1 extra large egg white

3½ tablespoons sugar

2 tablespoons unsalted pistachio nuts, chopped

Blueberry Coulis

1¾ cups blueberries

2 tablespoons confectioners' sugar, sifted

Preparation and cooking time: about
50 minutes, plus at least 30 minutes chilling

Each serving provides Ⓥ

cals 283, **protein** 10 g, **fat** 12 g (of which saturated fat 4 g), **carbohydrate** 38 g (of which sugars 34 g), **fiber** 4 g

✓✓✓	B$_{12}$
✓✓	calcium
✓	A, B$_1$, B$_2$, C, folate, niacin, copper, iron, potassium, selenium, zinc

1 Pour the milk into a skillet over medium heat. Split the vanilla bean along its length with a sharp knife and scrape the tiny black seeds into the milk. Cut the bean in half and add to the pan with the sugar. Bring to a slow simmer, stirring occasionally.

2 Meanwhile, in a clean bowl, whisk the egg white for the meringues until soft peaks form. Gradually whisk in the sugar, then continue whisking until the meringue is stiff and glossy, about 1 minute. Fold in the nuts.

3 When the milk is just simmering, spoon the meringue in 4 neat mounds on top. Poach slowly, turning once, until the meringues feel set, about 5 minutes. Transfer with a slotted spoon onto paper towels; set aside.

4 Strain the milk into a heavy-bottomed saucepan over low heat. Mix together the cornstarch and egg yolks, then whisk into the milk. Simmer, stirring all the time, until smooth and thick, 5 to 7 minutes. Do not let the custard boil or it will curdle; if it does start to curdle, immediately strain it through a fine sieve into a clean pan.

5 Remove the custard from the heat and pour it into a large, shallow serving bowl or onto 4 individual plates or dishes. Cover and chill at least 30 minutes or up to 1 hour.

6 Meanwhile, make the blueberry coulis. Put the blueberries and confectioners' sugar in a small saucepan over low heat with 2 tablespoons water. Simmer, stirring occasionally, until the blueberries burst and release their juices, 4 to 5 minutes. Press the mixture through a sieve and leave to cool.

7 Float the meringues on the custard and drizzle a little blueberry coulis over them. Serve immediately, with the rest of the coulis separately.

Plus Points

• As long as eggs are not overcooked, there is no protein loss and they retain all their content of vitamins A, D, and niacin. But if cooked for a long time there can be some loss of vitamins B$_1$ and B$_2$.

• Pistachios are a good source of vitamin B$_1$ and contain a small amount of carotene. Like other nuts, they are rich in potassium and low in sodium (unless salt is added during roasting).

• Blueberries, like all berries, are rich in vitamin C and also provide some beta-carotene. Both of these nutrients are important antioxidants.

Desserts

Some More Ideas

- Use frozen and thawed blueberries for the coulis.
- Omit the pistachios, if you prefer, or replace them with chopped pecans.

- For Lime and Passion Fruit Floating Islands, flavor the milk with the grated zest of 1 lime instead of vanilla. Make the meringues as in the main recipe, but without the pistachio nuts. Replace the blueberry coulis with a passion-fruit coulis: Halve 6 large, ripe passion fruits and scoop the pulp into a small saucepan over low heat. Stir in 1½ tablespoons sugar and simmer, stirring, until the sugar dissolves, 1 to 2 minutes. Leave to cool.

Pimm's Melon Cup

This slimline dessert is inspired by the classic British summer drink. Sweet melon, berries, pear and cucumber are marinated in Pimm's, which you will find in specialist liquor stores, and served in melon shells. A decoration of pretty borage flowers is a traditional finish.

Serves 4

1 small Ogen or Canary melon

1 small cantaloupe melon

7 ounces strawberries, sliced

1 pear, cut into 1 inch chunks

¼ cucumber, cut into ½ inch dice

1 star fruit, cut into ¼ inch slices

6 tablespoons Pimm's

2 tablespoons shredded fresh mint or lemon balm leaves

Borage flowers, to decorate (optional)

Preparation time: 20 to 25 minutes,
  plus 20 minutes' marinating

1 Cut the melons in half horizontally and scoop out the seeds from the middle. Using a melon baller or a small spoon, scoop out the flesh into a large bowl; reserve the melon shells.

2 Add the sliced strawberries, pear chunks, and cucumber dice to the melon in the bowl. Reserve some slices of star fruit for decoration and chop the rest. Add to the bowl.

3 Sprinkle the Pimm's over the fruit. Add the shredded mint or lemon balm and stir gently. Cover with plastic wrap and set aside in the refrigerator to marinate 20 minutes.

4 With a tablespoon scoop any odd pieces of melon flesh from the shells to make them smooth. Pile the fruit salad into the shells and decorate with the reserved slices of star fruit and borage flowers, if using.

Some More Ideas

• For a nonalcoholic version, omit the Pimm's and flavor with 1 to 2 teaspoons orange juice.

• Turn this into a luncheon fruit and vegetable salad, using just 1 melon (either Canary or cantaloupe), the strawberries, and cucumber, plus an apple instead of the pear and 3 ounces seedless green grapes. Omit the Pimm's. Make a bed of salad leaves, including some watercress and chopped scallion, on each plate and pile the fruit on top. Add a scoop of plain cottage cheese and sprinkle with chopped fresh mint and toasted pine nuts.

Plus Points

• This delicious combination of fresh fruit provides plenty of fiber and vitamins, especially vitamin C and beta-carotene (which is found in orange-fleshed melon varieties), both important antioxidants.

• While the latest research shows that women should avoid alcohol altogether during pregnancy, in the population as a whole moderate alcohol consumption is now associated with a lower risk of death from coronary heart disease.

• Pears contain plenty of natural fruit sugars, and are therefore a quick and convenient source of energy.

Each serving provides

cals 101, **protein** 1.5 g, **fat** 0 g, **carbohydrate** 12 g (of which sugars 12 g), **fiber** 2.7 g

✓✓✓	C
✓✓	A
✓	folate

Desserts

Blackberry Ripple Frozen Yogurt

Here creamy, custard-based ice cream is lightened with yogurt, instead of the usual rich cream, and flavored with a hint of orange. A fresh blackberry puree is stirred through for a pretty, purple ripple effect.

Serves 4

1¼ cups whole milk

Finely grated zest of 1 orange

1 extra large egg

2 extra large egg yolks

¼ cup sugar

1 teaspoon cornstarch

1 teaspoon vanilla

1 cup plain yogurt

¾ cup blackberries, to decorate

Blackberry Puree

¾ cup blackberries

2 tablespoons sugar

Preparation time: about 35 minutes, plus cooling and freezing

1 Warm the milk, with the orange zest, in a heavy-botttomed saucepan over medium heat until scalding hot. Meanwhile, put the egg, egg yolks, sugar, cornstarch, and vanilla in a bowl and whisk until pale and creamy.

2 Stir the milk into the egg mixture, then return to the pan. Reduce the heat and simmer over low heat, stirring constantly, until thick: Do not let the custard boil. Remove from the heat and set aside to cool.

3 When the custard is cold, beat in the yogurt. Pour the mixture into an ice-cream machine and churn according to the manufacturer's directions until the mixture is thick and slushy.

4 Alternatively, pour the mixture into a freezerproof container and freeze until it begins to set around the edges, about 2 hours. Tip out into a bowl and whisk with a balloon whisk or electric mixer to break down the ice crystals that will have formed. Return to the container and freeze 1½ hours longer.

5 Meanwhile, make the puree. Put the blackberries in a saucepan over medium heat with the sugar and 1 tablespoon water. Heat until the berries are soft and juicy, then bring to a boil to reduce slightly, 1 to 2 minutes. Remove from the heat and cool. Press the blackberries through a nylon sieve to make a smooth puree.

6 If using an ice-cream machine, transfer the frozen yogurt to a rigid plastic container, then lightly stir in the blackberry puree to make a ripple effect. If frozen in a container, tip out into a bowl and whisk well until softened, then swirl in the blackberry puree and return to the container. Freeze until firm, at least 3 hours longer, or overnight. (The frozen yogurt can be kept, covered, in the freezer 3 months.)

7 About 45 minutes before serving, remove the frozen yogurt from the freezer so it softens a little. Scoop into glasses and decorate with berries.

Each serving provides Ⓥ

cals 255, **protein** 10 g, **fat** 10 g (of which saturated fat 4 g), **carbohydrate** 34 g (of which sugars 33 g), **fiber** 4 g

✓✓✓	B₁₂
✓✓	A, calcium
✓	B₂, C, E, folate, niacin, copper, potassium, zinc

Plus Points

• Cornstarch is a good source of both starch and protein. It also supplies useful amounts of potassium, iron, phosphorus, and thiamin.

• This delicious frozen yogurt is much lower in sugar and calories than most commercial frozen yogurts.

Desserts

Some More Ideas

● Make Blueberry Ripple Frozen Yogurt, using fresh or frozen and thawed blueberries instead of blackberries.

● Instead of vanilla, add 1 teaspoon cinnamon to the egg mixture in Step 1.

● For Strawberry Frozen Yogurt, make the custard as in the main recipe, but omit the vanilla. Cool, then add the yogurt. Simmer 1 pound 2 ounces strawberries with the juice of ½ lemon and ¼ cup sugar until soft. Leave to cool, then press through a sieve. Beat the strawberry puree evenly into the custard-and-yogurt mixture. Freeze as in the main recipe.

Strawberry-Yogurt Mousse

This strawberry dessert captures the taste of summer. Mild yogurt with active cultures is used in place of cream for a lighter, lower-fat mousse, which is chilled until set and then served with a raspberry and currant sauce.

Serves 4

1 tablespoon unflavored powdered gelatin

1 pound strawberries

2 tablespoons sugar

2¼ cups plain yogurt with active cultures

Raspberry and Currant Sauce

1 cup red currants, plus a few extra on stems to decorate

2 tablespoons sugar

1 cup raspberries

1 tablespoon raspberry liqueur or kirsch

Preparation and cooking time: 20 minutes, plus at least 2 hours chilling

1 Sprinkle the gelatin over 3 tablespoons cold water in a small mixing bowl and leave to soak until spongy, about 5 minutes. Set the bowl over a pan of hot water and stir until the gelatin dissolves. Remove from the heat and leave to cool.

2 Meanwhile, put the strawberries and sugar in a bowl and mash with a fork. Add the dissolved gelatin and then the yogurt, stirring. Divide between 4 glasses or ¾ cup serving dishes. Cover and chill until set, at least 2 hours.

3 Meanwhile, make the sauce. Put the currants, sugar, and 2 teaspoons water in a small saucepan over medium heat. Bring to a boil, stirring to dissolve the sugar. Simmer 1 minute, then remove from the heat and add the raspberries. Puree in the pan with a stick blender, or crush with a fork. Press through a sieve.

4 Pour a little of the sauce over the top of each mousse and decorate with currants. Serve the remaining sauce separately.

Another Idea

• For Plum and Yogurt Bavarois, sprinkle 1 tablespoon unflavored powdered gelatin over 3 tablespoons apple juice and leave to soak 5 minutes. Bring ¾ cup plus 2 tablespoons low-fat (2%) milk to the boiling point.

Meanwhile, whisk together 1 whole large egg, 2 large egg yolks, 1 teaspoon cornstarch, and 3½ tablespoons sugar in a bowl. Pour in the hot milk, whisking. Return the mixture to the rinsed-out pan over a low heat and stir until thick, 3 to 4 minutes. Remove from the heat and stir in the gelatin until it dissolves. Pour the custard into a bowl and cool, stirring occasionally. Meanwhile, halve and pit 4 firm, ripe plums and put in a pan with 3½ tablespoons sugar and ¾ cup apple juice. Poach until the plums are just soft, 8 to 10 minutes. Remove them from the liquid with a slotted spoon. Simmer the poaching liquid until syrupy, about 5 minutes. Leave to cool. Stir ⅔ cup plain yogurt with active cultures into the cooled custard, then fold in ⅔ cup lightly whipped cream. Spoon a thin layer of the custard mixture into a chilled 1 quart ring mold, and arrange the cooled plums on top. Spoon in the remaining custard mixture. Cover and chill until set, at least 2 hours. Turn out and serve with the plum syrup.

Each serving provides

cals 175, **protein** 8 g, **fat** 1 g (of which saturated fat 0.5 g), **carbohydrate** 33 g (of which sugars 33 g), **fiber** 6 g

✓✓✓	C
✓✓	calcium
✓	B₂, folate, niacin, copper, potassium, zinc

Plus Point

• Yogurts with active cultures are good for the digestive system. Yogurt that has been heat treated will not have any live bacteria left. Read the label to find this out.

Desserts

Fragrant Mango Cream in Brandy-Snap Baskets

What could be more delicious than luscious fresh fruit blended with nonfat sour cream and lemon curd, and spooned into sweet brandy-snap baskets? This is a really special treat, wonderfully creamy without being too high in calories.

Serves 6

1 large ripe mango
2 passion fruit
2 tablespoons good-quality lemon curd
1¼ cups nonfat sour cream
6 store-bought brandy-snap baskets
1 tablespoon chopped pistachio nuts
Fresh mint leaves, to decorate

Preparation time: 15 minutes

1 Cut the peel from the mango and slice the flesh from the flat seed. Place half the mango flesh in a food processor or blender and process briefly until smooth; spoon into a bowl. Chop the remaining mango flesh into pieces; set aside.

2 Cut the passion fruit in half and scoop the seeds and pulp into the mango puree. Stir in the lemon curd. Add the nonfat sour cream and fold all the ingredients until well combined.

3 Spoon the cream mixture into the brandy-snap baskets and top with the chopped mango. Scatter a few chopped pistachio nuts over the top of each serving and decorate with fresh mint leaves.

Some More Ideas

• Look for brandy-snap baskets in gourmet delicatessens or specialty food stores. If you can't find any, serve the mango-flavored cream with bought plain brandy snaps on the side.
• Substitute a papaya for the mango.
• For Raspberry and Chocolate Cream on Panettone, add 2 tablespoons chopped toasted hazelnuts and 4 tablespoons chocolate ice cream sauce to 1¼ cups nonfat sour cream, and swirl together until the chocolate sauce marbles the sour cream. Cut 3 long slices of dried fruit panettone in half and toast under the broiler until golden. Spoon the chocolate cream over the panettone and scatter with 1 cup fresh raspberries. Dust lightly with confectioners' sugar and serve decorated with mint leaves.
• Slice 2 bananas and divide them among the brandy-snap baskets. Top with the chocolate and hazelnut cream above and finish with a fine drizzle of warm chocolate sauce.

Plus Points

• The ancient Indians believed that mangoes helped to increase sexual desire and prolong love-making. Whether or not this is true, mangoes are rich in beta-carotene. This antioxidant is easily absorbed by the body, because of the digestible mango flesh, and is then converted into vitamin A, which is essential for growth. Both beta-carotene, and vitamin C, which mangoes also contain, are antioxidants. The body is not able to provide its own protection against free radicals without the help of these and other essential nutrients from foods.
• Mangoes also provide useful amounts of fiber and copper.

Each serving provides

Ⓥ

cals 205, **protein** 5 g, **fat** 9 g (of which saturated fat 2 g), **carbohydrate** 26 g (of which sugars 22 g), **fiber** 1 g

✓✓✓	C
✓✓	A
✓	B₂, B₁₂, calcium

Desserts

233

Cinnamon-Banana Caramels

Any fruit—fresh, canned, or frozen—can be used to make this instant version of crème brûlée. The fruit is simply topped with nonfat sour cream—a low-fat alternative to heavy cream—then sprinkled with brown sugar and broiled to a rich caramel.

Serves 4

4 bananas

¼ teaspoon cinnamon

1¼ cups nonfat sour cream

4 tablespoons soft light brown sugar

Preparation time: 8 minutes
Cooking time: 1 minute

1 Preheat the broiler. Peel and slice the bananas, cutting each one into about 16 slices. Divide the slices between four 1 cup ramekins and sprinkle with the cinnamon. Spoon the nonfat sour cream over the banana slices to cover them completely. Sprinkle 1 tablespoon of sugar evenly over each dessert.

2 Place the ramekins on a cookie sheet and put them under the broiler, about 2 inches from the heat. Broil until the sugar melts into the yogurt, about 1 minute—keep watch to make sure it does not burn. Remove from the broiler and leave to cool for a few minutes before serving.

Some More Ideas

• Try peaches or nectarines, or a summer fruit mixture. Prepare the fruit in the same way as the main recipe. Gooseberries, plums, and rhubarb can be used, but they are best lightly stewed in the minimum amount of water until tender, then cooled before the topping is added.

• To make Crunchy Raspberry Dessert, use 1¾ cups fresh raspberries. Toast 2 tablespoons medium steel-cut oats in a skillet over medium-high heat, making sure they do not burn, 2 to 3 minutes. Stir the oats into the nonfat sour cream or plain yogurt with 2 tablespoons honey. Spoon the mixture over the raspberries and sprinkle the top with 2 tablespoons toasted slivered almonds.

Plus Points

• Bananas are great energy providers and one of the best sources of potassium (in terms of fruit), a mineral we need to keep a stable balance of water in our bodies. Apart from pure carbohydrate, bananas also provide fiber, plus useful amounts of vitamins B6 and C, magnesium, and copper.

• Cinnamon can help when fighting a cold, because it is a natural nasal decongestant.

• Along with starch, sugars are one of the main types of energy-providing carbohydrates. During digestion, sugars are broken down into glucose, which is released into the bloodstream and carried around the body as fuel for muscles, organs and cells.

Each serving provides

cals 210, **protein** 6 g, **fat** 5 g (of which saturated fat 3 g), **carbohydrate** 40 g (of which sugars 40 g), **fiber** 3 g

✓ B6, B12

234

Hot Apricot Soufflés

Keep cans of apricots packed in fruit juice in your cupboard and you will be able to make these light and fluffy dessert soufflés in minutes. They look impressive and do not contain the large amounts of sugar and eggs found in most sweet soufflé recipes.

Serves 4

1½ teaspoons sugar

1 can (14 ounce) lite apricot halves, drained

2 large eggs, separated

2 tablespoons heavy cream

1 tablespoon sugar

½ teaspoon vanilla

½ teaspoon lemon juice

½ teaspoon cream of tartar

To Finish

Confectioners' sugar

Unsweetened cocoa powder (optional)

Preparation time: about 10 minutes

Cooking time: 15 minutes

1 Preheat the oven to 400°F and place a cookie tray inside to heat. Lightly butter four ¾ cup ramekins and dust the sides with the sugar, shaking out any excess.

2 Put the apricot halves, egg yolks, cream, sugar, vanilla, and lemon juice in a food processor or blender and process until smooth.

3 Place the egg whites in a clean bowl and whisk until soft peaks form. Sift the cream of tartar over and continue whisking until stiff peaks form. Spoon the apricot mixture over the egg whites and, using a large metal spoon, fold together, taking care not to overmix and deflate the egg whites.

4 Divide the apricot mixture between the ramekins. Use a round-bladed knife to mark a circle in the middle of each soufflé; this helps the tops to rise evenly.

5 Place the ramekins on the cookie sheet and bake in the middle of the oven until the soufflés are well risen and golden brown on top, about 15 minutes. Immediately dust with confectioners' sugar, or a mixture of sifted confectioners' sugar and cocoa powder. Serve at once.

Plus Points

• Using fruit canned in lite syrup, rather than in syrup, cuts the sugar and thus the amount of calories.

• Eggs are a first-class source of protein—an essential nutrient for good health and wellbeing.

Some More Ideas

• For double-fruit soufflés, drain a second can of apricot halves and finely chop the fruit. Flavor the chopped apricots with a little minced preserved ginger or apple-pie spice. Prepare 6 ramekins, instead of 4. Make the soufflé batter as above. Divide the fruit between the ramekins, then top with the soufflé batter and bake.

• Substitute pear halves packed in fruit juice and add a pinch of ground cardamom. Or try sliced peaches and pears in fruit juice.

• Save the fruit juice to add to a fruit salad or make into a fruit drink.

Each serving provides (V)

cals 155, **protein** 5 g, **fat** 9 g (of which saturated fat 4 g), **carbohydrate** 13 g (of which sugars 13 g), **fiber** 1.8 g

✓✓	B$_{12}$, C
✓	A, E

Desserts

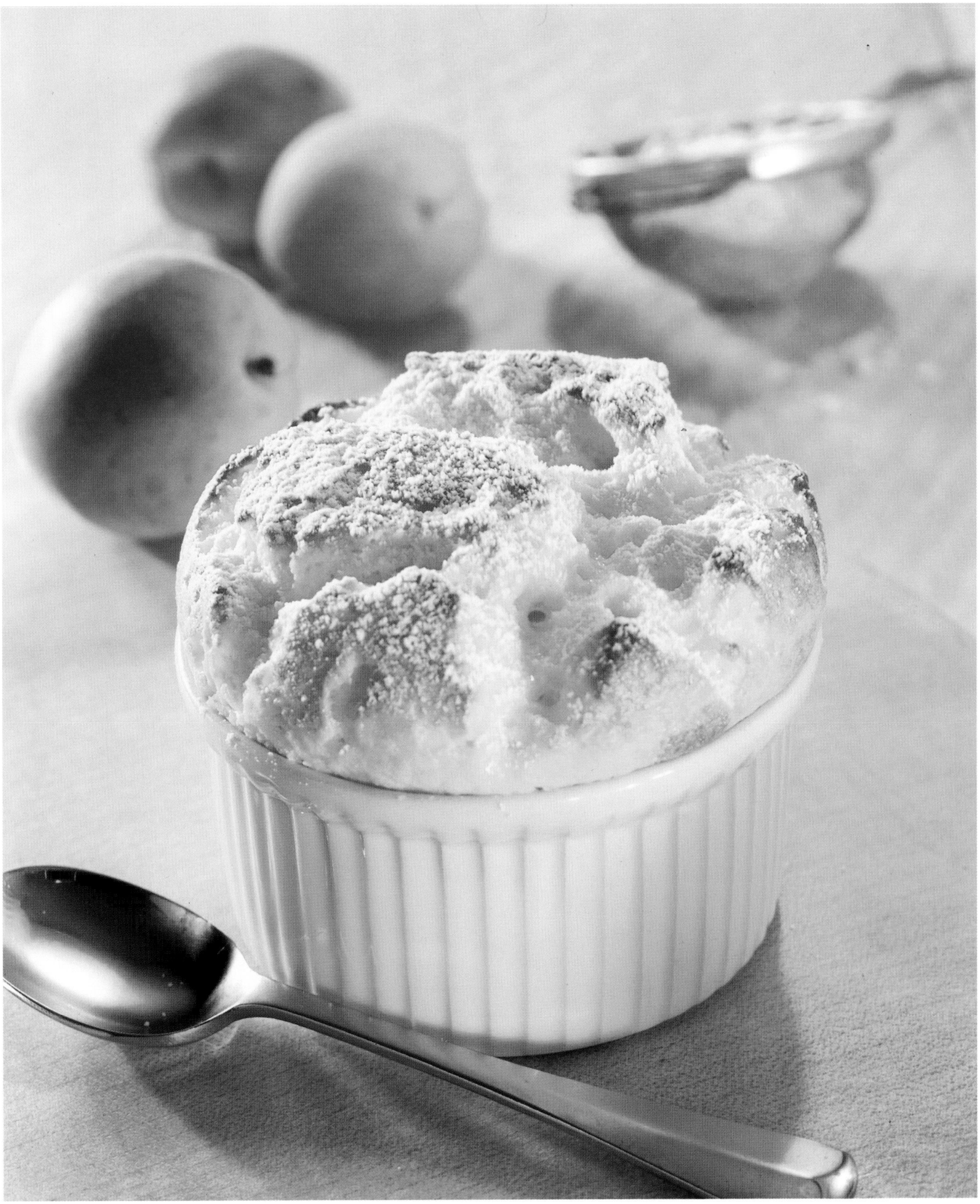

Summer Pudding

What an amazing dish the British summer pudding is—simplicity itself. The peaches or nectarines add a slightly different dimension to this version, a marvelous way of eating a large portion of ripe fresh fruit, not cooked at all so it retains all its nutrients.

Serves 6

1 pound 5 ounces mixed summer fruit (raspberries, blueberries, sliced strawberries)

2 ripe peaches or nectarines, pitted and diced

3 tablespoons sugar, or to taste

⅔ cup cranberry juice

8 thin slices white bread, about 7 ounces in total, preferably 1 to 2 days old

To Serve (optional)

Nonfat sour cream

Preparation time: 20 minutes, plus 2 hours macerating and 8 hours chilling

1 Crush the different types of fruit individually, to be sure all the skins are broken and the fruit is pulpy. Put all the fruit in a large bowl with the sugar and cranberry juice and stir to mix; leave to macerate 2 hours.

2 Cut the crusts from the bread and cut the slices into strips or triangles. Fit the bread into a 1 quart mixing bowl to line the bottom and side, reserving enough bread to cover the top. Fill in any gaps with small bits of bread.

3 Reserve 3 to 4 tablespoons juice from the mixed fruit, then gently pour the fruit mixture into the bread-lined bowl. Top with the remaining bread. Cover with a plate that just fits inside the rim of the bowl, setting it directly on top of the bread, and then place a heavy weight such as a can of fruit on top. Place the bowl in the refrigerator to chill, at least 8 hours or overnight.

4 To serve, turn the pudding out onto a serving dish. Use the reserved fruit juice to brush or pour over any parts of the bread that have not been colored. Serve with nonfat sour cream, if liked.

Some More Ideas

• Use an enriched bread, such as challah or brioche, instead of white bread.

• For a Fall Pudding, substitute raisin bread for white bread, and instead of the summer fruits and peaches, use 2 large diced eating apples, 2 diced pears, 2 tablespoons golden raisins, 2 tablespoons dried cranberries, and ⅓ cup chopped dried apricots. Put the fruit in a saucepan with 1¼ cups apple juice and ½ teaspoon cinnamon. Bring to a boil, then poach gently until the apples are tender, 5 to 7 minutes. Pour into the bread-lined bowl and weight as in Step 3. Serve decorated with diced star fruit and/or a scattering of pomegranate seeds, if you like.

Plus Points

• Cranberries and cranberry juice are good sources of vitamin C. They also contain a compound that prevents E. coli bacteria from causing urinary tract infections.

• Low in fat and high in carbohydrate and fiber, this is a delicious dessert in a diet for a healthy heart.

Each serving (pudding alone) provides Ⓥ

cals 160, **protein** 4 g, **fat** 1 g, **carbohydrate** 36 g (of which sugars 20 g), **fiber** 4 g

✓✓✓ C

✓ folate, niacin

Desserts

238

Golden Raisin-Lemon Cheesecake

Here is a delicious Italian-style cheesecake with a fresh lemon flavor. Cheesecakes are usually high in fat, but this recipe isn't baked with a butter-rich crust, and it uses lower-fat ricotta cheese rather than rich cream cheese, so the fat content is much reduced.

Serves 8

⅓ cup golden raisins

3 tablespoons brandy

3 tablespoons semolina

1½ cups ricotta cheese

3 extra large egg yolks

6 tablespoons sugar

3 tablespoons lemon juice

1½ teaspoons vanilla

Finely grated zest of 2 large lemons

Topping

2 oranges

2 satsumas

1 lemon

4 tbsp lemon marmalade

Preparation time: 20 minutes, plus 30 minutes
soaking and 2 to 3 hours cooling
Cooking time: 35 to 40 minutes

Each serving provides ⓥ

cals 220, **protein** 7 g, **fat** 7 g (of which saturated fat 4 g), **carbohydrate** 32 g (of which sugars 26 g), **fiber** 1.5 g

✓✓	C
✓	A, B₁₂, calcium

1 Place the golden raisins in a small bowl. Add the brandy and leave to soak until most of the brandy is absorbed, at least 30 minutes.

2 Preheat the oven to 350°F. Line the bottom of an 8 inch nonstick loose-bottomed cake pan with buttered parchment paper. Lightly butter the side of the pan. Sprinkle 1 tablespoon of the semolina into the pan, turn and tilt the pan to coat the bottom and side, then tap out any excess semolina; set aside.

3 Put the ricotta cheese into a fine sieve and press it through into a mixing bowl. Beat in the egg yolks, sugar, lemon juice, vanilla, and remaining semolina. Stir in the lemon zest and golden raisins with any remaining brandy.

4 Spoon the batter into the pan and smooth the surface. Bake until the top is browned and the side is shrinking from the pan, 35 to 40 minutes. Leave to cool in the switched-off oven with the door ajar, 2 to 3 hours.

5 For the topping, peel the oranges, satsumas, and lemon, removing all the white pith, then cut out the segments from between the membranes. Warm the marmalade sauce in a small saucepan over medium heat until melted.

6 Carefully remove the cooled cheesecake from the tin and set on a serving platter. Brush with a layer of the melted marmalade. Arrange the citrus segments on top and glaze with the rest of the marmalade. Leave to set before serving.

Some More Ideas

• Replace the golden raisins with finely chopped dried apricots or sour cherries.

• For a mixed citrus flavor, add grated lime and orange zests, and soak the golden raisins in orange juice. Replace the lemon juice with orange juice.

• Alternative fruit toppings include halved strawberries, blueberries, and raspberries.

Plus Points

• Many cheesecake recipes include finely ground nuts to help to bind the ingredients. In this recipe the nuts have been replaced by semolina, which is finely ground durum wheat, thus omitting the fat that nuts would have supplied.

• The fresh citrus fruit topping provides lots of vitamin C.

Desserts

Rich Chocolate Tart

A generous amount of good-quality semisweet chocolate makes this European-style cake moist and rich—just a small slice will satisfy any sweet tooth. It's perfect as a warm dessert, with a spoonful of sour cream and fresh berries.

Serves 10

6 ounces good quality semisweet chocolate (at least 70% cocoa solids)

⅓ cup unsalted butter

4 large eggs

½ cup firmly packed soft light brown sugar

3½ tablespoons all-purpose flour

To Decorate

Cape gooseberries, papery skins folded back (optional)

Confectioners' sugar

Unsweetened cocoa powder

Preparation time: 20 minutes

Cooking time: 15 to 20 minutes

1 Preheat the oven to 350°F. Grease a 9 inch springform cake pan and line with greased wax paper.

2 Chop the chocolate and put it in a heatproof bowl with the butter. Set the bowl over a pan of almost-boiling water, making sure the water does not touch the bottom of the bowl. Melt the chocolate and butter, then remove the bowl from the heat and stir the mixture until smooth.

3 Meanwhile, put the eggs and sugar in a large bowl and beat with an electric mixer until the mixture increases considerably in volume and leaves a trail on the surface when the beaters are lifted out. (If using a whisk, set the bowl over a pan of almost boiling water, making sure the water does not touch the bottom of the bowl.)

4 Add the chocolate mixture to the whisked mixture and fold it in with a large metal spoon. Gradually sift the flour over the top then fold in until just combined.　.

5 Pour the batter into the cake pan, gently smoothing the surface. Bake until the top of the cake feels just firm to the touch, 15 to 20 minutes. Leave to cool on a wire rack in the pan.

6 Remove the cake from the pan and peel away the lining paper. Cut into thin wedges for serving, decorating each with a cape gooseberry, if liked, and dusting the plates with sifted confectioners' sugar and cocoa powder. The cake keeps in the refrigerator 2 to 3 days.

Some More Ideas

● Use ground almonds instead of flour.

● If you're making the tart for a special dessert, drizzle 3 tablespoons brandy or an orange-flavored liqueur over the top after baking, then leave the cake to cool.

Each serving provides Ⓥ

cals 230, protein 4 g, fat 14 g (of which saturated fat 8 g), carbohydrate 24 g (of which sugars 21 g), fiber 0 g

✓✓	B$_{12}$
✓	A, copper

Plus Points

● Scientists at the University of California have discovered that chocolate, particularly with a high percentage of cocoa solids, contains significant amounts of phenols. These substances work as an antioxidant, helping to prevent the oxidation of harmful LDL cholesterol, which is the cholesterol that clogs the arteries. A 1¼ ounce piece chocolate contains about the same amount of phenols as a glass of red wine.

● Cape gooseberries contain useful amounts of beta-carotene, vitamin C, and potassium.

Desserts

Pannacotta

The traditional recipe for this "cooked cream," from the Piedmont region of Italy, is made with rich heavy cream. This lighter version, served with a pretty fruit compote, is still smooth and creamy, yet much lower in fat. Prepare it the day before serving, if possible.

Serves 4
2¼ cups low-fat (2%) milk
1 tablespoon unflavored powdered gelatin
5 tablespoons sugar
7 tablespoons light cream
Pared strip orange zest
1 vanilla bean, split
Rhubarb and Strawberry Compote
3¼ cups pink rhubarb trimmed and cut into
    2 inch pieces
Juice of 1 orange
2 tablespoons sugar
1 pound ripe strawberries, sliced

Preparation and cooking time: 30 minutes, plus
    at least 3 hours chilling

Each serving provides
cals 265, **protein** 10 g, **fat** 7 g (of which
saturated fat 4 g), **carbohydrate** 43 g (of
which sugars 43 g), **fiber** 4.5 g

✓✓✓	C
✓✓	calcium
✓	A, B₂, B₁₂, folate, copper, potassium, zinc

1 Pour ⅔ cup of the milk into a saucepan. Sprinkle the gelatin over and leave to soak, without stirring, until the gelatin is spongy, about 5 minutes.

2 Stir in the sugar, then set the pan over low heat. Warm slowly, without boiling, until the sugar and gelatin dissolve, stirring frequently.

3 Remove the pan from the heat and stir in the remaining milk, the cream, and the orange zest. Scrape the seeds from the vanilla bean into the milk mixture, then add the bean, too. Leave to infuse 10 minutes while preparing the compote.

4 Place the rhubarb in a saucepan over medium heat with the orange juice and sugar. Bring just to a simmer, then simmer until the rhubarb is tender, but still holding its shape, 3 to 4 minutes. Using a slotted spoon, place the rhubarb into a serving dish. Boil the juice remaining in the pan to reduce it slightly until syrupy. Pour the juice over the rhubarb and stir in the sliced strawberries. Leave to cool.

5 Strain the milk mixture through a fine sieve into a large measuring jug. Pour into 4 ¾ cup molds, cups, or ramekins. Leave to cool, then cover and chill until set, at least 3 hours.

6 To serve, run the tip of a knife around the edge of each pannacotta. Place an inverted serving plate over the top of the mold and turn them upside down, holding the two firmly together. Lift off the mold. Spoon some compote on the side of the pannacotta. Serve the remaining compote separately.

Plus Points
• A fruit compote complements a creamy dessert in taste and color, and also adds nutritional benefits.
• Although used as a fruit, rhubarb is actually a vegetable. It contains vitamin C and is a good source of potassium.
• The red coloring of strawberries comes from antioxidant anthocyanin flavonoids, which might help to strengthen the walls of small blood vessels.

Desserts

Some More Ideas

• If you do not have a vanilla bean, use a few drops vanilla.

• Serve the pannacotta with a fresh raspberry sauce. Push 1 pound raspberries through a fine sieve, then mix the puree with 1 tablespoon sifted confectioners' sugar.

• For Rose-Water Pannacotta, add 1 teaspoon rose water and the seeds from 8 cardamom pods to the milk and cream mixture in Step 2, instead of orange zest and vanilla; leave to infuse. Serve with Fresh Raspberry and Passion Fruit Sauce. To make the sauce, add the juice of ½ orange and the pulp scooped from 2 passion fruit to a basic raspberry sauce.

Fruit and Pistachio Baklava

Here is an update of the traditional Greek pastries, made with a cinnamon-spiced filling of dried dates, dried mango, and pistachio nuts, layered with phyllo pastry. Although this version uses less fat and honey than usual, it is sure to be a winner.

Makes 20 squares

4 tablespoons butter

2 tablespoons sunflower oil

½ cup finely chopped dried mango

½ cup finely chopped pitted dried dates

1 cup finely chopped pistachio nuts

1½ teaspoons cinnamon

8 tablespoons honey

20 sheets phyllo pastry dough, each about 7 x 12 inches

4 tablespoons orange juice

Preparation time: 40 minutes
Cooking time: 20 to 25 minutes

Each square provides Ⓥ

cals 196, **protein** 4 g, **fat** 10 g (of which saturated fat 2 g), **carbohydrate** 24 g (of which sugars 15 g), **fiber** 1.5 g

✓✓	E
✓	copper

1 Slowly melt the butter with the oil in a small saucepan over medium-low heat until blended. Remove the pan from the heat and set aside. Mix together the dried mango, dates, pistachios, cinnamon and 4 tablespoons of the honey in a bowl; set aside.

2 Preheat the oven to 425°F. Lightly grease a shallow 7 x 11 inch baking pan with a little of the melted butter and oil mixture.

3 Place one sheet of phyllo pastry dough in the bottom of the baking pan, leaving the dough to come up the sides of the pan, if necessary, and brush sparingly with the butter and oil mixture. Layer 4 more sheets of dough, brushing each one lightly with the oil and butter mixture. Spread the top sheet with one-third of the fruit and honey mixture.

4 Repeat the layering of dough and fruit mixture 2 more times. Top this final layer of fruit filling with the remaining 5 sheets of dough, brushing each with a little of the melted butter and oil. Trim the edges of the dough to fit the pan.

5 Using the tip of a sharp knife, mark the surface of the top dough layer into 20 squares. Bake 15 minutes, then reduce the oven temperature to 350°F. Bake until the pastry is crisp and golden brown, 10 to 15 minutes.

6 Meanwhile, gently warm the remaining 4 tablespoons honey with the orange juice in a small saucepan over medium heat, stirring constantly, until blended.

7 When the pastry has baked, remove it from the oven and pour the honey-and-orange mixture evenly over the surface. Leave it to cool in the pan. When cold, cut into the marked squares for serving.

Plus Points

• Phyllo pastry dough is a lower-fat alternative to piecrust and puff pastries.

• The sweetness of fruit is concentrated in its dried form, so no additional sugar is needed in the filling for this pastry. Dried fruit is also a significant source of dietary fiber.

• Dried dates are rich in potassium, and are a concentrated source of nutrients such as niacin, copper, iron, and magnesium.

Some More Ideas

• To make Peach or Apricot and Pecan Baklava, use 1 cup chopped dried peaches or apricots in place of the dates and mango, and chopped pecan nuts (or hazelnuts) in place of some or all of the pistachios. Spice with ground ginger, nutmeg, or apple-pie spice instead of cinnamon.

• For Pear, Hazelnut, and Almond Baklava, make the filling by mixing together ½ cup finely chopped hazelnuts, ½ cup finely chopped almonds, ½ cup chopped dried pears, ½ cup golden raisins, 1½ teaspoons apple-pie spice and the finely grated zest of 1 small lemon. Layer the filling as in the main recipe.

Steamed Kumquat-Honey Pudding

A pleasingly light, yet old-fashioned dessert for wintry days, this offers all the pleasure of a steamed pudding without the unhealthy saturated fat that is traditionally used. Layers of sliced kumquats add a deliciously tangy citrus flavor.

Serves 6

2 tablespoons honey

1½ cups fresh fine white bread crumbs

½ cup firmly packed soft light brown sugar

¼ cup plus 3 tablespoons self-rising flour

1 teaspoon baking powder

1 large egg, beaten

2 tablespoons low-fat (2%) milk

2 tablespoons unsalted butter, at room temperature

8 ounces kumquats, sliced (with skin)

Custard

2 large eggs

1 tablespoon sugar

1¼ cups low-fat (2%) milk

1 teaspoon vanilla

Preparation time: 15 minutes

Cooking time: 1¾ hours

1 Put the honey in the bottom of a 1 quart mixing bowl and turn it so the honey coats the bottom half of the bowl; set aside.

2 Put the bread crumbs in a large mixing bowl. Stir in the sugar, flour, and baking powder. Add the egg, milk, and butter and mix together to form a stiff cakelike batter.

3 Place a quarter of the batter in the bottom of the honey-lined bowl and arrange half of the kumquat slices on top. Add half the remaining batter to the bowl and top with the remaining kumquat slices. Finish with the last of the batter and press down lightly to smooth the surface.

4 Bring a steamer or deep pan of water to a boil over high heat. Cover the top of the bowl with foil and secure it firmly with string tied under the rim. Use some more string to make a handle. Place the bowl in the steamer: The water should come no more than halfway up the side of the bowl. Cover and steam 1¾ hours, topping up the water as necessary.

5 About 20 minutes before serving, make the custard. In a bowl, beat the eggs with the sugar and 3 tablespoons of the milk. Put the rest of the milk in a heavy-bottomed saucepan over medium heat and heat until bubbles appear around the edge.

Pour the hot milk onto the eggs, stirring. Strain the mixture back into the saucepan. Simmer over low heat, stirring constantly, until the custard thickens enough to coat the back of the spoon in a thin layer: Do not let boil. Stir in the vanilla.

6 When the pudding is cooked, carefully remove it from the steamer, lifting it by the string handle. Remove the foil covering, place a plate over the top of the bowl, and invert. With a gentle shake, the pudding will fall out of the bowl onto the plate. Serve hot, with the custard.

Another Idea
● Use sliced oranges instead of kumquats.

Plus Points
● Kumquats are not a true citrus fruit, but are closely related and so, not surprisingly, they are an excellent source of vitamin C. Although this vitamin is no longer believed to have a direct effect in preventing the common cold, it does help to maintain the immune system and might modify the severity and duration of infections.
● Milk provides both calcium and phosphorus— important for bones and teeth—as well as protein and B vitamins.

Each serving provides Ⓥ

cals 275, **protein** 6 g, **fat** 6 g (of which saturated fat 3 g), **carbohydrate** 53 g (of which sugars 28 g), **fiber** 1.3 g

✓✓ B₁₂, C, calcium

Desserts

Strawberry Shortcake

This streamlined version of a classic makes an impressive summer dessert. Based on a quick, light biscuit and filled with lots of juicy, fresh strawberries, it is easy to make and simply irresistible.

Serves 8

2 cups self-rising flour

1 teaspoon baking powder

5 tablespoons unsalted butter, cut into small pieces

3 tablespoons sugar

1 large egg, beaten

4 tablespoons low-fat (2%) milk

½ teaspoon vanilla

1 teaspoon confectioners' sugar

Strawberry Filling

12 ounces strawberries

5 tablespoons whipping cream

6 tablespoons nonfat sour cream

Preparation time: 15 minutes

Cooking time: 10 to 15 minutes

1 Preheat the oven to 425°F. Sift the flour and baking powder into a bowl. Cut in the butter until the mixture resembles fine bread crumbs. Stir in the sugar and make a well in the middle.

2 Mix together the egg, milk, and vanilla, and pour into the dry ingredients. Gradually stir the dry ingredients into the liquid, then bring the mixture together with your hand to form a soft dough. Gently pat the dough into a smooth ball and turn it out onto a floured surface.

3 Roll out the dough into a 7½ inch circle. Transfer it to a greased cookie sheet and bake until well risen, firm, and brown on top, 10 to 15 minutes. Slide the shortcake onto a wire rack and leave to cool.

4 Using a large, serrated knife, slice the shortcake horizontally in half. Using a large pancake turner, lift the top layer off and place it on a board. Cut into 8 equal wedges, leaving them in place. (For an attractive finish, trim a fraction off each cut so that the wedges are slightly smaller.) Place the bottom layer on a serving plate.

5 For the filling, reserve 8 whole strawberries, then hull and thickly slice the remainder. Whip the cream until soft peaks form. Stir the sour cream until smooth, then gently fold it into the cream until blended.

6 Spread the cream mixture thickly over the bottom shortcake layer. Cover with the sliced strawberries, pressing them into the cream.

7 Sift the confectioners' sugar over the top of the shortcake wedges. Carefully put the wedges into place on top of the shortcake. Slice each reserved strawberry lengthwise, leaving the slices attached at the stem end, then open the slices slightly to fan them out. Place a strawberry fan on each wedge of shortcake. Eat within a few hours of assembling.

Each serving provides ⓥ

cals 275, **protein** 5 g, **fat** 14 g (of which saturated fat 8 g), **carbohydrate** 34 g (of which sugars 10 g), **fiber** 2 g

✓✓✓	C
✓✓	A
✓	B_1, B_2, B_6, B_{12}, calcium

Plus Points

● Strawberries contain a phytochemical called ellagic acid, which is believed to help protect against cancer. In traditional medicine, strawberries are believed to purify the digestive system and act as a mild tonic for the liver.

● The action of whipping incorporates air into cream and increases its volume, thus making a modest amount go farther.

Desserts

Some More Ideas

• Raspberries, blueberries, and pitted cherries can be substituted for the strawberries.

• To make Spiced Shortcake with Fall Fruit, add 1 teaspoon cinnamon to the shortcake dough with the sugar. Halve, pit, and slice 8 ounces ripe plums. Reserve 8 neat slices for decoration, then use the rest to top the cream in place of the strawberries. Reserve 8 blackberries from 8 ounces and press the remainder into the cream with the plums. Finish as in the main recipe, decorating the top of the shortcake wedges with the reserved plum slices and blackberries.

• Instead of whipped cream and sour cream, fill the shortcake with 1¼ cups quark flavored with 2 teaspoons confectioners' sugar and ½ teaspoon vanilla.

Index

Titles in *italics* are for recipes in 'Some More Ideas'.

Project Editor
Rachel Warren Chadd

Art Editor
Jane McKenna

Assistant Editor
Rachel Weaver

Consultant Editor
Beverly Le Blanc

US Consultant Editor
Andrea Chesman

Canadian Consultant Editor
Pamela Johnson

Nutritionist
Fiona Hunter

US Project Designer
George McKeon

A READER'S DIGEST BOOK

Low Calorie Cookbook was published by
The Reader's Digest Association Limited,
London, from material first published in the
Reader's Digest Eat Well, Live Well series

First edition Copyright © 2003
The Reader's Digest Association Limited,
11 Westferry Circus, Canary Wharf, London
E14 4HE

Copyright © 2003 Reader's Digest
Association Far East Limited
Philippines Copyright © 2003 Reader's
Digest Association Far East Limited

® Reader's Digest, The Digest and the
Pegasus logo are registered trademarks of
The Reader's Digest Association, Inc.,
of Pleasantville, New York, USA

For Reader's Digest products and information,
visit our website:
www.rd.com (in the United States)
www.readersdigest.ca (in Canada)

Reader's Digest production
Book production manager: Fiona McIntosh
Pre-press accounts manager: Penelope Grose
Senior production controller: Sarah Fox

Origination: Colour Systems Limited, London
Printing and Binding: Toppan Printing
Company, Hong Kong

1 3 5 7 9 10 8 6 4 2

ISBN 0 276 42740 8
Book code 400-151-01

metric conversions

length

When you know:	If you multiply by:	You can find:
INCHES	25	MILLIMETERS
INCHES	2.5	CENTIMETERS
FEET	30	CENTIMETERS
YARDS	0.9	METERS
MILES	1.6	KILOMETERS
MILLIMETERS	0.04	INCHES
CENTIMETERS	0.4	INCHES
METERS	3.3	FEET
METERS	1.1	YARDS
KILOMETERS	0.6	MILES

volume

When you know:	If you multiply by:	You can find:
TEASPOONS	4.9	MILLILITERS
TABLESPOONS	14.8	MILLILITERS
FLUID OUNCES	29.6	MILLILITERS
CUPS	0.24	LITERS
PINTS	0.47	LITERS
QUARTS	0.95	LITERS
GALLONS	3.79	LITERS
MILLILITERS	0.03	FLUID OUNCES
LITERS	4.22	CUPS
LITERS	2.11	PINTS
LITERS	1.06	QUARTS
LITERS	0.26	GALLONS

weight

When you know:	If you multiply by:	You can find:
OUNCES	28.4	GRAMS
POUNDS	0.45	KILOGRAMS
GRAMS	0.035	OUNCES
KILOGRAMS	2.2	POUNDS

temperature

When you know:	If you multiply by:	You can find:
DEGREES FAHRENHEIT	0.56 (AFTER SUBTRACTING 32)	DEGREES CELSIUS
DEGREES CELSIUS	1.8 (THEN ADD 32)	DEGREES FAHRENHEIT

MM = MILLIMETER   IN = INCH   L = LITER   OZ = OUNCE   GAL = GALLON   LB = POUND

CM = CENTIMETER   FT = FOOT   TSP = TEASPOON   FL OZ = FLUID OUNCE   G = GRAM   C = CELSIUS

M = METER   ML = MILLILITER   TBSP = TABLESPOON   QT = QUART   KG = KILOGRAM   F = FAHRENHEIT